# SPACELING

# SPACELING

## By DORIS PISERCHIA

NELSON DOUBLEDAY, Inc.
Garden City, New York

# SPACELING

# 1

IT WASN'T THE THRILL of the chase that caused me to step out ambitiously but the fact that Gorwyn had sent his two best runners after me. Had I been blessed with the time in which to do it, I would have paused to marvel over that one. I, a common and ordinary—well, not so ordinary at that—brat, pursued by Pat and Mike who were the terrors of the school.

Down a grassy knoll I sped, full of confidence that the dum dums couldn't catch a long legged fourteen-year-old who didn't tire easily and who had a cunning and crafty soul. I ran with the wind in my ears and my heart a quickening drum in my throat. The world was good to look at; I was a healthy human female, though slightly insane, and there wasn't anything I couldn't do or anyone I couldn't outfox. Plus I didn't want to be taken back just then to listen to more of Gorwyn's lectures. Perhaps I would return next week or next year.

Pat managed to circle ahead of me to the left while Mike did the same thing on my right. Obviously they would converge and catch me before I arrived at the patch of woods for which I had been aiming. Angry and disgusted because they had gotten ahead of me, I took the only course open at the moment, raced up a sandy hill and stopped just short of the crest so they couldn't see me while I looked about for a ring. I hadn't planned to go into D-2, hadn't even wanted to because it would be like taking advantage of little children, but the dum dums were such good runners that I was forced to choose between Gorwyn's deadly-dull lectures and cheating a little.

A blue ring with a thin corona broke from a low lying cloud and drifted toward my hill. It came quite close to me, a vividly colored object brighter than the sky with a diameter about half a meter and with a center consisting of heavy fog. Pat and Mike didn't say a word or call out as they came at me from the other side of the incline but I heard the pounding of their feet. In fact, as I dived through the ring, one of them managed to touch my heel and tried to get a good hold on it.

I went on in safely, knowing they couldn't follow me because they were too big to fit through the ring. For a muter, which I happened to be, D-2 was habitable. Made up of treacherous ground, poison atmosphere and boiling sky, this was a world fit only for monsters or creatures called goths. Upon entering D-2, people transmutated into goths, exchanged their human forms for bodies that looked like nothing on earth. Their size and weight in either dimension was approximately the same. For some reason that rule of physics had never applied to me. As soon as I came out on the other side of that strange blue circle I hit the hot ground with four paws the size of basketballs. Attached to them was a goth that would have tipped the scales at two hundred kilos.

Perhaps it was my cunning and crafty nature that made me different from other people, or possibly it was my insanity. No matter, in D-2 I was, figuratively, a moose, and it was my intention that if Pat and Mike managed to find a suitable ring and come in after me they would regret it. A couple of swipes of a paw on my part or a little minor nipping with my fangs would help them to see the flaws in their reasoning.

They didn't come, at least not just then, so I relaxed and enjoyed my environment. D-2 was a vacation spot only for beings like me or the other odd organisms living in the rocks and labyrinths that made up this portion of reality. The world was like the belly of an active volcano, seething, murderously angry, sinister. Had I been human just then, I would have lasted about thirty seconds but as a goth I fit neatly into the landscape. Black and glistening, I had a long tail, two attractive red eyes, a blunt snout and a double row of healthy teeth.

Some goths ate in D-2. Some people did anything. I seldom stayed in the dimension long enough to work up a strong hunger, but there were a few places where I stored food just in case the necessity arose. Beyond a thick patch of fog was a valley with some deep crevices partially filled with ice. In frozen pockets I had placed the carcasses of dead animals I found. I hadn't killed them. It wasn't my idea of entertainment to invade a dimension on a whim and then slaughter something to satisfy my alien appetite, but things already dead were acceptable, to my way of thinking, and I doubted if anything could have made a goth sick.

If there was a sun in D-2 I never saw it. However, I believed it to be quite close since the world was so hot and fierce, except for occasional ice pockets, but the low cloud banks hid the sky. Looking up, I saw gray fog, black sleet, red mist and purple vapor all swirling and blowing in one big stew. It was all right with me. In my ebon and sinewy shape, I liked the way things were.

Loping from one hot hillcrest to another, lingering in glowing depressions in the rocks, I kept a weather eye peeled on one particular yellow ring overhead that dipped, bobbed and hovered but didn't really go anywhere. Blue on its other side, it was the circle through which I had dived to get to this dimension. Pat and Mike would have to enter it or one comparable to it in color if they expected to ground in this section of Gothland.

There were several yellow and green rings in the area and I could see them with no strain, which was why I was a muter. Or vice versa. The fact that I could see them was the reason I was able to travel through them and have my molecules rearranged.

I browsed through my universe and even took a short nap on a fiery stone. It wasn't that I hadn't soft animal flesh with good blood in it, but a goth's metabolism was alien and required ridiculously high temperatures for it to be comfortable. As a matter of fact, my blood was now blue while my internal cooling system prevented the rock from scorching me. It distributed the warmth in such a way that what I didn't need was discarded into the atmosphere. Most of the time I walked around with steam coming out of me.

D-2 was not a quiet world. There were underground explosions, loud hissing as water met hot rock, rumblings and grumblings in the sky. Now and then the rocks under me trembled and my human reflexes caused me to leap to another resting place. The inner core of the planet had deep and winding labyrinths everywhere in it, some hollow, some filled with lava or gas.

If there was such a thing as a native goth, I had never met one. Of course I was ignorant of too many facts, never having been educated about any world but D-1, or Earth, so there might have been goths indigenous to the place, but all I ever saw were transmutated people and furry little animals that looked like groundhogs.

For thirty minutes I ran at top speed through a deep labyrinth without coming across a single obstacle or impediment. To make that tunnel, a white-hot bore might have gone careening through the mountain without leaving a single chuckhole anywhere on the smooth walls. So many meters beneath the surface, it could have been black as pitch for all I knew, and it probably was, but my unique red eyes found plenty of light. In fact, the deeper I went, the better became my vision, somewhat as it usually was for me in Waterworld.

Loping, loping, a fantastic exercise in a fantastic body, and I knew all the time just how human I was inside yet it was so easy to appreciate the form given me by the ring or the dimension itself, or whatever. Being a goth was second nature to me in more ways than one.

The caves were enormous, their stalagmites looking like stony tree trunks, the stalactites resembling white waves. I ran a race with a stream of molten lava, bathed in a hot spring that spewed me out of a labyrinth and deposited me in a room that reminded me of an amphitheater. The ceiling was so high I could scarcely stretch my neck far enough around to gaze up at the breathtaking sight, the rocky growths erupting from the walls were seats awaiting monsters to fill them.

There was pure water that burst in torrents from holes in mountains, crashing in foam, exploding in falls, furiously attacking the planet's facade, sweet to the taste.

For hours I played, and then because I was restless I went

back to the area where I first entered the dimension. The rings that had been there had drifted away to be replaced by others, some large enough to accommodate adult humans, and Pat and Mike had come through with vines and natural nets made of roots.

Roaring in derision, I sped away to the amphitheater, settled down in one of the huge stony seats and waited for my would-be captors to arrive. It wasn't easy to sit. My spine wasn't rigid enough. My upper body sagged and put too much weight on my pelvis. Snarling my displeasure, I leaped thirty feet straight up to a horizontal beam that grew between two stalactites and there I lounged, waiting.

Even now Pat and Mike looked startlingly alike, small goths weighing approximately fifty-five kilos apiece. Where they got the vines and nets I didn't know. Likely they had stored them in the ice. As far as transmutation and rings were concerned, Gorwyn was a genius. Without a doubt, he had known exactly what to shove into a blue circle to get a length of vine or a net; perhaps he had used a leaf, carrot or a redwood seed.

They would have gotten me if I hadn't been so big and if the root nets hadn't been of poor quality. Pat and Mike methodically began climbing up after me and when I jumped down and entered the big winding labyrinth they followed. They behaved rather casually, as if nothing I was doing was any surprise to them, which made me nervous and inspired me to run even faster into their trap.

They had nets everywhere in the tunnel. When I rounded a corner and hurtled against one stretched taut across my path, another fell into place behind me and barred the way. They were held fast by hooks jammed into the rock. Back and forth against them I went, howling in anger and using all my weight as a battering ram. Feeling a weakness in the net behind me, I concentrated on it and literally tore my way through it. Pat and Mike were probably so stunned and alarmed that they forgot to use the anesthesia guns strapped to their chests. A little pressure with their tongues on the triggers and a pair of missiles would have buried themselves in my hide. Most likely the tunnel seemed to grow smaller from their viewpoint as I bore down on them at my best speed. For all they knew, I had turned raving mad during the changeover from human to goth and planned to rip their heads off as I went past.

It appeared that they also had cunning minds, had gone so far as to bury a net in my favorite pool and, when I rode down a hot waterfall and bobbed to the surface with the thing wrapped around me several times, I became so enraged I leaped back up the falls and kept climbing in high bounds until I was well out of the area. At my leisure I chewed the net to shreds only to realize a short while later that they had secreted pods of anesthesia in it. Locating a deceptively small crevice, I managed to squeeze into it and promptly went to sleep. They didn't find me and I had a long nap of several hours.

As luck would have it they were still searching when I finally awakened and staggered from my hidey hole. I had hoped they would think I drowned. It soon became obvious that their intent was to keep me away from rings of all kinds but more particularly the green ones. That created no special hardship for me. I would go into whichever dimension I pleased whenever I pleased and there was no way they could stop me. Unless of course they succeeded in capturing me.

I had investigated only a small portion of this planet, if indeed it could be called that. I assumed it had a sky though there was never any sign of stellar phenomena, no matter the time of day or night. As far as I knew, the dimension was made up of labyrinths and caves and not much of anything else. Now Pat and Mike tried to hem me in by stringing nets across all the tunnel entrances in my vicinity. Climbing up above a cave, I surprised one of them driving a hook into the rock with her bare teeth. She let out a howl as I used my hind feet to give her a horse kick that sent her tumbling down into a frothy pool.

The reason I was so anxious to get away from them at that point was my growling stomach. Not relishing the idea of a meal in this dimension, I nevertheless wasted no time loping in a roundabout manner to the ice pockets where I had stashed a few meals. Strange how hunger could alter one's philosophy in a hurry. The dree tasted just fine after being dipped in a nest of hot coals. Since it had been dead long before I dunked it, its cooling system didn't protect it from the flames and I popped it, sizzling and dripping, down my aching throat. Seven or eight more satisfied my appetite after which I took the time to kick a black goth into a yawning pit because she was climbing too close to me and preparing to lay her tongue on the trigger of the weapon strapped across her chest.

One place I had never gone was the valley of black sleet but I went there now with Gorwyn's runners at my back. The first thing the three of us did after entering a wall of flying pitch was to plunge to our shoulders in a swift tide. At least that's how deep I went. Pat and Mike probably went all the way under, being so short, but as they were swept away I didn't worry about anything dire happening to them since I had never seen anything die in D-2 from so mild an experience.

The driving sleet hadn't exactly blinded me, since my vision was fine in practically any kind of condition, but it threw me off course so that I waded out of it into unfamiliar territory. From where I stood in the valley, all the surrounding knolls looked alike. I began a series of experiments, leaping up to a hilltop and checking for some friendly bit of landscape before returning to the valley floor and then checking another possible exit point.

There were plenty of rings in the air but all of them were pale in color which warned me off. Light yellows usually exited in places such as eighty kilometers due south of the moon, ten meters from the bottom of the Mindanao Deep, the top of Annapurna, and the like. Besides, I wasn't ready to go back to D-1.

After waiting long enough to be reasonably sure Pat and Mike weren't going to be following me from the valley, I chose a hill at random, leaped to the top of it and sped through the yawning mouth of a tunnel. Completing a healthful and invigorating run, I washed in a pool, settled down beside a bubbling pit and went to sleep. For the next several days I intended to do nothing but loaf.

It was exactly seven Earth days later that I came across a ragged old man hiding in a deep labyrinth beneath a series of waterfalls. Any noise he made would have been muffled by the interminable pounding overhead, but I sensed him first and then caught a glimpse of him before he faded back into his hidey hole. Naturally he was in his goth shape but I had the distinct impression that an unkempt old recluse skulked around in his psyche. It wasn't anything I saw, just a feeling, or perhaps I picked up the strong aura surrounding him. At any rate, I guessed he lived in D-2 because he liked having a body that didn't creak and groan every time he moved.

He seemed to hate the sight of me, crawled out of his hole when he realized I had spotted him, and away he went in a hurry. He wasn't large or fast and I could have caught him with no trouble but I hung back on his trail and soon gave up. He whined like a hurt pup and I finally got tired of listening to him and took off in another direction. I had plenty of things to do and it was all right with me if he didn't want my company. I didn't want his either.

I did what I had been thinking about doing for a long time, made myself a fort and stocked it with provisions. The escape exit was a hole opening upon a corridor with half a dozen tunnels in it, not primary labyrinths which might have attracted attention but narrow bores barely wide enough to accommodate me. Emptying into widely divergent areas of the planet, they weren't likely to lure curious goths, such as a couple of runners sent by Gorwyn.

My cave, or fort, was roomy and relatively quiet, though occasionally something rumbled far underground, but there were no waterfalls or volcanoes close by. A corner served as the refrigerator, a deep crevice packed with ice and covered over with cool rocks. In order to fill it with food, I went to a dree graveyard.

Whenever a dree felt death approaching, he went to a high cliff and jumped off. I didn't know what the signal was that told them they were growing old. Possibly they simply felt exhaustion or began suffering from cold. A few of their corpses could be found at the bottom of almost any mountain so that all I had to do was scoop up the freshly killed ones.

One day I came across something puzzling and unsettling. Instead of dree corpses at the bottom of a long drop, there were chunks of fur lying about plus what seemed to be an enormous amount of blue blood. I knew drees couldn't have accounted for it since their blood was pale pink. A goth had died here, had done so in a peculiar manner and hadn't left any part of its skeleton or musculature to tell me what had happened. It seemed fairly obvious. Something had killed a goth and eaten it.

By nature a goth was slothful, accomplishing little besides satisfying herself with running, eating, exploring and just poking about. I think I subconsciously hoped to find a friend during my aimless wanderings for I remained essentially human with my former needs and desires constantly surfacing to plague me. I didn't do anything important, only loafed, dreamed and pretended I was out to conquer some vast kingdom.

While I was foraging one day, someone sneaked into my fort and carved an incredible message on the wall: LEAVE HERE, YOU ARE IN DANGER! So much for that. Being my own special kind of independent orphan, I didn't want to take the words seriously and even chuckled over them.

It irritated me when my food began disappearing. Naturally it had to be the old hermit who robbed me. While angry, I secretly marveled that he could sneak in and out of my fort without being seen. He was plainly a clever thief, possibly nearly as crafty as I, but only nearly.

I stored a few rotten carcasses to see how hungry he was. Either he ate them or threw them away because they were always missing from the refrigerator. This didn't happen occasionally but daily. I decided to remain in the cave, lie in wait for him and catch him in the act.

The warning carved on the wall must have reached me after all. At night I slept, but not soundly, and though I relaxed it wasn't a total surrender of consciousness because when the slok entered my fort one morning a part of my brain was aware of it and shrieked an alarm.

The creature got a piece of my tail but that was all. Still it caused me excruciating agony and sent blood flying all over the walls of my home. Soon I was fleeing for my life down one of the narrow corridors in the back exit and wishing it was wider so I could run faster.

The slok was an unusual specimen made up of springy body and teeth like kitchen knives. I didn't think he had any legs but I couldn't be sure. Our meeting in the cave had gone by in such a blur. I simply opened my eyes in the fort and saw him coming at me like some hideous kind of gigantic caterpillar.

As a matter of fact he had no legs but it was all I could do to stay barely ahead of him, and now and then I cast a glance over my shoulder to see what he was doing. He seemed to be both dedicated and mindless, sworn to catch and cut me to ribbons while he behaved as if he already had me in his grasp. He never closed his mouth while chasing me but continued clicking his teeth, snatching at me, trying to slice me into sections, grabbing at the air as if he didn't know the difference between emptiness and my substance. Full of eagerness and hunger, he pursued me.

The realization came to me that very shortly I was going to have to stop and make a stand. Somewhere ahead was one of the hollow caves that looked like an amphitheater and I knew I wouldn't have time to cross through it and climb one of the high walls. The thing behind me would make confetti of me before I got halfway up the nearest stalagmite. That he could jump I already knew. Like a maniac he zoomed up and down the tunnel sidings, seemingly defying the laws of gravity, leaping, bounding, writhing like nothing I had ever imagined, and all the while he clicked his teeth as if he were already devouring me.

My only chance was to be more savage than he, so as we both roared into the amphitheater, I did a low backward flip and came down to bite at his rear. He whirled with unbelievable speed and slashed my right thigh. His jaws clashed with mine for a brief instant and, luckily, I had a big enough mouth so that instead of getting anything tender and vulnerable, he managed to chip off a bit of fang.

He sounded as if he were chattering in some alien language as he made biting motions, click, click, snick, snick, and in a fit of rage I used a paw to knock him across the amphitheater.

His body consisted of several slender, steel-strong sections each with a hidden spring of its own and covered with dark green, pebbled hide. His head was way out of proportion, being large and round with rows of enormous teeth and small dark eyes. He stank of rot and evil. I guessed that he weighed one hundred and fifty kilos and, when stretched to full length, he probably measured three meters.

Instead of running back across the floor, he zoomed up a stalagmite and hurtled through the air at me. I kicked him ten meters straight up and didn't wait for him to fall but leaped and swiped at him with my teeth as we passed. He sprang while still far off the ground, seemed to brace himself against his back segments and buried his jaws in my left flank. I felt a searing pain and then we both hit the ground, hard. For a moment he was shaken loose of me and I began kicking him with first one hind foot and then the other and sometimes with both. No matter how he came at me, he was kicked.

The stalagmites in the room were spattered with blue and green blood, as was the floor. My breath was ragged in my throat, my chest burned, my head was a seething cauldron of pain and anger. For a little while I stopped being human and became pure goth, which might have been what saved me. By sheer instinct I managed to remain one gesture, one action, ahead of my dangerous foe, kicked before he could slash, ripped before he could tear at me, leaped at all the right times to counter his attacks, and at every opportunity I bit deeply into the back of his head. My teeth felt grisly and I could feel the bare bones of his neck.

Finally I was too exhausted to fight anymore. All I could manage to do was keep my fangs buried in that one spot on him. The rest of my body was utterly limp. In the meantime, the slok worried at my shoulder. With my teeth clamped the way they were, he couldn't really get into prime position, besides which I was heavier and lay on top of him. He didn't appear to be tired, which seemed incredible to me, but I could tell that my persistent gnawing was having an effect upon him.

Panic stirred within me. Soon I was going to fall unconscious, and in fact I could already feel it beginning to happen. When it did, the slok would tear me to pieces and then eat me. Summoning the last of my strength, I began closing my jaws, slowly and inexorably. The slok resisted, tore at me with increased savagery and then suddenly screamed as the bones in his neck gave way.

Reality seemed blurred after that. The amphitheater was dark around me and I had a vague awareness of being wrapped in a net and dragged somewhere, by whom I had no idea, nor did I care.

"You weigh a ton, little slok killer," somebody said in a very strange voice. "You saved my bacon and I won't forget it. I owe you plenty, sweetheart."

It was the old hermit, crooning to me in a bizarre fashion as he tried to make me comfortable in his cave. I didn't remember how we had gotten there.

"You're a mess, all torn up that way, but you're truly a beautiful sight to me," he said. "Here, now, move that leg a bit and I'll try and splint it with these flat stones and this net."

Once in a while I bit him. I longed to kick him but my legs were in a bad way and wouldn't do what I told them.

"Don't be cranky, kid, you're in too lousy a shape for it. At least I don't have to worry about that filthy slok anymore, and it'll take them a good while to learn it's been blasted to kingdom come. He had me pinned down good. Here's a nice drink of water for you. I can't figure out why you're so big. If I had the chance, I'd run a brain scan on you."

Even though the words came hoarsely and awkwardly from his throat, accompanied by hisses and snarls, I had no trouble understanding him. He was more dexterous with his paws than any goth I'd ever seen, could lift hollow rocks filled with water to my mouth, could clean my cuts.

Whatever work he had done before abandoning civilization and D-1, that old man understood his medicine. He knew he couldn't heal me and I wasn't fooled into thinking he could, but he held me together for a while. For three days he straightened bones and treated gashes to stop the flow of blood.

"If you're wondering how I can talk, well, if you lived in this dimension as much as I, you'd learn to split yourself and share personalities," he said. "I can talk as plainly as any human. Why don't you get well and I'll teach you how?"

I wasn't sure if that part of my delirium was real, his talking I mean. When my rotten condition took a turn for the worse, I somehow managed to make him understand that he was to take me onto the planet's surface. He objected in what sounded like a hoarse, human voice. I kept at him until he screamed at me and said he would do anything I asked because he owed me.

Draping me in a net, he took a part of it in his teeth and hauled me away, pausing whenever I yelled in pain, hovering anxiously and then swearing when I snarled at him. "I can't help the bumpy ride," he said. "In fact, I'm surprised I can even move you, big as you are." What seemed hours and much agony later, I lay under a sky of brimstone and swirling gas.

"Let me take you back down," said my companion, making as if to pull on the net. He noticed me looking at the sky. "Don't you think I already checked to see if there were any rings handy? I wish I could shove you through one and have you go out the other side whole and well, only there aren't any here!"

I snarled softly. A yellow ring danced in the distance. It was a long way off and I couldn't be sure it wasn't a figment of my fever. Again I snarled and it started drifting my way.

The hermit said, "Am I seeing this for real? Are you making that thing come to you?"

He never spoke another word, just squatted on his haunches beside me while the bright circle swam through the bruised air to pause near my head. He cleared the net off me and shoved with his paws and his rear until I was more or less standing on my splints, after which he crawled beneath me and used all his strength to raise me a bit. Then he rocked back and forth until we finally made the big effort in unison. He raised and shoved while I pushed with my sore legs. A cry burst from my throat as I left D-2 behind and tumbled onto the ground of my favorite Earth.

It might have been a bellow of anger. In my turmoil I hadn't paid much attention to the color of the ring as it came down to me. It turned out to be too much like the one I had used to travel to Gothland in the first place. Now I sprawled on the green grass of the school campus and there were Pat and Mike looking down at me with big grins on their faces.

# 2

DARYL WAS MY NAME and amnesia was one of my problems. Gorwyn had already had me analyzed six ways from Sunday but I couldn't remember anything that happened to me before the car wreck in Detroit. It seemed there was either a clot inside my brain or a permanent scar. The doctors couldn't be sure which it was without going in to see, and they didn't want to do that. If it was a clot it might disperse without killing me and my memory could come back. I was wearing an ankle bracelet when they found me. It had my name engraved on it, or at least everyone assumed it was mine.

I studied photographs of the driver in that wreck until my eyes watered but he didn't mean a thing to me. He was buried now but just about everything pertinent to his physical existence was on record. They had brain scans, fingerprints, tissue, blood and hair samples and complete photographs but none of it helped to match him with somebody who had once lived. There was nothing on him in F.B.I. records or any other records, which was slightly unusual since vital statistics and most local data were available in national or international computer systems.

The man was a stranger to me but he had died in the same modern, electrically powered auto that had thrown me onto a floor display in a department store. They said I must have been in the back seat and the earthquake hurled the fast-moving car through the plate glass window. That part wasn't so unusual since quakes were becoming an ordinary part of our lives.

Anyhow, the dead man and I had been together during his last moments but he remained a total stranger to me. Except for the chain on my ankle, neither of us had an iota of I.D. on us. As for the car, it was traced to a rental agency in Pennsylvania where the dead man, using the name Jno Jonz, had leased it for a week. No, the agency hadn't seen a girl with Jonz and no, they hadn't required fingerprints or anything else.

That was it. So much for my past. After I was taken to the hospital I talked a good deal about rings and dimensions while they were trying to bring me to consciousness, so they rightly assumed I was a muter which was why they shipped me southeast to Gorwyn.

The school was a tall skyscraper and the students weren't allowed below the third floor. Not just nobodies like me stayed at Mutat. There were also the children of the wealthy, not that our numbers were all that great. Gorwyn told me there were approximately two million muters in the world. That made me rare and valuable in at least one aspect, otherwise they would have kicked me out the door, or perhaps out one of the thirtieth-floor windows.

"I'm not staying," I told Gorwyn. "And don't tell me again I'm a ward of the state. For all you know I'm eighteen or nineteen."

"You don't even look fourteen which was the age the doctors listed for you. I can't imagine why you don't like it here, since you've no place else to go. Consider Mutat your home for a while."

"Consider yourself in error," I said. "I'm not staying."

I was walked about the grounds like a dog. On one end of the leash was Pat or Mike, or both, while on the other end I strained and pulled against the leatherwork strapped around my upper body. They only took me out because the doctors said I had to have plenty of green grass, fresh air and sunshine.

"Kid, I think maybe you're unique," said Pat or Mike. They were identical twins and I had never taken the trouble to try and distinguish between them. "If we did this to one of the other brats, treated them like slush, I mean, they'd be blubbering all over the place."

"Oh, I'm reacting," I said. "I'm biding my time. Another day I'll catch you in D-2 and then we'll see who puts whom on a leash."

"We aren't trying to be nosy or anything, but now that you've brought up the subject, tell us why you turn into a moose every time you hit a blue ring."

"Tell Gorwyn that's none of his business."

They laughed. They always did everything alike. Sometimes I didn't think they were two women at all but one very large one divided somehow into walking, talking halves. Tall, blonde and straight of feature, they were no doubt considered attractive by everyone but me.

"We don't think you really know how you do it, since you remember nothing about yourself, but we'd be interested in hearing your opinion," one of them said.

"Tell Gorwyn—"

"What makes you think we only do things for him?"

"Because that's what you are. Gorwyn-jumpers. You know. He whistles or grunts and you jump."

They grew agitated and wouldn't let me stop and pick daisies down by the brook. Yelling and straining against the leash, I called them names and kicked dirt at them. I wasn't supposed to get excited so they dragged me back into the building.

The elevators weren't guarded with the exception of the one on the third floor where four hefty women stood watch twenty-four hours a day. They liked to knock kids across the corridor.

"Why do you tell such lies?" said Gorwyn. "You know very well you got that black eye when you fell in the gym."

"They only hit me because I'm an orphan. They don't have to worry about getting sued."

"You really must develop a philosophy based on honesty, otherwise you'll reap nothing but trouble all your life. Come, it's time for the four o'clock lecture."

Transmutators had been showing up for the last hundred years or so. They could be anybody, just as long as their cells possessed an extra chromosome that showed up clearly on a slide as an irregular little donut. The secret, or talent, partially lay in the vision. If an individual could see the rings, he or she could travel into them.

Having a portion of the populace able to disappear into other worlds or dimensions created problems for the government. Rules and regulations were written, but they did no good as long as restraints weren't imposed on muters. One such step was to have them identified at birth and kept track of, though the extra chromosome wasn't always easy to detect in infants. Obviously one or two slipped by in the maternity wards. For instance, there were no records for me.

"There aren't going to be any for you, either," said Pat or Mike, when I brought up the subject. "Gorwyn's going to keep you for observation. Maybe forever. Who would care? You're such a worthless little freak."

"That's preposterous," Gorwyn said to me later. "What nonsense. One thing I happen to have is an active conscience. I've made records for you, most certainly, and they're in Washington where they belong. Personally I wouldn't mind dropping you out of a thirtieth floor window but I keep telling myself you're an affliction that time will cure. Incidentally, why did you bloody Tedwar's nose?"

"Can't you have somebody else guard me besides Pat and Mike? They get on my nerves."

"Their names are Padarenka and Mikala and they're doing what they get paid for. To tell you the truth, they get on my nerves too, but nothing is perfect in this world."

Most muters became chemists and physicists because their governments encouraged them to do so. If substances could be changed into other substances simply by switching them to another dimension, why shouldn't the process be made to be profitable? Why not find something useless in D-2 or D-3 that muted into something valuable when shoved into D-1?

"The secret is in gold and diamonds," Pat or Mike said to me one day as they dragged me through the flower beds on campus. It was spring and I would have felt fine if it weren't for my leather halter.

"That's dumb," I said, kicking dirt at them. "That's all anybody talks about. Who cares for gold or diamonds? Gorwyn has the right idea. I once saw him get a radish seed out of a hunk of D-2 junk."

I had a room of my own on the thirtieth floor but someone was always snooping in it and tearing it up. Frequently I came in to discover that my bureau had been searched, or my closet had been ransacked, or my bed had been stripped.

"Don't hit me and I'll tell you who did it!" said Tedwar, feeling his bruised lip and eyeing me with hatred. He was bigger and heavier than I but not half as earnest.

"Are you trying to tell me you didn't mess it up?"

"Pat and Mike did it. They're always in there. Don't hit me! I'm not lying! The last time I went through your things, they paid me a dollar to do it."

"What were you supposed to be looking for?"

"Nothing. I mean, I don't know. They just said to see if you had anything unusual."

I spoke to the elevator guards on the third floor. "You don't have to use your fists on me, you know. I'm not one of those people who are always trying to sneak away."

"We use our fists every chance we get," said one of them. "The fact is, we hate kids."

"Don't pay any attention to that slush," said another. "We have feelings the same as anyone. We also have bills we have to pay with our wages, and if any of you gets through this elevator without permission we get fired. Say, what's it like in D-2? What's it like in D-3?"

The law dictated that an American muter had to be educated at Mutat. Children with parents were allowed to go home on weekends. At the age of eighteen, a Mutat graduate could take employment with a company, or he or she could loaf for the rest of their lives. There was always money to be earned on the lecture-tour route, traveling around the country telling the sightless how elegant an experience it was to take a vacation from harsh reality. By the time the liars finished their work, the public thought D-2 and D-3 were Heaven with streets of gold and perfume for air.

Weekends were best for me because nearly everyone went home and I had the place practically to myself. I could have left for good anytime I pleased but the fact was, I knew if I didn't get educated I'd grow up to be an ignorant adult and, since I didn't want that to happen, my only alternative was to remain.

But not on weekends and holidays. Often on Friday evenings I went into D-2 or D-3, returning on Saturday or Sunday.

"I've used every kind of truth serum on you," said Gorwyn. "How do you account for the fact that I'm not getting any information out of you?"

"Does it ever occur to you that I'm telling the truth in just plain conversation?" I said.

"No, it doesn't. Somehow you're getting out of the building. Except for the channel, and I don't think you have access to that, the area is relatively free of rings, which is why the school was built here in the first place. You can't climb down to the ground with shoelaces or sheets any more because we moved all the extra supplies below the third floor. Could be you've bribed a guard, though I can't imagine with what. I suppose I should be grateful that you return of your own accord. Saves me the expense of sending Pat and Mike—I mean, Padarenka and Mikala—after you. However, the significant point is that truth serum doesn't make you spill the beans. Is it possible that blood clot in your brain has done something awful to you?"

My memory of the outside world was sketchy. Towns, cities and country roads drifted through my mind like scenes viewed from a train window. They weren't really mine because they weren't accompanied by introductions or farewells. In other words, I had no recollection of having approached or left them. My real memories were of a chaotic economy, corruption and hostile minorities. Detroit meant nothing to me. I didn't remember why I and the dead stranger had driven there.

"A break in your routine," Gorwyn said to me one morning after Algebra class. "A very important person is coming to see you today. He read my report to Washington regarding your immunity to truth serum, says you may be harboring a rare antibody, though I assured him you hadn't a blamed thing anybody could call rare. Except, that is, for your deep-rooted and neurotic hostility toward the elevator guards, Tedwar and every other human being who tries to help you. His professional name is Ectri. See that you're appropriately respectful to him."

My first glimpse of the stranger was from the end of a long corridor. A few days had gone by; I received the call and started walking to the main lounge. There was Gorwyn in the distance, his spare shape easily discernible in the shadows and then I saw another tall, broad figure, whereupon a stirring immediately began somewhere in my stomach. I sensed something about this tall, threatening individual. Thoughts flashed through my mind, startling me. Ectri, Ectri, the name seemed to mean nothing. I had no recollection of ever having met him, yet the farther I went down the hall, the more intense grew the foreboding that crept over me. Ectri was waiting for me where the shadows bunched. Like a slok he crouched and writhed in anticipation, and once I got near enough to him, he would step forward and take my throat in his big white hands. He would squeeze the life out of me.

Without missing a pace, I turned and casually entered the nearest doorway. It was a reading room, empty and full of windows. It also contained another doorway that exited into an intersection of several corridors. Swiftly I opened one of the windows by pressing a button on the sill. It was raining outside, a chill and bleak day that matched my new mood.

A bright green ring hovered in the sky a long way off and I ordered it, over and over again, to come to me. The thing was slow to obey because of its remoteness and because my mind wasn't sharp and focused. Footsteps and voices sounded in the hallway behind me. In another moment or two, Ectri would walk into the room and claim me.

I didn't wait for the ring to drift all the way up to me. It was directly below now, laid out flat like the rim of a swimming pool. Just as I dived out of the window, I pressed the button so that the pane would slide shut. At about the same instant, or so it seemed, I plunged through the ring seven or eight meters above the ground.

Waterworld, or D-3, was made of liquid. The only land in it consisted of floating mountains. A swimmer in Waterworld felt like a microscopic organism in a large fish bowl. There were decorative chunks of coral, rocks with caves in them, shells and clumps of sea flora all drifting independently in pale green fluid that seemed to have no boundaries. The planet was warm and quiet and full of mystery because it seemed to defy the laws of logic and physics.

I was a water-breathing, scaly-skinned swimmer forty-five centimeters long and weighing approximately four kilos. My legs were slender, my feet were little silken members. Since I loved Waterworld more than anywhere, I didn't come here as often as I went to Gothland. Here the silence was music, the currents were massage and balm while sporting in coral was a way of life.

When I woke up in that hospital in Detroit, I hadn't forgotten the different dimensions nor had I lost recollection of the fact that I was a muter with a difference. Amnesia cut all the people I had known out of my mind, plus addresses, scenes and activities and if there was anyone in the world who cared for me, I was unaware of it. At the moment I was also unaware of why I hadn't transmutated into a swimmer comparable to my human size. Instead of doing things like an ordinary person, I seemed to be way off the track, but I knew it was right for me to be tiny now. The ring hadn't done it. Something in my head caused me to turn out this way.

No matter where I swam, there were rings to be seen. Yellows, blues and other colored donuts hurtled or lazily floated through the water, their passage occasionally creating maelstroms that I deliberately avoided because they could suck me down into black pools where it was cold and full of loud noises that hurt my ears. It occurred to me that somewhere in the same universe occupied by Earth a planet of water orbited, glistening in the sunlight, rotating and growing warm. Then I wondered if my beautiful D-3 was Earth billions of years ago when she was nothing but placid fluid and gentle motion. I couldn't satisfy my own curiosity. Phenomena like Waterworld and rings kept all kinds of theorists engrossed.

A clear piece of coral afforded me a look at myself. My head and torso hadn't changed at all, except for their size and the skin condition. I had the same close-cropped, curly blond hair, the same blue eyes. All the other things were there, in a way improved upon. Especially I liked my scaled thighs and legs which were so slender and flexible that they could send me flashing through liquid space like an arrow.

I was still holding onto the piece of coral and admiring myself in its glittering surface when the world rocked. It wasn't a new experience and I didn't think it had ever particularly bothered me before, but it did now. I didn't like it at all. Feeling everything shift around me unleashed in me a keen sense of foreboding, as if I knew what it was all about and knew it was dangerous. Scientists said the dimension periodically passed through phases of reality and that the rocking sensation was created by the space between phases, similar to a person going from one bus and through a windy alley into another bus.

After all, it wasn't important. Nothing could make me pessimistic for long in my favorite world. Things soon settled down and I swam for hours, ate nuts and berries from floating shrubbery, played hide and seek in the holes and caverns in a rock, after which I curled up in a big piece of seaweed and went to sleep. I was never able to sleep in free float, probably a carryover from my human condition or perhaps I unconsciously feared floating away into nothingness or off the edge of reality, though I had never discovered anything but water when awake. It might have been the old human fear of falling; if I fell asleep without support, I might just drop out of everything. Anyway, the seaweed made a comfortable bed and hid me from prying eyes. Of course, I wasn't large enough to be easily seen and, furthermore, there was no one to see me. I and Waterworld existed quietly and happily while the dimension from which I had escaped consumed itself with its own inconstancy.

Avoiding each and every maelstrom that came along was nearly impossible, particularly since it didn't have to be a very strong one to take hold of me and toss me about. One day I ate too many sea nuts, was lying on a slab of coral groaning and moaning, when the slab took a fast flip under me and dumped me into a king-size eddy. Making like a bit of flotsam on its way down a sink drain, I reached out for any kind of support and banged my head on something big and solid. It was too massive for me to encircle it with my arms but there were pits in it deep and irregular enough for me to grab hold of. While black water churned all around me, I shivered from the sudden cold and hung on. Knowing my strength would soon fail, I felt around for more pits and cracks in the object, began crawling straight down into the churning water. At least it seemed down to me. I continued slipping until I came out of the black into green home.

My first act was to check the object I had descended. After hours of investigation, I knew no more than I had before. It was a rod or a beam that seemingly had no end. On my side it was more or less smooth and if I hadn't been so small I wouldn't have been able to hold onto the scraped and peeled places. Likewise it was smooth on the right and left sides while on the far side it was indented. The whole structure appeared to be some kind of giant metal girder.

Finding no end to it in what I considered to be a southern direction, I went north, fighting my way through several minor maelstroms that knocked me about until I realized it would be safer and easier to travel inside the indented portion. The walls on three sides protected me and my passage was considerably smoother. I must have swam a quarter-mile before venturing outside the indentation just in time to see a large net being hauled up from the depths.

The net continued moving upward and finally stopped. Whoever was doing the hauling must have thought the prisoners needed some calm water for a while, though they weren't taking their captivity badly. There were four swimmers in the net, a man, a boy and two women. They sat with their arms and legs sticking out through the holes in the mesh and their kicking wasn't too panicked. Their backs were to me so they were unaware as I swam through one of the openings and investigated the top of the contraption. In no way would I be capable of loosening the great knots.

Taking care that they didn't see me, I sped away to hunt for a chunk of coral, my intention being to provide them with sharp objects to cut themselves free. I could chip some pieces of coral from a floating reef, hide at the top of the net so the prisoners couldn't see me and drop the pieces down to them.

I suppose it was as good a plan as any and probably would have worked but the net wasn't there when I returned. I swam north and south along the beam but couldn't find it. It must have been taken east or west, or possibly I missed it in one of the many maelstroms.

Eventually one of those whirlpools grabbed me, sucked me down into a cold, black pit that was draining into a swift-moving current and dumped me into a warm ocean full of seaweed and floating mountains. I tried to find my way back to the metal girder. It was gone, hidden somewhere in the vast and unmarked space of Waterworld. Still, I searched for it for hours before giving up.

Feeling uneducated and not too confident at that point, I decided to return to Mutat. I didn't think the man named Ectri would still be there and now, when I thought about him, I couldn't see why I had been so afraid of him.

I had a photographic memory where color was concerned and I went on the hunt for a ring of the same shade as the one I had entered. It was a habit with me, checking the color of a ring after I left D-1. All around me in the water were dark yellows, ambers and pastels, and then there were sunny circles with subtle differences between them. After only a few seconds of study and concentration, I made my choice, swam forward and tumbled out onto the quaint old cobblestones of the quaint old town twenty kilometers from Mutat.

Feeling tired and out of sorts, I solicited a ride back to the school, got out of the woman's little electric car at the far end of the campus and began dawdling in the gardens.

I didn't pay much attention when Pat and Mike sneaked from behind two trees and crept up on me. They were always doing that and I figured they might as well get the credit for apprehending me. Like two golden bandits, they leaped on me and carried me away, but not to the school building as I anticipated. They had their own car secreted in a barn on the grounds, not the vehicle they used for normal business but a decrepit old gasoline burner with venetian blinds on the windows. In it we went back to town and then to a private airport where I was put on a plane.

I had been sold. It seemed that Padarenka and Mikala weren't satisfied with the wages Gorwyn paid them and earned extra by doing odd jobs such as kidnaping orphan muters and selling them to agents who represented corporations or individuals.

As I sat tied in a seat with a strip of tape across my mouth, it occurred to me that I hadn't asked the twins how much I brought them on the open market.

# 3

THE SWEET SMELL of contention permeated the log cabin much like the fragrance of pine needles, mountain air, wood smoke and my breakfast cooking on the electric range.

"Won't do you any good to cry," said Wheaty, eyeing me with a suspicious expression. He was probably wondering why I seemed so cheerful. For days he seemed to have been trying to make up his mind whether I was to be laughed at or avoided. "We eat a kid a day around here," he said. "Don't let anybody fool you, there are animals in this world."

I particularly appreciated the way he kept flicking glances at the ring alarm on the wall. There was one in every room in the cabin, one on the front and back porch and three down by the corral.

"I wonder what would happen if I rode a horse into D-2?" I said, noting his sudden pallor. I suspected that ever since the first moment we met, this man's blood pressure had been up, his pulse was rapid and his adrenals were miniscule geysers. "I think maybe I'll try it with Bandit," I said. "First I'll hogtie you to the saddle in front of me good and tight and then we'll travel at a dead gallop through a good old blue donut. You know, one of the house-size types. I heard, though, that the bigger they are the farther you have to fall on the other side."

"Is that a fact?" Having already partaken of a breakfast of one soft boiled egg and a piece of dry toast, Wheaty contended with indigestion and indignation while I did away with scrambled eggs, sausages, buttered rolls, jelly, juice and milk.

"Didn't they feed you where you came from?" he said. Pain contorted his features as I drowned my eggs with blackberry jelly. "Where *did* you come from?"

"Under a cabbage, where else? I'll bet I can tell you some things you don't know. For instance, I have a blood clot in my brain. Did you know I have amnesia? I admit there are times when I stretch the facts a little, but this isn't one of them. If your boss had been more astute, he wouldn't have done business with that agent. The guy was a crook."

"What do you mean, amnesia? What are you talking about, kid?"

"What's your name?" I asked.

"I told you a dozen times. Wierton."

"Mine's Daryl."

"Okay, kid."

"Okay, Wheaty. Anyhow, as I was saying, I'm ambulatory but that's about it. Shove me hard and I'm liable to go out like a green ring ducking inside this cabin."

He shot to his feet and checked the alarm on the wall, tapped it, placed his ear against it. The dial was pale pink. There wasn't a ring anywhere nearby.

"Could be I gauged you wrong," he said. "Could be you ought to be slapped silly and locked in a cage."

"Remember my blood clot."

"You remember it. It's in your head, not mine." He looked at me with his mouth slightly open but his washed-out blue eyes were steady. "Why do you tell such lies? You're in good shape. Admit it."

An old hound named Googs lived in the stable. She was supposed to hunt me down in case I found an opportunity to run. The idea had amused me but Deron assured me that Googs wouldn't forget her training no matter how friendly I got with her. In fact, so he said, the better the hound became acquainted with me, the easier I would be for her to keep track of.

Deron was some kind of professor-spy who liked nothing better than to put on dirty clothes and pitch hay or try to ride Bandit. Or maybe being a cowpoke-spy was his profession and donning the university cloak was the way he spent his vacations. Where Wheaty was of medium height and strongly built, Deron was tall and wiry. Where the former was possible to get to know, the latter wasn't.

"My ex-wife accused me of being unknowable," he said to me. It was later in the morning and he was looking off into the distance, squinting his almond-shaped brown eyes. "She said I had no pzing. When I asked her what that meant, she said it included everything ordinary."

He climbed onto Bandit's back, stayed there about thirty seconds, picked himself up out of the dirt and dusted his jeans with his big hat. "A psychiatrist once told me to father a child, or adopt one."

"Don't look at me. Your ex-wife was right. You're cold as a frog."

"I wasn't looking at you except in a clinical way. I doubt if Kisko will ever get any use out of you. You're a maverick like this horse."

I untacked the mount who was quiet now, scarcely heaving from the exertion of having cleared his back of unwelcome weight. "Do you know why you can't ride him?" I said to Deron. "You tell me."

"You're afraid of him." Taking handfuls of the coarse black mane, I swung astride the broad back and kicked hard with my bare heels. We jumped every fence on the place and took off across an endless plain of flowing grass. I kicked that animal black and blue and he loved every second of it, responded by bucking like a truck that had suddenly lost its shocks. More kicks and a few shouts and again we raced with the wind, ate up the ground as if it were speeding toward us and not the other way around.

I had good legs and knew just where to grip that specimen to diminish his speed. One thing a horse took note of was a rider who sat down hard and dug in with the knees. How did I know? It was just as well that no one asked me, since I had no answer. At any rate, when I eased the pressure, Bandit showed his appreciation by charging like an express train. Far behind us came the baying of a hound. Poor Googs. All she would get for her efforts today was a taste of dust.

I lay on top of a hill, sucking in air and sweating like a coolie. Bandit grazed nearby, tethered on a long vine. It had taken an hour of walking to cool him off. The sun tried to blind me, bugs made a strong attempt to eat me alive, my soul was in repose. I stuffed on apples, found a walnut tree and a hard rock and sampled several dozen, swilled from a brook, consumed red berries, blackberries, strawberries, crab apples and chewed sassafras bark.

That horse should have been named Took Off. It was all he ever did. Together we found an old mountain trail, climbed it in a hurry and descended even more rapidly. By then it was dusk and in a little while the sun would be gone. A car came winding across the valley toward the road leading to the cabin, turned in and increased speed. Bandit and I came off the mountain trail directly in front of it. My steed showed his annoyance at the intrusion by standing on his hind legs and pawing the wind. I caught a glimpse of a dark-haired man in the driver's seat, his expression frozen as he cut sharply to avoid us and plowed into some thick brush.

Bandit showed him a fat rear and we galloped back to the ranch ahead of a man who was undoubtedly the boss. That evening I lay in my bed and listened to them quarrel.

His tone icy and thick with sneers, Kisko said, "What kind of specialists have we here? Two grown men can't sit on a little kid for a few days. Maybe I should find less complicated work for you. Could be I should perhaps dislike the sight of your faces so much I wouldn't want to issue paychecks to you anymore."

Wheaty and Deron mostly mumbled their responses. They usually backed up whenever Kisko was angry or sarcastic, which was most of the time.

"I think you're fussing more than the situation warrants. She came back, didn't she?" I thought it was Wheaty who said that but I couldn't be sure. Actually, I didn't care.

"Sure, because she ate a gutful of green fruit and didn't want to be sick all alone in the big cruel world. What'll you do the next time she gets away? Send her a message? Please, kid, return to us otherwise we get our cans canned? That's the idea I'm entertaining at the moment. It's giving me indigestion. Furthermore, I want that dog out of the cabin and in the stable where it belongs."

Wheaty came in and took Googs away but I didn't object because I was too busy wanting to die. My belly stuck out like a watermelon and felt like a hot brick.

I was sick for three days. With Kisko at the ranch, the situation grew rife with strife. When I discovered I was going to survive my bout with wild fruit, I relaxed and fell back into my more slovenly ways. I loafed and was uncooperative about answering questions and expressing a willingness to earn my keep. For my efforts, Kisko put me in a cage, had Wheaty and Deron build one out of wood and hung it on the front porch.

"You shouldn't have done this to me," I said. "Just when I was beginning to think we could get along."

"You bet. Exactly what I was thinking. Like Socrates and his favorite thirst quencher." Kisko was calm, always calm, but his eyes glittered. Once in a while he rubbed them. His hair was black and so curly it looked like greedy little fingers clutching his head. His shoulders were too big, his waist too small, his hands too clean, his nose too narrow, his teeth too large, his mind too keen.

Making the cage rock back and forth on its rope, I said, "What's the point you're trying to make?"

"It concerns castles and kings and who gives the orders around here."

"It's easy to give orders but what if you have no takers?"

He smiled. "See the point?"

"I can get out of here any time I want."

"At any given moment?"

"Like spit from between my teeth."

He stopped smiling. "The first time you touch that horse without permission, I'll put a bullet in his brain."

It took me a couple of minutes to digest that. "I won't ride him without permission," I said, finally.

"You see? Already we're making point after point."

"You should have bought someone else from that slave block. I hold grudges."

"You're going to get even with me for locking you up?"

"No, for threatening an animal that never did you any harm. You can lock me up but you can't keep me locked up."

"We'll see," he said harshly. "Speaking of threats, as long as you make them so eloquently and convincingly, stay where you are. Live in a cage like a monkey. Eat like a brute. Learn your lesson, muter. My name is Kisko. You work for me or you don't live like a human. For all I care, you can stay in there for the rest of your life."

"There's such a thing as the law."

"Forget it. I'm the law."

That evening Wheaty came to see me. "Go away," I said. "I know he sent you to soften me up."

"Since when could I soften up a rock? I just brought some insect spray to make sure the mosquitoes leave enough of you for me to feed breakfast." He squirted from a can and I complained about the fact that he got some on me. "We'll give you good schooling if you cooperate with us," he said. "Deron knows his business. You'll have the best food, you can ride that maniac in the stable and keep the dog in your room. There are a lot worse jobs you could be offered."

"Which one is the expert about rings? You or Deron?"

"Neither, but he knows more than I do. Why?"

"There's something I can't remember. Ask him a question for me."

"Sure."

"If a person is injured in D-2, comes back to D-1 and then returns to D-2, will she materialize with the same injury?"

"I'll go ask him." Wheaty hesitated. "What do you mean, you can't remember? How could you forget something like that?"

"I told you. If you don't believe I have amnesia, I can't help it."

He went away and returned in a few minutes. "He says you won't have the same wound." He peered through the wooden slats at me. The light from the window played across his anxious face. He reminded me of the dog. "What's on your mind?" he said. "Are you brewing more trouble?"

"Give my regards to Kisko."

The secret was in the color of the rings and not in one particular spot of turf. For instance, if I wanted to go to my old camping ground in D-2, I had to find a ring the right shade of blue. Going back to Mutat wouldn't make the task any easier because it didn't matter where the rings were. As for the sky outside my cage, there were more colored circles now than there had been during the day, and a blue one changed course at my silent suggestion and dropped within range of the alarms in the paddocks. There were scrambling movements inside the house before Wheaty and Deron broke through the doorway together.

"Nothing to worry about out here, boss!" Wheaty bellowed as he shone a flashlight on the wall alarm. "There's nothing within a half-mile!" To me he said, "Listen, I see no reason for you to bust a gut laughing over this. You want us to pull you out of there and give you a beating?"

"I have to go to the bathroom."

"That's too bad. You don't get free until your manners improve."

I hunched in a corner and whined.

"Cut that out," he said.

"You're reacting to her," said Deron.

"Just shut your educated mouth."

"You know better than to think twice about any of them. I can't see how this one could possibly reach you. She's the worst I've ever seen."

Wheaty just looked at him and then went back inside. Deron watched me for a while with a smirk on his face.

"You're mad because I know how to ride Bandit," I said.

He didn't say anything, merely smirked some more and then followed Wheaty.

The lights in the sky were colored moons with smokey coronas, not enough of them to blot out the stars but sufficient to make it look like Christmas. Resembling candles, some of the lights hung low and burned to flickering little sputterings as they receded into the distance, or they smoked and did awkward dances like flashlight beams on a wall. The one that had inspired the commotion was long gone.

Lying in a corner of the cage, I bided my time and watched for something useful to come along. Being the restless type, I needed something to do so I began rocking the cage. It squeaked like a rusty gate and by and by I heard low mutterings from in-

side the cabin. Eventually the three of them came outside. Kisko
was in a smoldering mood but his voice was cool as he ordered
Wheaty and Deron to take the cage inside. They complained
that it wouldn't fit through the door while he assured them in his
best hatchet tone that it would, and it did.

Wheaty stood outside the bathroom door and when I dawdled
too long he kicked open the door, picked me up and put me back
in the cage that was now in the middle of my bedroom.

As soon as they all got soundly to sleep again, the ring alarms
went off. "You're enjoying every minute of this," Kisko said to
me. His glittering eyes were droopy-lidded and dangerous.

Deron was studying the wall alarm. "There's a ring right outside the window."

"What are the odds it or another one moves inside the house
and straight through that cage?"

"About a million to one. We're worrying for nothing."

"Shut off the alarms. Let's go to bed. I can sleep with odds
like those."

They went to sleep and I went to D-2, waited until the cabin
was shadow-quiet before beckoning for the ring to come to me.
It was blue, not the exact shade I would have preferred but good
enough to get me out of the cage and the cabin and away from
the three human hard-hearts. I timed it accurately. The blue
donut didn't drift slowly but came at a rapid pace, upended so it
seemed to stand on edge as it sped across the floor. It was big
enough so that I didn't need to do anything but just sit there and
give it permission to close over me. It continued on through the
house and probably flew skyward while I landed on a hot rock in
Gothland.

Of course I had taken a chance traveling. The last time I left
this planet I was in extremely poor condition. While in the cage
my prime worry had been that Deron was wrong and I would
revert to my former state. Fortunately that didn't turn out to be
the case. My two-hundred-kilo mass was healthy and whole and
because I was so appreciative I ran fifty miles without stopping.

Where rings and muting were concerned, I had an almost infallible memory, therefore I knew this particular spot had never
been one of my favorite landing places. The fact that I often
grounded in unfamiliar territory in D-2 was the reason I

believed the planet was immense. At any rate, I didn't have a cache of food here and there wasn't much of anything to do that was interesting.

After a few days I was restless, felt out of sorts, even experienced odd stirrings in my psyche. Or was it in my stomach? I found myself listening for the baying of a foolish old hound and the clop clop of a horse's hooves. Where was the sweet wind here, the burgeoning orchards, the green apples that tasted so good and made me feel so bad? It seemed I could almost taste the perspiration on my upper lip as the sun beat down on my human body. I didn't recognize the feeling but I was homesick.

Shrugging off ennui, I stashed some drees in an ice pit, went swimming in a lake of black pitch, rambled through miles of labyrinths until I eventually gave up the pretense and flopped down beside a bubbling volcano to mourn. The thought of going to D-3 lent me no inspiration. The truth was, I had no desire to grow scales and swim in an endless ocean. I seemed to have lost my appetite for living. If I had any will at all, it was to ride a horse and kiss a dog.

Kisko was charging the battery in his car when I came walking up the road. He straightened as if the cable in his hand had given him an electric shock. Finally he turned and bent again to his task, ignoring me. When I got within hearing range, he said, "I'm going to do you a favor and tell you to leave. I'm giving you the best opportunity you'll ever have in your life. Go back wherever you came from. Hide under a cabbage or go to the devil, only get away from this ranch."

Later he showed me a stray cat that had taken possession of a corner of the barn. In the nest with her were six black kittens. They looked like tiny goths. While I sat and watched them, I thought about Kisko. Had he known all along that I would come back? Could he have been so clever that he knew how strong an appeal there was in a horse, a dog and a piece of country?

# 4

I LAY IN MY BED and listened to them fight. Wheaty was yelling, something he did a great deal of these days.

"You heard her yourself! She doesn't even remember about ring channels. That proves she really does have amnesia. Since when do we use sick kids?"

"You mean wise kids," said Deron.

"So you don't like her, so shut your mouth! You, Kisko, what do you think you're doing? What are we running here?"

"A ladies' benevolent sorority, or didn't you know?" came the rasping reply. "Every day we succor the underprivileged and bind up the wounded. In our spare moments, we counsel the confused. We go out of our way to keep people from getting their tender toes stepped on."

"But a sick—"

"Are we at war or a garden party? Since when do I have to contend with my own men? What do *you* think we're running here?"

"This isn't right."

"Then go find me somebody who is right. That's what I sent you out for in the first place. I didn't tell you to bring me a runny-nosed brat."

"There are no more. Every muter is strictly accounted for. Except for her, the market is dried up. I've watched the papers.

Not a word, no advertisements, no reward offers, no nothing has turned up. I don't think anyone is looking for her."

"Which makes the situation here even sadder, I can tell by looking at your face. Except that it makes it better for us. A muter maw doesn't like the taste of anything but muters, right? Isn't that what you think we are? A mouth that eats children?"

The argument ended there but only for the time being. While Wheaty was usually noisy these days, Kisko was almost always angry. He didn't like it that he couldn't pump my brain after giving me a shot of Pentothal.

"What is it with you?" he would say in his most impersonal fashion while I sat being a runny-nosed brat. "Maybe I ought to get a specialist in here to excise that blood clot in your head, or was that little story a lie? Don't bother to answer because it might be a lie, too. How did you get away from us that night? It was a million to one shot against the ring coming into the room yet it did. I'd be gratified if you explained."

"Deron isn't all that good at mathematics."

"How do I get you to work if you remain so independent?"

"In other words, you went looking for a puppet but came up with a real live person."

"Take a ride on Bandit and break your neck. Play with a wolf and contract rabies. I suddenly don't delight in your presence."

I could only guess why he wanted me in the first place. He seldom answered questions, particularly when they were mine. As for ring channels, Deron explained them to me. They were the method by which most muters operated since waiting for a ring of a specific color to come along consumed too much time. The channels were flowing streams of circles of different shades and shapes and could be found in many areas. Their positions remained more or less constant and there was one in the town east of the ranch.

"Why should I bother telling you anything?" Deron said to me. "You don't intend to cooperate. You only hang around because of the animals and Kisko."

"How did you work with the others before me?"

"Hypnotism, brainwashing, drugs, whatever worked best. The first two have no effect on you while the third puts you to sleep."

"Physiological difference?" I said.

"Not a permanent one. I think you really are sick. The X-rays I took show a definite mass in a critical area of your brain. By a rare stroke of luck, it might disperse with time. If it goes gradually, you'll return to normal, whatever that is. If it moves all at once, you're gone."

He took me to see the ring channel. "As far as I'm concerned, there's nothing there but blank space, but it's been described to me by plenty of muters. What does it look like to you?"

"It's a stream about three meters high," I said. "Most of the rings are small but some are fairly big. They're all moving in a more or less straight line at about ten kilometers an hour. There are reds, greens, blues, browns, grays and plenty of off-shades."

"I'm sick of your lying," he said. "Why don't you confine it to certain periods throughout the day? It's difficult to tolerate it all the time."

"Anything you say," I said, not having the faintest idea what had set him off.

I thought it was uncanny that the majority of people couldn't see rings. The people in the town walked right through the flowing channel as if it didn't exist. Had I done something like that—now that the question occurred to me, I discovered I didn't know the answer. What would happen? Would I be distributed in D-1 and D-2 in several portions, would several of me appear in several places in those other dimensions, or would one of them capture all of me?

"It depends," said Deron, when I asked him. "What that means is, I don't know. The few cases I've heard of where an infant wandered into a channel, they landed whole in either D-1 or D-2. The better the vision, the more control over rings a muter has, or so I've been told. Somebody who doesn't really see them clearly hasn't a great deal of resistance to their lure. Animals are like that."

That evening he tried to ride Bandit and broke his arm when he landed in the water tub. Instructing Wheaty as to how to set it and mount a cast, he sat disagreeably through dinner.

"Does she have to sniffle like that?" he said.

"She has a cold," said Wheaty.

"Why don't you adopt her?"

"I should have filled that cast with poison ivy. As soon as it comes off, I'm going to break your jaw. And another thing. If you damage one hair of that horse, I'll break your other arm and both your legs."

I studied maps in front of the cold fireplace. Lying on a thick rug, I perspired and looked at rings and blueprints of labyrinths. It was nearly eighty degrees inside. The air-conditioners were off because of my cold.

"This is too much work," I said.

"What good are you to me if you won't learn your assignments?" said Kisko. Even when sitting in an overstuffed chair he managed to look tense and unfriendly.

"I mean it isn't necessary for me to bother with these maps. Show me a color and tell me what to do."

Throwing a photograph of a blue ring at me, he said, "Run down the tunnel you find on the other side of this."

"Is that all?" I started to get up.

"Not now. In the morning." He rubbed his eyes.

I grinned. "After a good night's sleep? When I'm rested?" Non-muters kept forgetting we changed bodies when we traveled.

"Deron was right. You're wise. Go now, go tomorrow, go to the devil. I'll have him drive you to the channel."

"I don't want the channel."

"I can't wait all week."

"You turned off all the alarms, otherwise you'd know there are about a hundred rings outside."

"It has to be the right shade. How can you learn the color I want by just glancing at it? You can't do it."

"I have a good eye. No, don't come out with me. I couldn't bear to watch you grieve."

"Wise, wise, but take care. If you want to live . . ."

"I shouldn't go at all?"

He was angry when I came back into the cabin ten minutes later. "What's the matter? Was I wrong or wasn't I? You couldn't find the right color. Great. At this rate I'll have you trained in at least ten years."

"I don't know why you're mad. I did the job. What more do you want?"

"Naturally. You went to the correct place in D-2 because it

took you only a couple of minutes to find the correct ring in the yard outside and then you hustled down the correct tunnel and came back to me to report."

"Sure."

"And I suppose it was a multi-colored tunnel with silver sequins on the walls?"

"It was red with scar marks all over it. It was shaped like an hourglass."

He blinked three times and threw another photograph at me. "Of course I'll expect you back in ten minutes."

I was back in nine. He timed me by his watch, listened to me describe a short, wide corridor with a white arrow painted on the right side.

"That's enough," he said. "Go to bed."

The next day he had Deron examine my eyes. "What's the matter with him?" I said. "Why is he always so suspicious of everything?"

"Of course it isn't in your vision," said Deron. "He knows that. We all know it. It's in your mind. Maybe the explanation is that you have a photographic memory for colors. But that's no answer for the other mysteries, such as why you don't require the channels to find the rings you want. Could be you'll tell me one of these days?" When I didn't reply, he said, "Have you always been able to operate this way?"

Cheerfully I said, "I don't remember."

Wheaty had a fit when he found out my assignment for the day would be tunnel number ten. I didn't even know what it was.

"You haven't even prepared her!" he said to Kisko. "Can't you work her up to it like the others? If you're that anxious to get rid of her, take her up some country road and dump her out. She's at least as good as a cat!"

"She's ready now. Go work on the generator. It's not functioning properly and neither are you."

"Tunnel eight!"

"Ten. Every hour counts." Kisko had some words for me before I left for work. He repeated himself when he said he didn't like the fact that truth drugs seemed to shut my mouth rather than open it because that was how he had always interviewed his scouts after their stints in D. Their answering simple, straightforward questions wasn't reliable since the grave possibility existed that they might miss some little detail.

"Sorry about that," I said. "Every time I think about blabbing from my subconscious something slams shut in my head, like a door. Maybe that really does happen. You know, if you don't trust me enough to tell me what I'm supposed to be looking for in D, I'll most likely overlook it. I'm beginning to think my best course would be for you to give me possession of Bandit, Googs and the cats and bid me adieu."

After blinking, rubbing his eyes and wiping several thunderous scowls off his face, he agreed to describe a few landmarks in which I should take interest that afternoon when I went to Gothland.

He did and I wasn't pleased about it. "I'm supposed to estimate the height of a ledge at the end of tunnel ten and estimate the circumference of the tunnel entrance above it?" I looked at him and kept looking until he averted his gaze. "We're right back where we started and you haven't told me a thing. You're saying I don't need to worry about points of landscape because what I'm supposed to notice will be so noticeable I can't miss it. Okay. So long." I walked down the road, went behind the barn and looked through the mess of rings hovering over a swamp. I called one to me.

Upon my return from Gothland, I stopped in the barn to see why Maverick was making such a fuss. That was the name I had given the mother cat. She snarled and growled until I chased away a big groundhog, after which I sat down to play with the kittens. It was warm and quiet and before long I fell asleep.

Deron awakened me by yelling his head off. He stood over me looking amazed and frustrated. Wheaty came running, Kisko came running, Maverick began squalling and then I was dragged away to the house like a truant.

Why had I fallen asleep in the barn? Why had I gone into the barn in the first place? Didn't I take this business seriously? Never mind my trying to answer that, why hadn't I reported back immediately? All the questions coming at me at once served to shut my mouth better than truth drugs had ever done it. Hadn't I been aware that they thought I was dead? Why should they think such a thing? Because I hadn't come back!

"Why shouldn't I be all right?" I bellowed when I had the chance. "There wasn't anything there, just the tunnel, the ledge and another tunnel above it, and there wasn't anything in the second hole besides a bunch of black rocks."

"You weren't supposed to go in that one!" Wheaty yelled.

Kisko made Deron take Wheaty away and then he and I sat in the living room and discussed my journey. I assured him both tunnels had been uninteresting and even boring.

"In fact, it was even annoying because of the noise made by some waterfalls somewhere overhead," I said.

He found that interesting.

"There are a lot of falls in D-2, and some of them are really huge so you can't expect total silence anywhere in the dimension," I said.

Since he asked, yes, the noise had sounded louder at the far end of the second tunnel. Sitting in the chair cross-legged, I supported my chin in my hands. "Why didn't you tell me in the first place that what you were really interested in was the noise? You think it's something besides waterfalls, don't you? After I ride Bandit, exercise Googs and feed Maverick, I'll go track it down. Never mind all those dumb routines of checking out tunnels one at a time to see if I know what I'm doing. I'll just go and find out what the noise is."

His eyes must have bothered him fiercely, the way he dug at them with his knuckles. "That sounds like a reasonable idea," he said, not looking at me. "However, I don't want you going beyond the pit. Not this time. Do you understand?"

"I assume I'll recognize the pit when I see it. Okay, I won't go beyond it."

Wheaty followed me around all the rest of the afternoon. "I'm only making sure you're comfortable. That's all right, isn't it? I mean, that's my job. I'm a nursemaid, a wet nurse."

"Which means I'm a baby. Listen, Wierton, just because I can't find my birth certificate doesn't mean a thing. For all you know I'm much older than I seem."

"Don't call me that. I like Wheaty better. About the trip to the pit later, I'm telling you to call it off. In fact, you're going to get on a bus and hightail it out of here. This is no place for you."

"How many have the three of you put in that meat grinder?"

"What are you talking about?"

"Haven't you been yelling that you're killing kids?"

His homely face reddened and his voice rose. "How dare you say a thing like that? Nobody's killing kids!"

"You send them on missions into D-2 and they don't come back. What do you call it?"

He groaned. "Never mind that. Kisko's kidding you, as usual. He doesn't expect you to come back, once you reach the pit. He wants you to make it because he needs the information but he doesn't expect it. Neither do I. Meet me at sundown at the end of the road and I'll drive you to the bus stop."

Before sundown, I was in D-2 chasing and being chased by sloks. How I had hated going into that tunnel. To begin with, it was too narrow. Three meters into it, I knew it wasn't for me so I backed all the way out onto Earth to find one more to my liking. Materializing behind the barn on the ranch, I ran across the field in pursuit of a smaller circle that was an almost perfect match for the first. This time in Gothland I found a series of tunnels each of which could have accommodated three goths my size. The openings were side by side in a straight line and, since the middle one appealed to me, I went in at an easy trot.

The noise was so loud I couldn't hear anything else so I kept a weather eye peeled on my fore and aft. About fifty meters into the tunnel, I rounded a bend and came to a dead stop. Several meters ahead of me a slok fed on the remains of a goth. It was balanced on its bottom tip like a fat, round accordion, its neck extended and bent to the carcass, its teeth clicking as it tore the flesh to pieces.

Carefully I retreated and left that particular tunnel. The second one I tried was narrower and straighter so that I could see into it for at least a quarter-mile. The way looked clear so in I went at a fast lope.

Everything appeared to be fine and I was making good time, with nothing threatening, when all of a sudden the hackles on my neck rose. Without pausing or losing my coordination, I performed the most graceful horse kick of my career, braced on my front paws, let my great weight go forward for a moment and then swing backward as my big feet went up and out. I connected with something, kicked it against the tunnel ceiling with all the force of which I was capable.

Feeling pleased with myself, I looked down at the unconscious slok. It would be asleep all night. Directly above me was a deep niche in the stone where the creature had been crouching. Luckily my timing had been perfect and my feet had caught and hurled it even as it plummeted toward my back.

The sloks were stupid, or maybe that was a shortcoming of whoever gave them their orders. They were stationed in niches at quarter-mile intervals along the corridor and they weren't difficult to detect. I dispatched six ugly specimens before arriving at the pit. Four were gotten rid of quite simply. Making sure of a niche's location, I deliberately loped beneath it and then abruptly sprang backward while the slok leaped for my nonexistent back. Before he landed, I was astraddle him and gripping his neck in my jaws. As for the two remaining creatures, I kicked them into insensibility.

I don't know why the machinery in the pit astonished me because even innocuous Gorwyn had managed to transmutate common objects into harnesses and anesthetic guns.

The machinery was immense, as was the pit itself. Knowing that the tunnel behind me was at least temporarily free of sloks, I lay on the ledge and looked down at about two hundred sloks and goths who worked in what appeared to be an open factory. The machinery, which dominated everything, seemed to be an engine with double bores that disappeared into two mountain walls. If I hadn't known better, I would have said it was a cannon.

The goths appeared to be doing what they did voluntarily. They weren't being forced or coerced, at least not that I could see. In harmony they and the sloks worked on small machines in a cleared area, or they climbed in and out of the big engine, polishing, lubricating, testing parts, putting the monster into operating condition, or rather improving or maintaining that condition, because it plainly functioned. The entire area shook and vibrated in response to the power being generated and unleashed there.

I was alternately counting machines and personnel and looking back over my shoulder when a troop of sloks came down the corridor on the hunt for whoever or whatever had knocked out their sentries. They spotted me at about the same time I spotted them, but they were too late and merely chopped the air where I had been lying. I leaped to a ledge directly above and outside the tunnel where I crouched, reached down and swiped them into the pit, one by one.

In a short time every slok and goth in the place was climbing a ladder after me. As soon as they were all off the pit floor, I did some climbing of my own, in big leaps and bounds downward until I reached the bore on the right side of the excavation. I ran across the top of it.

Some sloks came out of the door in the giant engine while a single specimen followed me across the metal pipe. Wondering what to do next, I spied a green ring speeding from inside the mountain wall and into the clearing. Stepping up my pace until I was moving parallel with it, I skipped sideways and flung myself through its center. As I was doing this, a goth dropped from a low ledge in the rock wall and followed me.

My entrance into Waterworld was accomplished only a second ahead of it but it was enough time for me to grab hold of a shell and swoop inside it. I and the shell's tenant, a pink wormlike creature, both watched a male swimmer come through the blue donut in a hurry. He looked about with anticipation and did a double take when he didn't see anyone. Swiftly he whirled, even shaded his eyes with his hands for a few minutes while he shoved water out of his way. The shell drifted in front of him and he pushed it aside.

A clump of seaweed came within easy reach so I waved goodbye to the startled worm and changed my hiding place. While the swimmer looked about in puzzlement, I got a good look at his face. He was a stranger but at least I would recognize him if I ever saw him again. That was the second important thing I would think about when I had time. The first was the worm in the shell. As far as I could recall, there wasn't supposed to be anything alive in Waterworld but flora and muters.

So much for friends and associates. The only one of the three back at the ranch who hadn't wanted me to go on this suicide mission was Wheaty. Only the fact that I happened to be bigger than anybody in the neighborhood had prevented me from ending up in a slok's belly.

I felt low. I felt hated and neglected. I decided I needed a vacation so instead of returning to the ranch I went to Paris. It wasn't difficult. I'd been there before and knew all the right rings to take.

I was wearing a stetson Wheaty had given me and people stared at it. A muter always came out of D wearing the same things she had worn during or prior to her entry. My cowboy outfit was a bit out of place here. With the wages in my pocket I bought some Japanese pajamas and thongs and was thereafter ignored by everybody.

The Boulevard Voltaire didn't match its reputation which was primarily sustained by those who saw only picture postcards or travel brochures. In actuality the street was an anachronism existing for the tourists who liked to be reminded that once upon a time the remainder of the city and, indeed, the streets of most cities resembled this. Inside, the buildings were bulwarked with modern steel and plastic while outside, the decaying brick and clapboard were periodically sprayed with a strong, transparent glue that kept them from falling onto the pavement. At an angle overhead, the skyscrapers reared. The street's tenants only lived in the ramshackle buildings during working hours, hurrying to their modern apartments at dusk. They were professional live-ins.

The Bastille on the Rue St. Antoine had collapsed long ago and the ugly red structure rearing in its place was totally artificial. Tourists didn't mind that it wasn't genuine, nor did they stop visiting Paris simply because everything worth seeing had been copied and rebuilt in many places on the globe. The Bridge of Sighs was also in Chicago, the Tower of London jutted from the tundra of Siberia, a plastic pyramid marred the landscape of Oahu.

Having viewed the sights to my content, I decided to conduct an experiment, located a ring channel beside a filthy river and brashly walked into it. It was a good-size channel, seemingly appearing from thin air inside a thicket and rushing for several yards along the river bank before plunging into nothingness beside a tree. At any rate, I wanted to find out whether or not I could be broken into a dozen parts and distributed haphazardly about the countrysides of D-1 and D-2. How I'd extricate myself from the situation if such turned out to be the case didn't occur to me.

Feeling a hundred little fingers pressuring me as the rings swept by, I finally began to grow nervous. I kept telling them in my mind that I didn't want to enter them, and I didn't enter any of them, but their desire for me was tangible. A red circle rushed straight at me like a scarlet maw and, suddenly terrified that it wouldn't heed my wishes, I sucked in my stomach and jumped all the way out of the channel.

So much for friends and vacations. An hour or so later I trudged up the dusty road to the ranch. Googs was sleeping on the front porch and didn't awaken as I sat down beside her. I stayed there for a long time, just looking at the dark horizon, and by and by someone pushed upon the screen door and came out. Kisko didn't say a word, merely stood staring at me as if at an apparition.

# 5

THE OLD HERMIT was still in Gothland, though he made himself
difficult to find. I tracked him for three days and finally cornered
him in a cave. I think he was expecting a slok or an unfriendly
goth because he almost fell over in a dead faint when I stepped
into view. So shaken he couldn't speak, he lay gasping and waving me away with a paw. I tried talking to him but it was no
good. It must have taken him a long time to learn how to do it.

"You had no right!" he said later, indignant and most of all
afraid. We were now in D-1.

"Stop looking around like that. There's nobody here. Don't
you think I have any sense? This is a cornfield in Peoria. Who
would think of looking for anyone in this spot?"

"Ignorance is a big problem with you!" he snapped. "And quit
gawking at me."

"I can't help it. You look like a diplomat or an aristocrat or
both. The aura around you in D-2 was plain bum."

"And yours was of a great lady, so we were both wrong." He
kept glancing about, primarily at the sky. "I have to go back immediately. How dare you take me by the scruff of the neck and
haul me out of my home? If I wanted to live here on Earth, you
wouldn't have met me in the first place. And what's the meaning
of your turning into a pint-size moppet after being as big as a
rhinoceros?" He was thin and balding, dressed elegantly in a

striped suit with stiff white collar and shiny shoes. It was uncanny how his aura disagreed with his actual self. "I can't stay,"
he said. His large eyes were doleful, reminding me of Wheaty.
Extending his right arm, he pushed up his sleeve and showed me
a narrow scar. "There's a radio implanted in there. They'll be
here within five minutes and that will mean the end of me."

"So will the sloks."

He shivered. "I'd rather take my chances with them. Let me
go back. I'd prefer to stay here and spend a few years examining
you but when it's my life you take second place."

"Who's after you?"

"Believe me, names wouldn't mean a thing to you."

"How about Ectri?"

"Never heard of him, her or it."

At least he needn't go back where the sloks were busy hunting
for him. While I called a fat blue ring of familiar shade to me, he
explained that five minutes had never been enough time for him
to exit onto Earth and then find a more suitable place in Gothland. Like other muters, he had to rely on ring channels or the
rare coincidence of a useful circle happening by.

The ring paused beside us, hovered. "I've never heard of anyone like you. How long can you hold it there?" He sounded clinical in spite of his anxiety.

"At least long enough to find out if you're telling the truth
about the radio." No sooner had I said it than two fast ships
hurtled out of the clouds and headed in our direction. They were
small cruisers, streamlined and official looking.

"I'm not a fugitive, or not the kind you're thinking," said my
companion. "Incidentally, you may call me Croff."

"I'm Daryl."

"How do you do?" With that, he fled into the ring and I followed.

A week later I ran away from the ranch, rode Bandit and held
onto a box containing Maverick and her kittens while Googs ran
along behind us. We got about twenty kilometers beyond the
town before Deron came with the trailer to take us back. I had
nothing to say and refused to answer any questions.

"Of course I did nothing to make her angry," said Kisko. It

was night and I lay in bed staring at the dark ceiling, listening to them.

"Must have," said Wheaty. "She wouldn't get mad about any-thing Deron or I did. You went to Spain on your vacation, didn't you?"

"What of it?"

Wheaty sounded tired. "You pay me to keep an eye on her, which is an out-and-out impossibility, but I think I understand a couple of things about her so I'm asking you what you did on your vacation."

"Loafed in the sun, surfed, made some business contacts. That's it."

"Are you sure? No other contacts?"

"What's that supposed to mean?"

"Ladies happens to be the subject I'm sidling around the bush about."

"None. Oh, I ran into a woman I used to know. We had din-ner and I drove her to the airport."

"And you kissed her good-bye."

"What is this?" said Kisko. "What are you driving at?"

"The kid must have followed you," said Deron. "She found out where in Spain you were going and then she followed you."

"How could she do that?"

"Today you're wearing the dunce cap. We're talking about a ring-hopping flea, not an ordinary girl. She saw you playing the ardent acquaintance and now she won't work for us anymore. She won't even tell us about that last trip."

Wheaty and Kisko left the cabin and Deron came into my room. Turning on the light, he sat down in a chair. "Wheaty said to tell you he was glad you decided not to go into D anymore. He also mentioned that if he had known I was going after you, he'd have sabotaged the trailer. Next time, he said, do it at night while we're all asleep."

"I'm not particularly interested in this conversation," I said. "I hardly ever believe anything you say."

"Yeah, I know. How did the pit look?"

Weary of resisting, I said, "Deep and noisy."

"How many little machines?"

"Twelve."

"They've added two. They're power pods. They drive the engine."

"What does it do?"

"Nothing, yet, except make noise."

"What will it do?"

"We don't know. That's why we have you. I appreciate your telling me. Why don't you just scram away from here by yourself and let Wheaty send the animals to you later?"

"You'd get another kid," I said.

"What do you care? Besides, I don't think so. The market is all dried up." He looked at me with almond-shaped brown eyes that were steady, unfriendly and deceptive. "You can fool them but not me. You're here for kicks, not those animals that you could have swiped a dozen times. You're not here for money or an infantile crush on a man old enough to be your father and then some. All those things enter into your thinking, but that's all. D doesn't scare you. Nothing does. Why is that?"

The library in New York had volumes of words about transmutation but very little that I wanted to know. What was a muter? Why did they have an extra chromosome? What were the other dimensions? There were answers galore in that largest of libraries in the world but none seemed accurate or to the point. A goth couldn't talk? I knew one that could. A muter was dependent upon the chance movement of rings? I knew one who wasn't. Muters simply traded one body mass for another? Indeed?

The list of those who were expert in the field of transmutating was small. Biographical articles were accompanied by photographs and I was surprised and amused to see a young Croff staring up at me from a glossy page. Beside his well-bred features was the name of Ja Parl. I didn't know or recognize any of the other faces, though one looked slightly familiar, a man named Bud Jupiter. Heavy bearded with a shock of gray hair, somewhere in his sixties, he reminded me of someone.

"You lied to me," I said to Croff later in Gothland. I didn't speak with my vocal cords but made marks in the dirt beside a volcano.

No, he hadn't, he said. He appreciated that I had brought him here to a safe place empty of sloks, and he hadn't lied. Parl was the name he had used at the University. It was his professional name. His real name was nobody's business.

To my displeasure, he soon developed a sore throat and couldn't talk to me anymore. Meanwhile I was wearing down the claw on my right forepaw. Our communication was brought to a forced halt so I waved good-bye to him, left the dimension and went back to the ranch.

"You're an educated fellow," I said to Deron, flattering him not at all. "Did you ever hear of radio implants?"

Ever cautious, he said, "What kind?"

"So the law can keep track of fugitives and other enemies of the realm. Don't bother to tell me it's illegal since I already know that. I also know it's done all the time."

"If you know so much why are you bruising my skull with questions?"

"You know those two bores in the pit?" I said. Immediately he grew tense and I took satisfaction from the fact. "I'll run the left one down if you do me a favor."

He wanted to know what I meant by running down the bore so I explained that I'd find out where it went. He then said I probably wouldn't be around to appreciate it when he did the favor if I embarked upon such a foolhardy venture.

"Which is why you have to do your part first," I said.

A few days later Croff was stupefied when I went bounding up the side of a low volcano in D-2, took the scruff of his neck in my jaws and climbed through a conveniently placed yellow ring. Wheaty and Deron were there in the room waiting for us. Wheaty tore off Croff's fancy coat, yanked up the shirt sleeve, found the scar I had described and swabbed it with antiseptic and anesthetic. Deron was ready with a wicked little knife, slit Croff's flesh and deftly scooped out the tiny receiver which was taken by Wheaty and crushed in a pair of pliers. A few swift stitches and a bandage slapped in place concluded the operation, and the dazed Croff was left staring in bewilderment at his arm.

Wheaty and Deron exited from the room and headed downstairs. From the open hotel room window, I saw their car speed away. "Come here," I said to Croff. A blue ring waited about ten feet below.

"They fixed our position," he said. "They had time. They can still find me." He looked at the ring and then at me. "You're joking, aren't you?" He turned pale. "My aim was always terrible. You could lure it closer, I know, but then you've a mean streak in you."

A police cruiser dropped from the sky, swung around the building and disappeared over the rooftop for a moment, just long enough for Croff to fall, bellowing, through the blue ring. I went head-first after him. One nice thing about going into D-2 was that a drop of twenty or thirty feet, or even more, was nothing to a goth. Our bodies were flexible enough to absorb a great deal of shock.

The rest of that day was tedious. We weren't in Gothland very long before Croff skipped out on me. He spied a crevice in a mountain and popped into it. I was too large to squeeze in after him. For a while I sat with my snout in the crack, snarling and spitting as I asked him what he thought he was doing, reminded him of the virtues of gratitude, but finally I realized he wasn't coming out. He had probably already gone through another opening in the rock and escaped out the other side of the mountain.

Back at the ranch, Wheaty and Deron made me irritable with their questions. They had agreed to help me get the radio out of Croff's arm but now they wanted to know the wherefores of what they had done.

"The only thing I know about him is that he was afraid of the police," I said. The complete truth was none of their business, not that I knew it either. Filling them in on every detail hadn't been part of the deal.

"Where does he come from?"

"I don't know."

"What's his full name?"

"I don't know."

"Why would anyone choose to live in D-2? What do the police want him for?"

I couldn't answer the first question to their satisfaction because they weren't muters and, as for the second, I suggested they probably knew as much about it as I, which was practically nothing.

"About the bore," said Kisko, but I didn't want to hear and

walked away. He followed. "I have my doubts that you can even get into it. There are too many . . ."

I didn't say it either, but I was thinking it. Not once had any of them ever mentioned the sloks. I wondered if they had an idea of what the enemy looked like. Not much at art, I made a stab at painting a big specimen on my bedroom wall that turned out to be realistic enough to make Wheaty yell at me.

"Why do you always have to do weird things? You do it all the time! Look at that nightmare!"

"What are you so upset about? They're not so bad when you get to know them. On the average they weigh a hundred and fifty kilos, own about eight dozen teeth and travel a hundred kilometers an hour when they're perturbed, which is ninety-eight percent of the time."

After they decided to let me alone, I sneaked away via a ring and visited Mutat. There I ransacked the living quarters of Padarenka and Mikala. The small bungalow sat in a grove of trees on the north edge of the campus.

Trying to describe the conglomeration of objects that would transmutate into a holster and loaded anesthetic gun was like trying to itemize the things a hard wind blew into a stairwell. There were little bits of debris all hanging on a shiny piece of string, including slivers of brick and quartz, some hardened glue, a scrap of paper, a drop of water encased in wax, an aspirin tablet and some things I didn't recognize. Either Gorwyn was a genius or he had to be crazy to have had the patience and tenacity to figure this out. All the junk on the string had to be there in its particular order or the process wouldn't work.

Very carefully I removed a loaded string from a box under Padarenka's bed and tied it about my waist, leaving so much slack I had to hold onto it. Even so, when I landed in D-2 a few minutes later, the gun and holster were so tight on my chest I wheezed.

Kisko was wrong when he said I wouldn't get inside the bore in the pit. The fact was, it turned out to be a matter of agility and deception on my part plus my own private brand of recklessness. There was nothing so thrilling as a chase in D-2. The goth physique was made for just such a pastime.

I could have found the proper ring and materialized on top of the bore but I chose to do it the tedious way, or the most interesting. Down the tunnel I prowled, dispatching the sloks hiding in the ceiling niches as I had done during my previous journey along this route, with one exception. No enemies would come down the corridor behind me for, having taken advantage of the engine's noise, I rolled several large boulders into the tunnel and then stacked them, plugging the passageway. I had a sore nose and paws when the job was done.

I emptied the pit by standing in the tunnel exit and spitting and snarling until all down below were inspired to climb up after me.

One of the half-dozen or more things I should have done before going into the engine house was to practice my aim with the sleep gun. I shot a slok in the tail and it didn't even faze him. He leaped for me so eagerly that he sailed clear over me and got kicked into the pit.

I ought to have found out what conditions were like inside the engine house, whether or not there were doors or overwhelming odds. A single archway was open, the one leading to the left bore. Its door was sliding shut as I entered the big, shiny concavity. The goth leaning his nose against a button on a banked panel received a sleeping dart in his ear, another in the fur on his back and another in his chest before he went down. The door stopped sliding shut.

There was only a moment or two for me to look around before I scampered through the half-open archway. During those few instants, I saw a great deal of expensive, ultra-modern equipment in the form of computers, temperature dials, pressure gauges, energy scales, and the like. There was also a small arsenal on one wall, a collection of guns, knives and bludgeons. Evidently each weapon had a magnetic attractor built into it because a goth wearing a metal harness tapped a button with a claw and a gun flew from the wall and across the compartment to lodge against his shoulder. With a twist of his head he used his tongue to activate the trigger and pellets began ricocheting around me. One singed the fur on my tail as I went beneath the half-closed archway. I galloped down the seemingly endless bore.

The place was like the inside of a cylindrical mirror, a dull gray, lambent lights reflecting dozens of images of myself, full of booming echoes that threatened to knock me down. Behind me came sloks and farther behind them came goths. The distance between the two groups lengthened so I slowed down long enough to see how a slok reacted when kicked against a metal wall. My specimen ceased troubling me almost at once, bounced off the ceiling like a limp bag and went skidding into the path of his associates.

It was easy to run in the bore. There wasn't a flaw anywhere in the shiny surface and my weight was sufficient to create traction. About seven meters in diameter, the cylinder seemed to stretch for miles. I knew I was in no danger as long as the situation remained as it was. I simply had to run faster than my pursuers.

Straight as an arrow the bore or pipe raced through D-2, vibrating, nearly dancing as the power pods back in the pit fed it with mighty juice. As I ran, I thought about the power of the machine. It wasn't doing anything but making noise but my imagination conjured up dire visions of what it could do. I saw the bore as a gigantic cannon aimed and ready to fire. At what? I couldn't think of a single answer. There seemed to be no reason in the world why the engine and its tubes should exist.

Patterns in my life seldom remained static. My sojourn through the metal hallway was disrupted by an optical illusion appearing ahead of me. By the time I saw it I was convinced I had run eighty or ninety kilometers.

The change in the landscape caused me to slow down. My enemies gained ground. Unable to make sense out of the intense light, I slowed even more. A slok made a grab for my tail, grabbed again. I wasn't too busy to give him a kick.

The light was green, a familiar enough shade and one that I saw every day, but this had a gray center that completely disoriented me. The scene was like a circular buzz saw embracing a center of darkness with everything whirling and swirling as if in a strong wind.

I hadn't much time to make up my mind, what with sloks preparing to surround me, but the fact that they didn't seem disturbed by the strange lights lent me courage. I barged ahead and waited to see what would happen.

The center of the circle changed to a glittering black. I didn't realize I was within the perimeter or corona of a large green ring until I fell through one of the openings in the pipe. Actually, I jumped. There was nowhere else to go unless I plunged into the maelstrom of blackness or unless I turned to fight the sloks and goths who seemed to have increased in numbers and ferocity. With the disorienting lights behind me, I faced the enemy, meanwhile looking for a way out.

On both sides of me, the holes suddenly came into view. At first I didn't think they were real, but as I began kicking sloks as fast as they attacked, I saw that the shapes in the steel didn't change position. For some reason, I thought of air vents. The holes were big enough and inviting and at the last minute, when it was obvious that I had to make a choice or go down, I took my option and backed through the nearest one.

One second I was a big, hairy goth and in the next I vanished. The green light had been the corona of a green ring and the holes in the pipe were entrances into the third dimension or Waterworld. All of a sudden I was a swimmer seven centimeters long. Instinctively I made like a wraith, ducked down along the side of the bore and lay flat against it while adult swimmers floated everywhere, searching.

Ever so slowly I drifted farther under the bore. Now and then a swimmer passed below me, but they were looking for a human-sized prey and not one who could fit herself around a few barnacles on the metal. I faded into the anonymity of familiar flotsam and while I waited for them to abandon their hunt, I thought about what I'd learned. What kind of people could build a pipe that extended through a green ring? Why had they done it? Also, what kind of people turned into sloks when they traded dimensions?

# 6

I WAS WALKING down a hot and dusty street in the town near Mutat when Pat and Mike sprang out from behind a tree to take me prisoner. They tied my hands and stuck tape across my mouth so I couldn't yell. After thrusting me in the back seat of their old gasoline burner, they rattled out of the territory and rode through the countryside for what seemed like years. It was actually only a few hours but I couldn't see through the venetian blinds on the windows and there was nothing for me to do but endure the stifling heat and brood over my past mistakes.

Grunting and groaning weren't satisfying pastimes but I had to do something, besides which the noises inspired my kidnapers to make occasional comments such as, "Shut up, brat," or "You're neck-deep in friction, kid," or "Your rotten little remains are going to save our hides, beast." Conceivably, they might eventually tell me something I could use.

From their mutterings I gathered they had made a nearly fatal error by selling a certain human property and now they intended to get back into someone's good graces by locating and snatching the same property. Trouble was, she was immune to truth drugs and was difficult to catch and hold onto.

Languishing in the hot automobile, I groaned and made garbled threats behind the tape. Who wanted me? Who had ordered them to pick me up? To whom were they delivering me?

They stopped to eat but didn't offer me anything. I could have used a cool drink, some fresh air and my freedom.

When the ground first began to shake, I wasn't aware of it. In a half-swoon from the heat, I gradually realized that Pat and Mike were concerned about something. Hope filtered through my sagging psyche. If they were in trouble, it could only mean the opposite for me.

It was late afternoon. Pat suddenly jammed on the brakes and she and Mike got out. The ground under me moved almost rhythmically, making me wonder if we were on train tracks. Perhaps they intended to kill me by stalling in front of an old transport. Or maybe we sat on the wobbly edge of a cliff.

Struggling up, I shoved aside the venetian blind with my head, peered through the back window and saw, to my surprise, that we were on a superthroughway in green country. Why, then, was the world gyrating? I noticed fresh air coming into my section and knew Pat and Mike had left their doors open while they gawked at the rippling turf beyond the road. Immediately I attacked a back door handle with my teeth. First I pulled up the lock after which I clamped the handle in my jaws and slowly applied pressure in the wrong direction.

Someone outside was yelling. Tires screeched, alarms sounded as drivers pressed buttons, horns on old models honked. I changed direction with my jaws, moaned in pain, pushed upward, choked and gurgled, all at once fell from the car as the door opened. Instead of falling onto macadam as I anticipated, I dropped into a culvert that had been created when the street split. Now the air was filled with such a thunderous roar I thought the sky was cracking open. It was only the earth breaking up around me in several places, and I landed in one such spot. Panic came when the culvert shuddered and threatened either to close in on me or widen and drop me even deeper. The ground couldn't make up its mind as it yawned and buckled, and I waited no longer but bounded erect and started climbing. I used my feet and when they weren't enough, I dug in with my chin.

Eventually Pat and Mike noticed me going at full speed across an untouched field. They came after me. Once in a while I fell when the ground dipped or heaved. The earthquake continued and so did I, through high grass with the twins hot on my trail, until I spied a blue ring in the sky. Any ring would have done. I directed it to swoop toward me in a swooping arc so that as I went through it in a sloppy dive it probably flew skyward where Pat and Mike couldn't reach it.

If I had anticipated tranquillity in D-2, disappointment awaited me. The tape over my mouth muted into a snoutful of foul smelling gook while the rope on my hands fell to the ground in little white flakes that disintegrated. Almost eagerly I landed in a pool of hot tar that began heaving in exactly the same manner as the surface of the dimension I had just fled. Not only was Earth having an earthquake, a like disturbance marred the peace of the second world.

Plowing through the tar pool to the lower rocks of an escarpment, I attempted to climb to a solid looking ledge. If the mountain fell on me, I might never get out from under the debris.

A tremor dropped me back into the pool which abruptly plunged into a chasm as its bottom fell out. I hurtled and continued to hurtle within the mass of spewing liquid until finally I was washed into a labyrinth and carried through it at breakneck speed. Everything, including me, rushed down a hot falls and was temporarily submerged in a pool within the confines of an amphitheater. I hung around no longer than was necessary. Beaching and finding my way to the surface through various labyrinths, I started hunting for a green ring. I had to know if anything was happening in D-3.

Waterworld was having one of its common maelstroms, only now I knew they weren't so common and never had been, and I also knew the experts were wrong in their cautious explanations that the rumblings and movement in the wet dimension were mere settlings. This was an earthquake, or a waterquake, and it was the same one that disrupted Gothland and Earth.

"The trouble with you," Kisko said to me later, "is that you drop bombshells as if they're handkerchiefs. Pardon me while I react."

"Squirm," said Wheaty. "You've pulled an indescribable from your magic hat."

"Could it be mining?" said Deron.

Kisko shrugged. "Sounds like it, though I don't know how."

"Not gold or diamonds!" I said, prepared to be disappointed. When the three urged me to tell them again, I did. The bore began in D-3, went straight through a ring into the pit in D-2 and continued elsewhere. No, I had never seen or heard of anything or anyone holding a ring stationary.

I went riding into the hills. It was hot and Googs limped along behind. The earth was good but I felt depressed. There didn't seem to be anything going for me. I knew, even then, that the most important thing in my life was and would be the human relationships I established.

"You and I, Bandit, we're two of a kind," I said aloud. "We come on too strong and people think we're smart alecks." Intent and act. No matter my intentions, I would probably never be the belle of the ball.

It suddenly started to pour and we sought shelter under a big tree. Bandit liked cool water dripping on him so I sat on the ground between his legs with Googs hunched against my side. My one regret at the moment was that I couldn't take them into D with me and get lost. I didn't dare. Who knew what they would be like on the other side or if they would even survive the transition?

Pondering the question gave me an idea so, after the rain stopped, I exercised Bandit and then went back to the house. Deron wanted to talk about the metal bore but I walked away from him and headed for the barn. When a suitable blue ring happened by, I went into D-2 and hunted for a live dree. One popped from a tiny hole in the ground, saw me and started to pop back in. Too quick for it, I snagged it with a claw and, with it dangling from my teeth, jumped through a yellow ring and promptly had a fat white rat trying to eat my head off. I lay on my back and watched it race across a narrow meadow toward a cluster of old barns. So much for that.

The next dree I caught turned into a small bobcat that took one look at me after we entered D-1, screeched and took off at flank speed toward a convenient patch of woods. So much for that.

Back in Gothland I examined several drees. There seemed to be six or seven varieties, all similar as far as size and body fur were concerned but with definite differences in shapes of eyes, ears and tails. They all seemed to be natives of Earth and they had either accidentally gone through blue rings or someone had deliberately forced them through.

Returning to the ranch, I discovered that my three caretakers were having another quarrel about me. Wheaty wanted the others to stop sending me into D—as if their orders really motivated me—Kisko wanted me to take it easy for a while and lay low in case the sloks were mustering a defense against intruders, and Deron wanted to know why I hadn't been captured or killed. He was all for locking me in the cage again until I came up with some satisfactory answers. How had I managed to get farther into the enemy complex than any other muter who had ever worked for them? Why didn't I use ring channels like everybody else? Why wasn't I dead?

"Sometimes I think that's how you want her!" said Wheaty. "If you ever had any ethics you've lost them." To Kisko, he said, "You're no better. I didn't sign up to tag along while a kid constituted the first assault wave. What kind of human being are you?"

"The kind who finds it difficult to work without a second in command. Are you sure you're not part of the resistance? Because you're better at resisting than anything else."

Wheaty looked sullen. "When a full grown guy doesn't come back from one of our assignments, I feel bad. I tell myself it's a lousy world. I haven't been able to create a bromide for her. What'll I say when she doesn't come back?"

"When do we eat?" I said.

Wheaty came in to talk to me after the others had gone to bed. "I know the only reason you work for us is the animals," he said. "I got a good place picked out for them. It's a nice farm in Ohio, little, but you'll think it's great, and it's all paid for with your name on the title. What do you think of that?"

"I wish you hadn't done it."

His sagging chin drooped even more. "What does that mean? Do you want to get Bandit away from Deron or not?"

"I'd rather buy him with my wages."

"Then do it. Who do you think owns the papers on him and everything else around here? That's part of my job, buying hunks of territory so we can work out of them."

"How much does he cost?" I said.

"Who?"

"Bandit."

"What's the matter with you?" he said. "Don't you understand what I'm talking about? This is your life. You don't have to buy the horse. He's already yours."

Getting out of bed, I crossed to my bureau and took out my money envelope. Coming back with a stack of bills, I said, "Is a thousand dollars enough?"

His pale blue eyes looked defeated. He appeared to be exhausted. "I don't understand you. You aren't like any kid I ever met in my life. You want to give me all the money you risked your neck for to buy something I'm trying to hand over to you for nothing."

"You have your methods of operation, I have mine. Where's the paper?"

He went away to the money box hidden behind some wallpaper in the living room and came back with the registration. "Here's the thing, all signed. The horse is yours."

"And this money is yours."

He felt his forehead with trembling fingers. "Maybe I'm too old." He glanced at the slok I had painted on the wall. "I should have been born a hundred years ago. I can't tolerate the bad weather we get these days."

"How much did you pay for the farm?"

"You can earn that much by putting your life on the line a few more times, is that it? Didn't you ever hear of charity?"

"As long as I can work—"

"Shut up," he said. "Don't talk. You're the kind of person who has to be looked after. For some reason you have no normal human caution. Do you want to spend the rest of your short life running from monsters? What is it, a thrill or something? Isn't ordinary living exciting enough for you?"

"It's just that everybody lies to me and that includes you. If people told me a few truths, I'd probably be satisfied to retire."

"People don't tell you truths because there aren't any. Don't you know this is a lousy world?"

He gave me plenty of time to move the animals before he betrayed us, for which fact I was grateful since I wouldn't have

wanted to leave them there where no one would be around to
care for them. Maybe he thought that since I was usually away I
wouldn't be caught along with Kisko and Deron. Or maybe he
believed it would be better if I died of a quick bullet or a bludg-
eoning than in the jaws of a slok. It was a long time before I
had the chance to ask him which it was.

I had no intention of using his farm in Ohio. Hiring my own
driver, I left Wheaty's man somewhere in Pennsylvania while I
and the new employee drove to Jersey.

A woman named Olger lived on the farm I leased. She had
walked away from an old folks' home and simply moved in. My
coming was no surprise to her since it was a good piece of property and she probably knew that sooner or later someone would
come along and claim it. Anxious to stay on, she agreed to take
care of the horse, the dog and all the cats. I gave her money and
permission to find good homes for the kittens. When I was fully
satisfied that everything was in order, I left and went to work.

There would be no more blunderings or reckless boltings into
danger. Such was my decision, so I floated cautiously into Greenworld somewhere near enemy territory, more particularly in the
vicinity of the vents where the metal pipe rammed through a
ring. If I hadn't decided to be careful for a change, I probably
wouldn't have entered D-3 practically in the middle of a drifting
clump of seaweed and then I wouldn't have found Mike.

While I clawed and fought to get free of a great deal of cloying vegetation, a dead face popped into view followed by a slender female torso and a pair of scaled legs. Her expression was
one of pain and fright and her eyes were wide and staring. No
doubt the seaweed had snagged and held her while she floated.
No blood leaked from the jagged wound in her throat which
meant she had been dead a while.

It was no easy task to free her of the weeds, since she was so
much larger than I, but I managed and then began shoving her
through the water. There didn't appear to be anyone else about
but I was afraid her killer might come along to check and see
how the corpse was doing, so I got out of there in a hurry. Only
when I was certain we had the area to ourselves did I shove her
through a yellow ring and onto a familiar cornfield in Peoria.

I had no way of knowing what would happen but simply

hadn't wanted to leave her there to decompose in Greenworld. I did have a hope or two, and they were confirmed when both of us landed whole, human and clothed between rows of corn. Transmutating was always miraculous but that day it seemed more so when the slashed and ugly throat of the twin suddenly became milky smooth.

"Which one are you?" I asked.

She was all right for a second and then the shock hit her. Her hand went up to her neck while her old terror came back. Finally realizing she had no wound, she sat up and looked around. Again she felt her throat. Then she croaked her sister's name. "Pat!"

"You were the only one I saw," I said. "Who did it?"

"You mean who killed us?" she said, shuddering as if someone had dropped an ice cube down her back. "Her name was Erma. She said she'd be sure and put our bodies where they would never be found. Her friends held us in the water and she took a knife . . . Pat!"

"Come on, maybe we can find her in the same area."

The twins had been taken into Greenworld and killed because the woman named Erma was annoyed with them. She had wanted to interview me and they let me escape. Mike told me this while we searched.

We found the second body stuffed in a cave in a floating mountain. Pat also woke up hale, hearty and scared out of her wits when shoved into D-1.

They might have been grateful to me for saving their bacon but they weren't very informative. All they knew about Erma was that she cornered them on campus one day and threatened their lives if they didn't get me back. Naturally they complained to Gorwyn who declared they were making it all up.

"There isn't any use in your asking us," said Pat. At least I think she was Pat. "We don't know anything about Erma other than that she's big and has a mind like a wolverine."

"Let me switch the subject for a moment," I said. "You snooped in my room at Mutat. Why?"

"Gorwyn told us to."

"Did he say why?"

"He probably didn't have a reason. You know how silly he is.

We were supposed to hunt for anything at all out of the ordinary. It was an easy job because you didn't have any property extraordinary or otherwise."

"Did you ever tell him or anybody about me?" I asked.

"You mean about how you mute into such a big goth? No, we never told him or anyone else. Gorwyn thinks we're morons and doesn't engage in real conversations with us. Mostly we're just his runners."

They were scared and they had no funds. I told them to stay where they were and I'd go and fetch them some money.

Circumstance got in my way and it was a while before I saw them again. Running through the corn until I reached a deep culvert, I jumped down and sped along the curve of ground. Out of their sight, I located a blue ring, plunged into Gothland and then entered a yellow one that would put me back on the ranch. I walked up the road, whistling, my hands in my pockets, not anticipating anything unusual but finding plenty.

The sight of a group of people congregated in the living room startled me so that I lost my calm. Kisko sat in a straight-backed chair with a strip of tape across his mouth and his hands bound in front of him, while directly to his rear stood a huge woman who kept nudging his neck with a gun. Deron lay on the couch nursing a bleeding scalp. The rest of the strangers were men who sat or stood and regarded their leader with blank faces.

"Hi," I said. "I was wondering if I could use your phone. My mom's car broke down—"

"Grab her before she gets out the door," said the big lady, just as I went into action.

I didn't go far, about three meters backward before someone took me by the neck and tossed me onto the middle of the carpet. "Wait'll my mother hears about this!" I said. "You people need a lecture on the law!"

Erma hustled around Kisko's chair and poked her gun in my mouth. It tasted of powder so I knew it had been fired recently and that made me start looking around with anxiety uppermost in my mind.

"We hear there's a muter around here who can really hop rings," said Erma.

"Is that so? Well, I wouldn't know anything about that. My mom's car—" It was difficult talking around the gun.

The steel started clicking back and forth across my teeth. She wasn't a kid lover, I could tell. "You'll be better off saying nothing at all than lying. Except that you'll say plenty later when we squeeze your empty little skull in an iron vise."

They must have been afraid they would miss somebody, and obviously they hadn't trusted Wheaty all the way which was why they hung around for two more days before pulling out and taking us with them.

"There's gotta be someone else," said Erma. "Someone a lot bigger than these two guys. I figure maybe a wrestler or a side-show freak." Occasionally she came over to my chair and played drums on my head with the gun. "Where's the big muter, buzzard? You know who I'm talking about. The hippo. Gargantua. The one who's been running us ragged in 2."

# 7

ON THE WAY to a private airport I sat on Erma's lap in the back
seat of an electric car. Her left hand was loosely clasped on my
hair. She was never tranquil but wriggled, writhed and sniffed
like a hound on the scent. The fingers of her free hand drummed
against one knee. Now and then she applied pressure on my
hair but I could tell her heart wasn't in it. She probably wasn't
even thinking about me or the others. Possibly I was wrong.
Maybe she dreamed of strange treasure, such as making a pan-
cake out of my head and mincemeat of Kisko and Deron. She
wasn't the cerebral type and didn't talk much.

The plane trip was brief and afterwards we took another car
to a ghost city that had only four or five tall buildings still standing in it. The air stank of old pollution and yellow smoke rose
from a chemical dump a few blocks away. Stumbling on the broken sidewalk, I took wings as Erma elevated her right arm. The
high structure into which I was carried was cold and smelled
like a crypt.

They kept me in the basement and out of the way. I wondered
if some former tenant had kept a large animal there since the
chain to which I was attached was embedded so securely in the
concrete wall that only an elephant or some other behemoth
could have pulled it loose. I wore a metal necklace that rubbed,
chafed and grew as chill as a collar of ice. Squatting on the floor,

I tried guessing how long it would take me to catch pneumonia. Each time one of my captors came in to look at me, he or she carried a naked light bulb attached to what seemed to be an endless cord. Usually it was Erma who came.

"Do I get any food or water?" I said once.

"Shut up."

"I just like to know—"

"Shut up. We know you have an unusual companion who can hop rings like crazy. We only want to know his name and whereabouts."

"How do you know it isn't a she?"

Erma bent down and stuck the bulb against my arm. "It's somebody big. I'm told we can't get any information from you with drugs but that's something I'll have to discover for myself when I find the time." She played a game of seeing if she could stick the hot bulb on a bare spot on me before I jumped out of the way. She was quick and the chain wasn't very long.

"What if I don't have a companion?" I said, backed against the wall with my eyes on the light.

She took me by one leg and upended me in the air. "You mean you've been doing that stuff in 2 all by your little self?" Dropping me on my head, she said, "Before I'm through with those two upstairs I'll know the secrets of their innermost souls, which happens to be a nauseating thought now that I think about it."

"Deron and Kisko don't know anything. Let them go and I'll tell you all you want to know."

"You're a mosquito. Be quiet before I swat you."

After she went away, I wallowed in a puddle of self-pity. They didn't intend to let me go, not ever, otherwise they would be providing me with items to keep my body and soul together, such as a blanket and at least something to drink.

Night or day, I lost track of time and didn't know what it was. Once Erma plunged a hypo into my arm and I went out like the bulb when it was switched off. She was mad when I came back to consciousness, burned me good and yanked out a few wads of hair.

One day she brought in Deron, lit up the place with a dozen light bulbs so I could see everything and beat the daylights out of him. He didn't have a chance. I think her soul was so hostile she could have whipped anyone, but then she was larger than a normal man and strong as a bull. When Deron finally got the idea that nobody else was going to come into the room and interfere, he got some grit in his expression and started boxing with her. She knew how to do that too, cracked his face with rock-like fists that split his mouth and brows and bent his nose first in one direction and then another. For such a big person she was fast on her feet.

She didn't quit even after his right wrist snapped and dangled when she kicked him, just kept on blasting at him with her dynamite fists and boots until I backed into the corner and closed my eyes. I could hear him fall, hear her haul him up and knock him down again, over and over, repeating the carnage until at last she lost interest and kicked him out the door.

I knew why she hadn't started on me yet. I would probably last all of fifteen seconds and she wasn't quite ready to make me a corpse. After the first two days, I would have told them anything they wanted to know but they didn't ask me and wouldn't even listen to me. It was as if I were an incidental in the situation, someone who had lived at the ranch but who hadn't done much of anything of significance.

What I learned, during their brief and violent excursions into my dank and dingy quarters, was that they believed Kisko had hired a whiz of a muter and that all I did was act as a red herring to keep snoopers off the real trail. I had gone into D where there was danger, but not as the main spy. If Erma and her crew hadn't believed something like this, they probably would have dissected me into microscopic proportions to get at the truth. As it was, they left me alone and concentrated on Deron and Kisko who finally broke, and no wonder. They babbled out the truth that I was the only muter working for them, which truth wasn't accepted by Erma because of her many and diverse misconceptions, besides which her superiors would have done better to commission someone who took less delight in their work. She became so engrossed in what she was doing that she lost sight of her first goal and, before she realized it, her victims were beyond giving information of any kind.

Not knowing what was happening to Kisko, I lay on cold concrete and wondered if Deron had survived his beating. I hungered and thirsted, shivered with fear and influenza and tried not to let the darkness take over my mind.

Then Erma came in to finish me off. Their job was almost done and they hadn't learned what they wanted to know. My captor was full of disgust for humanity. She spent the next thirty minutes twisting my fingers out of their sockets, and I either yelled or promised to tell all if she just brought in Kisko and Deron so I could see they were still alive. She didn't wheedle or beg and neither did she bring in my friends, which was evidence to me that there was nothing left of them for her to show me. After she broke my thumbs I couldn't talk anyway so she must have decided she was through wasting time. Either that or she was carried away with blood lust.

When she poked the light bulb in my face, I saw her big right fist coming at me like a meaty avalanche and believed the blow was intended to kill. There wasn't much time for me to react. Mostly I was trying to get my eyelids unstuck so I could see which way to sway. Her dark eyes were hooded and full of resentment while her fat lips pursed with displeasure. The lid of my left eye came unstuck just in time for me to perceive the white boulder whizzing through space to knock my head off. I didn't move intentionally, just instinctively. Because she was so infuriated and couldn't see much better than I, she probably didn't notice or care when I went backward in a hurry, rode with the blow as best I could and, before all my internal lights went out I hoped my brains wouldn't decorate the walls.

The old dreg who woke me up said he had been scouting the neighborhood for goodies and saw the whole bunch of us come in six days before. He had hung around, skulking in and behind the skeletons of buildings, and saw five people leave. That left three still inside. He said there had been a lot of noise during those first days, but then after the five left, there wasn't so much as a squeak from the windows. That had made the dreg curious so he investigated with caution.

I don't know how he broke my chain. I kept passing out. Maybe he gnawed it in two. As a matter of fact, I think he told me later that he found a hammer and chisel and took his time about getting me loose from the wall. He kept telling me he had a wheelbarrow outside in which he intended to haul me to the hospital twenty kilometers down the road. For a price. I kept telling him he couldn't haul three people that far in a wheelbarrow and, over and over, he said I was the only living thing in the building besides himself.

He walked and I crawled up three flights to a room where Kisko and Deron lay, shone his light on their naked bodies and while I cried he ran another mirror test to see if their nostrils created any fog. Finally he said maybe one of them had a little air left in him, but he added that hauling both of us all those kilometers would cost me what I had in both pockets of my jeans, which he had already cleaned out.

In his better days he must have been a weight lifter. I never found out because he didn't linger long, left us on the front stoop of Mercy and took off with about four hundred dollars of my money.

The doctor told me I had a blood clot in my head that might kill me one of these days, and I said was that so and what was it still doing in there after all these months, and she said was that so and maybe she had better run some more tests since clots usually didn't hang around. I told her not to bother.

I wasn't overly concerned about myself since I was mostly all in one piece and hadn't been fatally injured by Erma's love tap, so again I advised the doctor not to mind about my sore skull because it was Kisko that worried me. She said she didn't blame me for being worried about him. Though he and I were charity cases, we would both receive the best medical treatment humanity was able to offer in this century but there was no use my anticipating miracles. Doctors were just people, not magicians.

Three months later Kisko and I walked out the front door in time to greet an early snow. We went hand in hand because he couldn't navigate any other way. For the past few days I had swept floors in a slaughterhouse down the street, so there was enough money for a bus ride to Jersey.

Olger was glad to see me since her funds were running low. I had a crew come from town to fix up a rubber room for Kisko and then I locked him in and traveled back to the ranch via rings. It had been vandalized so there was nothing worth carrying away other than the money box secreted in the living room wall. Everything was either broken or gone. All the fences had been taken, likewise the lumber from the front and back porches. Since the money was what I had come for, I wasn't too disappointed. A cold winter was predicted by the weathermen so the outbuildings would probably be carted away for firewood, and perhaps even the ranch house itself. By spring there would be no evidence that I had ever lived there with one friend, one half-friend and one traitor. Strange how the three kept getting mixed up in my mind.

Between the two of us, Olger and I managed through the winter and let Kisko get away from us only once. That day she kept a good coal and wood fire going in the open hearth while I put on heavy clothing and went out hunting for him. I found him lying in his pajamas on a mound of snow, screaming his head off. He was too worn out to struggle, having already fought a legion of demons with his bare and bloody fists, so I led him back to the cabin, cleaned him and dressed him in long underwear and put him back in his room. It was heated with a fine electric grill hidden beneath the rubber lining.

He couldn't be trusted to have a sink or toilet in the room. Olger would wait until he was in one of his tearful moods and then she would clean him and his environment, all the time bawling him out because he was such a pig. He wasn't always bad. At times he was calm and even looked rational, though he never spoke, and then he was permitted to sit with us at the table. Toward spring the last of his casts were taken off.

There wasn't much Olger and I could do that winter but sit by the fire and try to keep from freezing. The house wasn't like the one at the ranch that had boasted of a generator large enough to power all the machines and light fixtures. Our old farmhouse in Jersey owned the one small generator that took care of the rubber room but other than that, we had no real comforts. Our lights were candles, the heat and cooking fires came from coal and wood. We did have running water. After the first real thaw, someone from the city would come by in a tractor to see how we had fared. The driver's job would be to haul away bodies and report deaths.

Kisko grew quieter as the cold weather wore on, or he did until we had an earthquake, and that set him back so far he had to be locked in his room for a week. He rushed out of the house as soon as the tremors began, slogged through the snow as though he were anxious to get to some particular spot, and I chased him a mile before his adrenalin stopped spurting.

It wasn't what the experts called a severe quake, but of course that depended upon one's point of view. People who watched bridges collapse thought it was the worst disaster they had ever been a party to, which was the same sentiment expressed by those whose homes were destroyed. The government people said it wasn't anything to get alarmed over, that what with the second and third dimensions moving around outside of ours and possibly even through us, we had to anticipate a little ground settling, or something. I knew better and so did Kisko. He might have been deep in psychic trauma but his soul wasn't so paralyzed it couldn't respond when a sleeping leviathan stirred.

I had been hoping spring would have a healing effect upon him. It turned out to be one of those long and gorgeous seasons with trees and bushes budding and blooming until the world looked like a garden.

Olger carried out the last bucket of ashes and started cleaning walls while Kisko and I took leisurely walks. I kept waiting for him to wake up and begin living again.

"Worst case of walking withdrawal I've ever seen," said the doctor in town. "Usually when they're this bad, they just lie down and begin dying so earnestly we have to stick them in a life support unit. Of course when they do that these days, they do die since we haven't the power to run the machines."

"Tell me something cheerful," I said.

"He's in top condition, if you discount the fact that his brain isn't working right. X-rays show that all his broken bones are healed, except for his right shoulder which will always be a trifle weak. You haven't told me how he got all those breaks. Did he have a run-in with a corn chopper or something?"

"What can be done for him?"

"Nothing. There isn't anything wrong with him. He has to focus his attention outside his private fog, is all. I'd say the likelihood of that happening within the next fifty years is zero. My advice is for you to take him up to the home on the hill over there and leave him. It isn't a bad place."

"Thanks."

"I'm only being friendly. I don't know what happened to him. Pain is the most subjective thing in the world, more so than taste or opinion. Some other person might have taken his punishment and walked away from it whole while somebody else would have lost his marbles halfway through the ordeal. The human mind can't be messed around with. I have a machine in my lab that can knock you off your shelf just by shining a little light in your eyes. Take your daddy to that home on the hill and say good-bye to him."

It had been a while since I visited D so after returning Kisko to the farm, I went to Waterworld for a good soaking. Floating and drifting in green water helped me to think. There were many things I thought I should do, but it seemed like too much of an effort to even consider them. There was the metal girder that needed investigating, also the net that made prisoners of swimmers, besides which Croff had to be hunted down and questioned. So many situations pending, seemingly innumerable solutions to problems skulking just beyond reach or vision, and what was required was action.

Making myself do it, I left the third dimension and went to the second, popped noisily into what I thought was going to be the engine house in the pit in Gothland. Good fortune remained with me but it wasn't good enough to spare me a hefty fright or a wild ride.

The engine house had been a temporary thing with the sloks and it had either been converted into a corner station for the pipes or disassembled altogether and replaced with a junction.

I no sooner materialized as a goth than I found myself in the midst of a black maelstrom. I was immediately disoriented because Gothland wasn't the place for such a thing. Regardless, I was hurled from wall to wall by some kind of thick fluid that gushed from the first pipe into the second so rapidly I had no time to think about getting my footing. That I was in for a hectic ride was obvious so I relaxed as much as possible and let myself go careening down the pipe. Sometimes I was scraped along the ceiling or side but always I was thrust forward by the fluid. It wasn't water, mud or tar. It tasted like a combination of acid and clay.

An advantage of being a goth was that I could see in and through almost any kind of substance. Somewhere ahead of me the environment was bound to alter and, since I couldn't anticipate whether or not it would be pleasant or even tolerable, it would be better if I got out now.

I had only one chance and took it without hesitating. I didn't know where the gushing acid was headed, didn't want to know at that moment, and so when I saw what looked like a yellow light off to my right, I twisted as strongly as I could and dived for it. A second later I pitched onto the top of a high mound of sand on Earth, rolled down the side of it and landed on the rough ground of a quarry.

Immediately I regretted having left the bore. Possibly nothing drastic would have happened to me had I remained in it and I also might have discovered what the acid solution was for. Now I couldn't find my way back into the metal pipe because the ring that had handled my passage had ducked away and was gone by the time I landed at the bottom of the sand pile. I hadn't seen what color it was.

The next day I made a phone call and placed an ad in the *Big City Bugle*: CROFF, MEET ME TUESDAY NOON IN PEORIA. After that, each Tuesday I ring-traveled into the cornfield to see if my old hermit acquaintance was there. Usually I lingered for thirty minutes or so and then left.

Having heard there were some ring experts in Boston, I paid a visit to one of their institutions of higher learning and was told in haughty tones by a young secretary that Doctor Ectri didn't grant many interviews, particularly to juveniles. I thanked him and left in a hurry. It seemed Washington wasn't the only place Ectri liked.

Brooding in Waterworld one day, wishing I were a single-celled creature without the brains to worry about more than where my next meal was coming from, swimming and drifting along with currents created by minor maelstroms, I came across a large clump of seaweed serving as a graveyard for the bodies of two women and two men. They were securely bound and probably never would have drifted loose.

One by one I untied them and shoved them through a yellow

ring onto a street in Nebraska where they were resurrected whole, horrified and full of bad memories.

My advice to them was to go home and forget what had happened. It seemed they had been swimming and minding their own business when a net came up from nowhere, grabbed them and carried them to a platform on a metal girder where an extremely large female water breather shot them with a spear gun.

One of the women borrowed bus fare from me and took off for distant parts while the others headed toward a police station down the block. As for myself, I made like the woman and traveled a distance.

"The trouble with you is that you aren't happy as an orphan," said Gorwyn. "Subconsciously you're searching for a family."

It was several days later and I was smelling the faint musty odor coming from the school's headmaster. I was here because I had gone into a department store to buy some candy and an eager truant officer had put the tag on me. It was either Mutat or the police so I gave him the school's address.

"Which I haven't the faintest hope of finding here," I said to Gorwyn. "How are the third-floor bouncers these days? Still beating up on the inhabitants?"

"As if they ever did."

"You could do a lot better around here without me."

"No doubt, but there's such a thing as law and it protects creatures such as yourself. Welcome back."

"I don't see Pat and Mike around."

"They seem to have flown the coop, probably to a higher paying job. I regret their absence since they're fairly good runners."

"As long as I'm back, I guess I'll take some courses in rings."

Though I kept a close watch on the newspapers, I found nothing regarding the woman and two men who had gone to report their kidnaping and murder to the police.

A week went by and I was walking through the pasture at the farm with Kisko, both my hands tightly clasped on one of his so he wouldn't run away. He was always calmer when someone took the time to touch him and talk to him.

"It's time for the big experiment," I said. I stood in front of him while he sat on a tree stump and stared at the sky. Once in a while he blinked. "You can't go on like this," I said. "The doctor tells me it isn't good for your brain."

Rings drifted through the air and I called a bright blue one to me. Its corona reminded me of a marble, dark and solid in some places and striated in others. "You know what peripheral vision is," I said to the man seated in front of me. He didn't know much of anything those days but I talked to him because I was nervous. There was a possibility that he would be dead in a few minutes.

"Sometimes we see a lot of things that are beyond our direct line of sight, such as from the sides of our eyes," I said. "Like shadows, they don't always appear to be substantial, but if they're there, they're real and if we see even a little piece of them then they mean something to us."

The wind stirred our hair, chilled me through, made me worry about his catching cold. Would he be better off dead than as he was? "The only reason we're out here is because you blink so much," I said. He was looking at the sky as if it was something he had never seen before. "It's no disgrace on your part to have been beaten up and tortured by a maniac," I said. "She'll get her reward, don't worry. Just because she showed you what hell looks like is no reason for you to curl up and resign from the human race. Anyway, you keep blinking, and for a long time I've noticed you only do it when there's a ring close by. Like right now. Do you understand what I'm saying?"

The doctor said he had to get outside himself. I couldn't think of a more positive way for me to try and make that happen. My idea was to have him stand directly in front of me, his back to me, with my arms tight around his waist.

The ring grounded ahead of us and then moved slowly to our left where Kisko could get his best glimpse of it, if indeed he could see it at all. If he didn't see any part of it, I'd step into Gothland alone as soon as I took a step to the left. What would happen to him or both of us if he saw only a part of the ring as we went through was a mystery. I didn't want to worry about it. Whatever, in my opinion he wouldn't want to or couldn't resist its lure.

He tried to break away from me, refused to step to the left. I forced the ring to stay parallel with us as he dragged me along.

Gripping him tighter, I yelled at him to stand still while I made the ring swoop at us. He cried out and started to stampede just as the inner blue donut enveloped us.

Of course he had always been able to see at least a shadow of the rings; of course he didn't know how to say no and of course he was transmutated into a goth, just as I was. The difference between him and other people was that he had a brain or a mind that could be called unique. When he landed in D-2 he wasn't an ordinary goth. What he was I didn't find out that day. All I heard was a shriek of terror and then somewhere ahead of me a huge dark shadow disappeared around a hill of rocks.

# 8

"It's ALL ECONOMIC and always has been," said Croff. He glanced uneasily over his shoulder at the cornfield, at the sky, back at me, continually on his toes and ready to bolt. "The only reason I responded to your ad was because I owe you something, but I can't help you track down your friend. I don't know that much about the mutating process. The rings themselves were my specialty and I can tell you I wasn't overly knowledgeable."

"Tell me about that receiver we took out of you."

"We were all on the staff at Burgoyne. There was Trundle, myself, Appy, Orfia and the others. Something was placed in our drinks at a faculty party on campus one night and we woke up in a hotel suite with those mechanical devices in our arms. There was a crew of musclemen who brainwashed us with drugs and tape recordings of gibberish. We weren't supposed to do ring research anymore. They suggested that we change our field of work and concentrate on something else. They wanted us out of the way but they didn't kill us because each of us had attracted considerable attention with our work. It took me six months to decide to go to the police. The same for the others. We were picked up again and given shock treatments and some more hard conditioning. They removed our complaints from the police files so there was no evidence that we had ever told anyone what happened. I don't know what became of the others. I only realized what was expected of me. Every time I came back from D that gang picked me up. I simply decided not to come back anymore."

"Who are they?"

"That's just it. I haven't the faintest idea. No hullabaloo was raised because I quit my job and kicked over the traces. Now the whole thing has been forgotten. Nobody cares. I know I'm still not free. There's a guard stationed outside my home in Atlanta and one outside my office at Burgoyne. I can't go back to anything or anyone."

"What do you plan to do with the rest of your life besides look over your shoulder?"

"Be smug and critical if you like. I've developed a thick skin. I figure I might as well be a dreg or a hermit if I'm not permitted to do the work for which I was trained."

"Get the law to help you."

After looking around again to make sure we were still safe and unobserved, he said, "I did that exactly twelve times. The gang must have some kind of computer tie-in with everything because each time I went to the police I was picked up, taken somewhere and either beaten or forced to listen to their stupid tapes, or both."

I hid in a culvert after we parted, watched while Croff disappeared among the corn stalks, followed him to a ring channel half a mile across dry pastures. Trailing him from there to his shabby dwelling place in Queens was easy.

Back at Mutat I sat in a thirtieth floor lounge and gazed out the window. It was a gray day that matched the shade of my spirit. Somewhere in D a mad goth roamed and prowled and I was responsible for his being there. Or at least I assumed he was a goth. As if that weren't a serious enough problem to occupy my mind, there was also something wrong with the world. During the past five days there had been at least four earthquakes somewhere, no minor tremors but disturbances severe enough to destroy property and lives.

Rings were like the plates that made up the upper crust of Earth's surface. Just as the latter floated and created a viable layer upon which living things grew and moved, so the rings drifted and formed the perimeters or surfaces of other dimensions or worlds.

Gorwyn told me that. He helped me to see the rings, seemingly bobbing haphazardly through air and ground, as organized and orderly crusts of Dimensions One, Two and Three. They needn't spin or float in an observable orbit to maintain a dimension's outer substance, though they might have been moving in such a manner for all anyone could tell. No one really knew the shape of any dimension, not even that of D-1. For instance, Earth seemed reasonably round but instruments measured and accounted for only certain types of matter and were incapable of tracing the drift of substance moving toward or through rings. In order to do that, special instruments would have to be devised that penetrated Two or Three and then came back through yellow rings because those rings were the corona or perimeter of One. More and more, fact seemed to depend upon perspective.

So much for the outsides of the colored donuts, what about their cores? According to Gorwyn, the rings were adaptors, no more and no less. A living organism or a substance stepped from an environment into plastic surgery or a dressing room, was made over or made up so that he, she or it could exist or function in the next environment. The phenomenon wasn't something that had simply begun without precedent one day. As a matter of fact, nobody really altered or influenced the universe. One only discovered it.

Gorwyn's laboratory held a fascination for me, more particularly the animals in their cages. "Never just shove something into a ring," he said to me one day. "It's liable to back out and eat your head off."

"You mean it might get mad at you?" I said.

"Not precisely. Ring travel sometimes opens doors in the mind that might better have remained closed. I once had a guinea pig that came back from D-2 as wild and ferocious as a wolf."

"Did you go in and out with it?"

"Now you're asking if I can travel through rings. You already know the answer. I can't see them, therefore I can't penetrate them. No, I devised a type of leash that stayed on it after it went into D and all I had to do was apply pressure to retrieve it. The thing was so hostile I got rid of it, gave it to a former colleague who was interested in that phase of the business."

"About the mind—" I began.

"You needn't ask because I don't know that much about it. The mechanical monitors tell me exactly where the rings are so I can work with animals that see them, but you can appreciate my limitations. What I've learned has taken me a long time. As for your question, some people take tranquilly to the rings while others fall completely off their shelves, have drastic changes in personality, develop all sorts of manias or neuroses, etcetera. Usually those last types go into D once or twice and then spend the rest of their lives in therapy."

"Suppose there was a crazy person who went in and got lost?"

Gorwyn shrugged. "Sheer speculation even discussing such a thing. It would depend upon how crazy he was, the amount of brain stimulation at the time of entry, his body metabolism, adrenalin level, but mostly it would depend upon what he was thinking and who he believed he was when he went in. Why? Do you know someone who's wandering about lost in D?"

"I was just wondering."

"I see. Watch out for the monkeys, please. If you play with the hasp on the cage door you might loosen it and then they'll get out."

After dinner that evening I sat in my favorite lounge and thought about Kisko and Erma. For some reason the two seemed to go together in my mind those days. Why hadn't she made a more concerted effort to kill me? In my mind's eye I saw myself once again chained in the dank cellar, sick and shivering while I imagined how she was killing Kisko and Deron. Wheaty hadn't believed there was an accomplice with me in D who did all the dirty work while I took the credit and the pay envelopes. He didn't know exactly how I operated but never in our acquaintance had there ever been a mention of a secret associate of mine.

That was the crux of the puzzling items that kept coming back time after time to nudge my consciousness. The idea of a partner for me was a fabrication dreamed up in whose mind? If it had been Kisko's or Deron's fantasy, Erma learned all about it when she had them propped on the brink of death and ready to shove them over. What about Wheaty? No matter what he told Erma, she had listened to the whole truth, as they believed it, from the lips of her crushed victims. That she would prefer the tale of a whole and untouched traitor rather than suffering men didn't seem reasonable.

Whom did that leave? Only Erma herself. She could have broken me like a stick of chalk yet here I sat hale and hearty. She could have arranged for my corpse to lie in some deep grave to the end of time yet I sat in Mutat with indigestion from eating too much ice cream.

As I sat and thought about it, an odd idea came to life in my head. Erma had never intended killing me, not from the first moment we met in the living room at the ranch, and perhaps before that. My broken fingers and the punch on the jaw had been no more than brief sport to her.

Tedwar came up behind me and interrupted my reverie. "If I didn't know for a fact that you have only empty space between your ears I'd swear you were thinking," he said.

"Disappear before I beat you up."

"This is as much my lounge as it is yours."

"Who told you that nonsense?" I said, getting up and preparing to do something meaningful. He quickly sidled out the door, stood in the hallway with his arms akimbo and a smirk on his face.

"You're the ugliest girl I ever saw."

"You're the fattest slob I ever saw," I said.

"You're the stupidest dummy who ever lived."

"I make better grades than you so that puts your I.Q. on the same level as a dead person."

He drooled on purpose, formed a lot of spit that dripped down onto his chest. "I had a candy bar on my bureau but it's gone now."

"Oh, yeah, I meant to thank you for that. Next time get one with more nuts."

"Next time I'll sprinkle one with arsenic." He rubbed a knot on his head, acquired earlier in the day in the gym when he tried a street-fighter chop on me and tripped over himself. "You're scrawny and hideous and not even your parents wanted you, otherwise you wouldn't be an orphan. I'll bet they dumped you as soon as you were born."

I chased him down the hall and got in one good punch before he flew into his room and locked me out. For a fat pest he could move as if on wings.

Groppo was good at helping me to relax and think so I went to see him, let him out of his cage and played catch with him. His tough, gnarled fingers dug into the beach ball and once or twice I thought he was going to sink his teeth into it. For a chimp he was very brainy, brown-faced and snub-nosed, about a meter and a quarter tall and fast on his feet. Gorwyn always raised the devil when he discovered I had let one of his pets out. I never told him I preferred Groppo's company to Tedwar's, though he undoubtedly already knew this. I hadn't too many friends my own age in the school and they had gone home for summer vacation, so there was only Tedwar with whom I waged continual war because he seemed to want it that way, and there was also Groppo for whose existence I was grateful since he was at least intelligent enough to know that company was better than solitude.

We sat on the floor and shared a banana and then he went to sleep with his head on my lap while I leaned against the wall and thought about my problems.

I had to be particularly on the watch for Tedwar during physical fitness class. He could be formidable when in full flight, like a battering ram, and every so often during body building period I would look around and see flapping red curls, wet mouth and furrowed brow as he tried to run me down. There weren't so many students present that I got lost in the shuffle. I was good on the ropes and bars and could match anyone my size at running and team games. However, nobody else in the class was my size so I fell behind in track and went back to my room every day to count my new bruises acquired during contact sports.

I knew Gothland was too big to search but I tried anyway, first visiting all the familiar haunts and then branching beyond into strange territory. I prowled through that dimension until I was sick of it.

"It was madness that broke up the group," said Croff. It was late afternoon and he was displeased because I had known how to find him. "I told you I don't know anything about a conspiracy. To do what, for heaven's sake? Create earthquakes? Come now! Yes, there were six of us but I spoke of that before. The others were much closer to each other than to me. I sort of stayed out of things. The madness came quite a while before we were rounded up and served with the radio receivers. It was Appy, seemed to have his brain blown out by ego or something. I believed it was a treatable condition but the idea was beneath him. No, I don't know what happened to any of them and I've never met anyone named Ectri, Erma or Kisko. One thing I do know is that a man named Bud Jupiter was tied into it but I have no idea how."

Croff wasn't having a difficult time of it financially as he had earned a considerable amount while he was one of the world's leading authorities on dimensions and had possessed the foresight to transfer some of his bank accounts to his private name before disappearing into Gothland. Now he lived an obscure existence made interesting only when he felt the need to avoid a certain store or other public place.

"Yes, I care about what's going on but all my contacts have been broken," he said. We were in a diner twenty kilometers from his apartment, eating spaghetti and practically gagging on the smoke coming from the candles all over the walls. It wasn't that dark outside so they weren't really necessary. "I used to be a person of consequence," said Croff, sounding like an old hermit or a bum on the skids. "What are you grinning about? Never mind. Eat your dinner, which brings me to remark that you should put on some weight, else how can you experience a normal pubescence?

I liked him and wished he were my father. How simple my life would be if there were someone to whom I could bear my troubles, confess my sins and make earnest but vain promises. Across the street the bank people lit their candles and made ready for the evening rush. They didn't have too many fans so the interior was probably like an oven. Their computer stood in a corner, an energy-gobbling necessity or luxury of twinkling lights, infallible patterns of electronic activity and platinum facade. Banking made fun, or so their ads claimed.

"Tell me about the madness," I said.

"Appy? He was always a bit eccentric, as sociable as a post and not half so friendly, but forever in the thick of things. We all thought he got the way he was dosing himself with dope before mutating. I don't know. It was such interesting work, doubly so in retrospect and especially when I compare it with my accomplishments and activities of today."

"What did you learn about D?"

Frowning, he stopped eating. "It's an enigma, or I should say D are enigmas. It'll take time to learn about the worlds and even more time to account for individual human differences. As for the earthquakes you seem so concerned about, they might be caused by the deep ocean drilling for oil but there isn't anything I can do about it since I'll be clapped in irons the moment I show my face. If I knew one honest policeman. . ."

"How many dishonest ones have you approached?"

"None, lately. I value my anonymity, my freedom and my health. Actually I prefer living in D-2, but the lure to go there is too strong to be altogether wholesome so I resist."

We discussed my peculiar talents or rather he did most of the talking while I listened. He was especially keen after I told him green rings mutated me into a tiny swimmer. Of course it wasn't natural, he said, which made it even odder that I had no recollection of my background. The supposed clot in my head, still present after all the time that had passed, could be an implanted instrument, but he knew of no one who could do a thing like that and he had been in a position to know everybody who was somebody in the field of ring research. Second-guessing such an instrument's effect would be impossible. As he had mentioned once or twice before, if he had the time he would love to study me.

He gave me the addresses of his former associates, not that they would do me any good as every one of them had likely fled into D with receivers in their flesh. At least I might gain some information about them from their neighbors.

"Obviously you don't know who you are for a good reason," said Croff. "Why don't you leave it alone for a while?"

"I can't. It's practically all I ever think about."

"Of course you'll be making an error if you assume your personal predicament is tied in with mine or the others or with the inexplicable machinery in D."

"Why do you say that?"

"Too coincidental."

He was only making noise to mollify me, to alter the direction of my inquisitive nose, to divert me into a more sanguine state of mind. It was all right for him to do that and I appreciated it and never asked him how he would feel if he were young and faced with the realization that no matter what he did there was no one behind him.

We parted outside the diner. He was apologetic because he had talked away the remaining daylight and now it was getting dark. No amount of indoor candlelight and outdoor torchlight could illuminate the wide street or its alleys. I watched Croff hurry away with his hands in his pockets and his shoulders hunched, one of the best minds in the country relegated to obscurity, nonentity and idleness by a criminal with no name. Who was Erma's boss?

A youth gang passed me by, began breaking the burning torches off their posts and tossed them at buildings. There weren't many torches and after they were extinguished total darkness descended over the block. Keeping an eye out for furtive followers, I strolled along and watched the rings in the sky. They shone like strange suns that had blundered into this alien system and were looking for a way of escape. Now their coronas were invisible while only their cores glowed with color, blues, greens, reds, browns and here and there I detected orbs so ebon they were easy to spot against the sky.

Around the corner a green glow beckoned me and I knew a ring had either grounded or was skimming the surface of the street. In fact it was parked between two buildings several meters above a youth gang who were having a confab about the evening's business. Not one of them looked up at the gleaming green moon, no one seemed uneasy, not a member remarked over it but rather they peered through the night at one another as though there was no genuine illumination in the world, never had been and never would be.

Generations of the dole had almost literally altered genes so that their minds worked only a certain way. There had to be a great many hours of vacancy or emptiness in their days. They called them leisure. During this time they existed. Mug, assault, do something really gray, get plenty of fun and a little dope, run errands for junior members of the local syndicate, find some action just so long as it was mostly passive action, and everything would be just fine until it all ended with a bullet, bludgeon, knife or overdose.

They scattered when the earthquake hit, literally went in every direction as the buildings on both sides dropped rooftops on their heads, sent mortar, brick, plastic, glass and steel hurtling down through the green ring that might never have existed for all they had known or cared.

While I helped a rescue party uncover them I thought of what Croff had told me about his having heard of other people with my special talents. "Think what that means," he had said. "The species is building toward genetic greatness. One with such a talent might be a freak but more means natural progress."

Who were those people? No names, just that Appy had mentioned them once upon a time.

Was Croff talking through his beard? Certainly the boys under the rubble hadn't been thinking about special talents when they died and I doubt they believed the world was on its way up and out of its ghetto of misfortune.

# 9

ECTRI TRAVELED down into Jersey to a comfortable-looking estate that wasn't exactly a horse farm. As a matter of fact he raised ponies and dogs. The former were smaller than the latter which were the long, sleek, gray racers that liked nothing better than to chase after artificial rabbits dangling from track arms. Ectri himself never did anything much but oversee the place, or at least that was all I ever saw him do. Once in a while he rode one of the larger ponies, not industriously because they weren't of a size to be used as mounts but were decorative oddities, housebroken like puppies and not even kept in the stable but in a corner wing of the house. The high chain link fences discouraged thieves who might otherwise snatch up the animals and stick them in their cars.

The fences did nothing to impede the activity of a spy like myself who skulked in high grass and watched to see what the tall, menacing owner of the property was up to. How discouraging it was for me to discover he wasn't up to much of anything and that he had obviously come there for a vacation. I watched him play with the miniature ponies, wash dogs and clip their nails, trim bushes and trees around the house, all the mundane things a menacing person wouldn't normally do. It would have seemed more natural for him to take up a weapon and go after somebody, perhaps me.

While I kept a more or less glum watch on him, I still had to show up in Mutat occasionally, so I often left the estate and ring traveled back to the school. The elevator guards on the third floor didn't keep a record of people riding to the upper levels, otherwise Gorwyn would have jumped all over me.

Tedwar was usually somewhere in the background, watching, demanding to know where I had been and what I thought I was doing, threatening, predicting dire fates for me. I told him I thought it was very considerate of him to miss me so much. He took to dogging my footsteps, undoubtedly to find out how I was getting out of the building. If a ring infrequently happened to come through the walls into our living quarters he hopped right into it and went away but he couldn't make a ring do his bidding and come to him when he wished to go somewhere.

One day I climbed into Ectri's dog compound which was simply a fenced-in pasture where the animals roamed and stretched their legs. They stretched after me that day and I didn't wait around to see whether or not they thought I was a rabbit but took off running toward the nearest fence. Having twenty-five greyhounds on one's trail made for good speed but I wasn't that good and they began making headway toward my heels. They weren't nice, tame dogs. A trainer couldn't obtain a competitor from a creature that laid around all day munching tidbits and enjoying fond pats. The hounds behind me were fiercely independent and only manageable in a cage or runway.

I didn't actually see the dark ring. I had never really seen any rings but the greens, blues and yellows while all those others resided somewhere in the corners of my awareness, as if they didn't exist in the substantial world but in a misty limbo. This particular circle lurked in a niche in my psyche like a vague hint of light at the far end of a tunnel, like a trickle of water in a desert, like a patch of blue in a thunderous sky. It was hiding behind a tree stump and I didn't see it except with a miniscule part of a corner of my eye. There was no time to find a familiar-colored ring, no time for anything but the expectation of being grounded by Ectri's dogs.

The forbidden ring left the vicinity of the tree stump and swooped close to me, not in front of me because then I wouldn't be able to see it, but I made it sidle up and then I barged on in.

Immediately I felt like a wet rag sliding down an embankment of mud. Not surprisingly, the world of this ring had no light and in fact was darker than any place I had ever been. I sensed rather than saw that this was a planet of shifting, slippery surfaces surrounded on every side by inky emptiness. My body was long and soft and created little friction between it and the slick surface upon which I lay.

Using my seal-like appendages, I attempted to pull myself up but all the while I slowly slid down the slag, mud or slime under me. There was no one else in this part of the unlighted dimension so it wouldn't do me any good to call for help, not that I possessed the physical equipment to do any calling. There didn't seem to be any assistance for me anywhere.

Having climbed Ectri's fence to see if his dog pasture would afford me an interesting bit of information, I might have been better off taking my chances with his gray racers. In my present condition and position all I could do was struggle to raise one weak fin to a level higher than my head so that I could do the same with my other front fin and thereby stave off sliding another centimeter toward the abyss.

The world had no sound, or perhaps I had no ears. The wet stuff beneath me was inert, noiseless. My breath? There was no such thing here, only effort as I attempted to stave off annihilation. Blackness and silence worked against me. I wasted energy peering and listening.

The mound suddenly swelled and I heaved myself upward just as a whole section fell away. I sensed a little unevenness in the surface now and hugged it almost with fondness, lay as flatly against it as possible. For a while nothing changed but then movement began again and the thought came to me that I was on a giant mound of jello that wobbled when someone poked it. No, I was on an alien planet and it couldn't have been more real or alien if I had boarded a spaceship, traveled to a distant light in the sky and landed on this satellite.

When I finally fell, or was thrust off the pile by the senseless motion, I decided I was in hell. It would be a place like this, not fiery and flecked with hurtling brimstone but empty, lonely, black, hungry as a never-ending pit, deep as a chasm, quieter than any grave. There I was, falling and uselessly flailing fin-arms and fin-legs in a place where no friction could be generated and where there wasn't anyone to hear or care.

The fact that I knew I was falling helped. At least I wasn't drifting which meant I had left somewhere and was headed elsewhere, though the latter might turn out to be infinity. Examining myself helped pass away time as I moved through the dark dimension. I had no ears, or that was my impression. There didn't seem to be anything on or in my head but a pair of enormous eyes and a sharp little snout. About a meter and a half long, I weighed in the neighborhood of fifty kilos, mostly blubber or soft, resilient flesh, much like a seal except that I wasn't a water animal. Neither did I need air or any other gas to sustain me. What I seemed to thrive on was vacuum.

The quivering pile onto which I had first landed must have been some kind of launch pad, doorway, first step or whatever for creatures entering the dimension. Initially they had the slag with which to contend and during this activity they became somewhat oriented to their new selves and environment. I didn't believe I or the dimension was being manipulated but this was the way I explained things to myself. There was little else to do. For a while.

If I hadn't been afraid or if I hadn't been human by nature I might have enjoyed being a space skimmer. Darkness was all right, likewise silence, and who missed oxygen or any of those other things? Just me, but I knew it was because deep inside my mind the spark of humanity was ignited and would remain so as long as my spirit survived.

It wasn't so bad drifting nowhere and doing nothing. It was even possible to do calisthenics, to cavort and twirl like a motorized feather or bit of fluff. All of space was about me and though other objects probably existed somewhere I needn't worry about overcrowding. It seemed my new nature ran more toward the isolated state than the gregarious.

All this went through my mind before I landed on the plank. What it really was I never found out but it was my guess that it and others like it jutted here and there in the black dimension and a space skimmer who happened to land on one had all her problems suddenly condensed into one big tough situation. Perhaps the planks served to make life in the black more interesting. A little conflict never hurt, not even when it lasted a thousand years. Fortunately my confinement didn't last that long.

Falling through vacuum and having done so for an hour or a day, I stopped moving as something was suddenly thrust under me, breaking my fall, not jarringly but so unexpectedly that it brought me new alarm. Right away I didn't like it. Right away I knew bad luck had touched me with a random probe.

Hunger or thirst weren't problems to be reckoned with here for they simply never occurred. Possibly time was distorted or perhaps there was an invisible trough from which I unknowingly swilled. Stranger things had happened to me and it was true that a sense of unreality accompanied me every moment I was on the plank so I couldn't give a positively accurate account of the things that occurred.

Mostly nothing did. Boredom became a terrible enemy as I crawled ever forward looking for an end to the surface under me or at least something different. It was solid, smooth, impersonal with nothing to recommend it to a space skimmer. My mouth was capable of yawning and I did a great deal of that after a long while. Not so fearful as before, I cracked my jawbones with huge, spiritless gapings, blinked at the sky, whacked the floor with my fins and wondered which way it was to the egress.

My prison without bars had some definite measurements, was approximately infinitely wide and infinite in length, which was too bad for me as I didn't relish the idea of a stroll toward forever though I did in fact crawl in that exact direction for a time. Sometimes I went back the way I had come but it didn't help. Time, effort and boredom squeezed my mind dry, made my jaws ache, rubbed my belly raw and threatened to drive me maniacal or catatonic. For what seemed hours I lay on my back soundlessly groaning. If only there had been a little squeak of noise, something, anything to disrupt the tedium.

Having thought myself into a nearly incurable state of ennui, I began crawling again, gaining a centimeter or a meter, forward with the left front fin and then the left rear, right front next, etcetera, and I would have imagined that so much activity would get me somewhere.

By accident I noticed the warm area on the otherwise indifferent surface, vaguely realized I had slithered across it before, not just once but many times and, yes, touching it with my fins, belly and snout told me they were familiar sensations. I couldn't be wrong about such a significant item. I had been over and over this same route before.

I had nothing with which to mark the spot, besides which it wasn't all that noticeable, being merely a slight heated area on the plank, somewhat like a spot on a rug where a sunray landed. At least one thing was in my favor throughout the odd exercise. I seemed to have infallible aim and was capable of moving in straight lines, scarcely veering from my intended path.

It took me hours or possibly days or weeks to figure it out and even then I couldn't believe it. Crawling took on genuine purpose because it was the only way I could determine the dimensions of the plank or whatever it was, using the warm spot as my marker. At first my measurements made no sense. Until doomsday, though, I could have traversed that surface and gotten nowhere. The puzzle had to be solved with luck and logic. Traveling forward, I came across that warm spot, traveled two meters and came across another, found still another four meters ahead and then a fresh one two meters beyond that, and so on and on until I lay down in exhausted bewilderment.

After resting I changed direction, traveled directly left and crawled six meters before finding another warm spot. Two meters ahead of it was another and six meters beyond that was yet another. I lay with my snout on the warmth and wondered what it was. Possibly a faraway star was sending me a feeble ray. The fact that I didn't see the light made no difference because my eyes weren't like those I used to have. Conceivably there was illumination all around me and sound everywhere although I didn't believe there was. Still the warmth existed under my snout, easily discernible through my soft skin, and as a matter of fact I was sensitive enough to note that the heat wasn't evenly distributed over the area, being more noticeable on the right end than the left.

This new discovery inspired me to movement so that I crawled forward two meters to a new warm spot and examined it. How strange, but this one had more pronounced heat on its left side yet seemed to be similar in every other way to the first spot. On I went, six meters ahead, and found the spot with a warmer right side. Turning left, I went four meters and there was a spot with a warmer bottom side, went ahead two meters and the warm side of the spot was on top.

If I hadn't known better I would have finally sworn I was lying on a flat plank approximately three by four meters with a single warm spot near one corner, about a meter from both edges. There I was, and naturally my calculations had to be incorrect because if I was on a plank of that size it would be a simple process for me to find an edge and get off the thing.

That last thought inspired me to sinister imaginings such as, it was a distorted world I was in and what if the plank kept swinging around beneath me each time I reached the edge, or what if I myself were turning without even realizing it?

From the warm spot I went at a right angle one meter and stopped. If I were indeed on that plank which I had imagined, then I was now perched on the edge and should be able to leap, fall or roll off into the chasm which seemed to constitute most of this dimension.

It didn't matter. Roll, pitch or scramble as I might, all I did was move one meter forward to the old warm marker. I was on a plank I couldn't get off because something had happened to its depth. My prison had length and width but that was all. As far as progress on it was concerned, it would either be nonexistent or imaginary. I couldn't get off an edge because there wasn't any. Every time I traversed the length or width of it I just kept going in the opposite direction without any other change ever having taken place.

Mine seemed to be an environment where solutions didn't happen. Only circumstance changed, if one were lucky. I believe to this day that planks like the one I was on jutted out all over that dark dimension, and I can conceive of all sorts of people in the shape of seals lying on those planks wondering if they're ever going to get off them.

Deliverance was such a simple thing which was why I don't think many people ever managed it. After deciding I was on a two-dimensional enigma approximately three by four meters, and after deciding that crawling was a waste of time and I'd never escape the wretched object, I surrendered mentally, emotionally and physically and expressed my contempt for accident and coincidence by slamming the warm spot one last time. I hit it hard with a back fin after which I planned to lie down and die or do whatever else I had to do.

It was like dumping a truck, unloading the marbles in a toy, unfooting the unwary. The warm spot was struck by me and immediately something flew through space and collided solidly with the plank. Perhaps it was another plank, come to straddle mine and form an attractive line I could have spent a lifetime investigating. Rather than do that or anything I let inertia take its course, rose off my flat jail like a bit of down and began plummeting at a decent rate of speed through vacuum.

Having already done a foolish thing by leaping into a dangerous situation while trying to avoid another, I behaved stupidly again, spied a forbidden ring in the darkness, forced it to come to me and plunged through it. Anything to escape before another plank came along.

It was an off-colored ring, pale yellow and therefore to be shunned but I was so demoralized that any circle would have looked inviting to me.

One instant I was an odd little seal creature and in the next I was submerged in liquid and about to give a healthy snort of relief for having misjudged the ring's color and landed in Waterworld. Instead I began choking. I was submerged in fluid but there wasn't a single scale or gill attached to my body. Not a tiny swimmer, not any size swimmer, I was Daryl Nobody somewhere on Earth and in need of air.

The thought flashed through my mind that I might be at the bottom of Loch Ness. Or the Atlantic. Or Old Faithful. In fact I was in Rock Lake, state of West Virginia, about to be snagged by a fisherwoman sitting on a dock thirty meters away. Her startled face grew more so as I surfaced but she was calm enough as she reeled me in, hauled me out and sat on my back. It seemed she had never heard of other methods of resuscitation. Her name was Deider and she wasn't about to believe I was a ring traveler.

"Scared me some, seeing you float up like that, but a good swimmer could make it underwater from the other side to where I pulled you out. It isn't all that big a lake."

"Like a submarine?" I said.

"Just eat and don't try me with any tales. I've been here and there and it's my opinion that people who say they see rings in the air are big liars."

I tried to imagine that her three-sided shack was something created by the staggering economy but she assured me folks in those parts had lived thusly for better than three hundred years.

"We're like the original settlers of the country while everyone else are foreigners," she said. "Except that I'm Christian. It's live and let live and don't talk about anybody."

"Thanks for the food and saving my life."

"You're welcome. Next time don't fall in the lake with all your clothes on."

Deider, her six children and ailing husband weren't suffering from the energy crisis because they had never had any energy to miss. They owned an outhouse, a clean well with a hand pump, open fireplaces and enough candles to last a decade. Three of the children had scholarships and attended the college fifty miles away while the other three brought home books from the library and tutored themselves. At age eighteen they would apply for high school diplomas and scholarships to the college. Deider assured me they would be successful. All her children had whopping minds. They just didn't have any money.

I stayed a few days. Woods so dense they could scarcely be walked through lured me. Chewing sassafras bark, I tramped for miles through the most beautiful country in the world. Sitting beside a slow-moving creek, I watched crawdads burrow in the soft mud, blues and reds that scurried and dug with frantic motions. Squirrels played tag just out of reach, birds held socials, thunder cracked over my head like war, rain broke like shattered diamonds, spiders skulked and watched, apples rotted to make strong perfume, pears dropped like heavy stones.

To be a nonentity wasn't exactly my goal but it seemed to work for me decently well those few days. I lived in the woods like an Indian and though I didn't hunt game I did track down nuts and berries. Now and then I showed up at Deider's shack or one of the children searched me out in the wilderness.

"The best thing to do after you find something you enjoy is to stop and figure out why everything else is so bad," she said to me.

"Figuring out stuff like that can take a lifetime, and then what's left to enjoy?"

"Memory. That's all that's fun anyhow. Don't you know it isn't the doing that's so great?"

"I don't want a life of just thinking and remembering," I said.

"What a funny thing for a little old hermit like you to be saying. You don't do anything but think, alone the way you always are, not unless you have an invisible friend."

"I don't know if he's invisible or dead or what."

Mutat was waiting for me in the pale sunshine, a prison of bricks, steel and formalized minds, a halfway house where unwanted persons were fed and kept track of. If kids like me weren't loose in the streets we weren't getting into trouble which meant we weren't bothering adults, so they stuffed us in buildings like Mutat where other adults bored us to death with their outpourings. Who cared if somebody sailed around the world in a rotting ship? Had the man known how to ring travel? Had he ever seen a ring or had he once dreamed such a thing existed?

Something that never failed to annoy me was having my things snooped through. Somebody had had fun while I was gone, managed to pick the lock on my door and then ransacked in a reckless and abandoned manner. Even my bed was torn apart and the mattress lay on the floor, gutted like an old doll.

The strings of junk that had constituted sleep guns and harnesses in D-2 were gone from my closet. Looking around at the mess, I suddenly got so angry I wanted to dismember someone so I went stomping down the hall toward Tedwar's room. His door was ajar which made it all the easier and quicker for me. The carpet muffled sound so I got as far as the door itself before coming to an abrupt halt.

Apparently nothing in the world could be expected to work in a normal fashion. I heard Tedwar crying big racking sobs that came from deep inside his soul. My wrath left me that quickly. I couldn't hold onto it.

I leaned against the wall and listened to my mortal enemy cry his heart out. What had ever made me think he was an unfeeling monster? How could I nurture hatred for someone who suffered even more than I?

# 10

TRYING TO TRACK down Croff's old associates wasn't as easy as I anticipated. Orfia was my first choice for investigating since she had been a particular thorn in Appy's side, seemed to have gone out of her way to scorn him, had been his avowed target for revenge. So Croff had said. He didn't know what caused the antipathy between the two. It had something to do with professional jealousy. The situation had gotten so that nobody could get along with Appy or pacify him once he went into one of his frequent rages but Orfia was special, especially toward the end before they were all taken captive by the hoodlum. Had Appy been captured along with the others? No, but that didn't mean anything. There were a few people who hadn't been picked up.

Croff was only sure of Orfia's address at Burgoyne, and he hadn't known if she was using her professional, domestic or real name. People did so love their anonymity.

After I finally got to see the university records, I found them scant and uninformative. In fact they had been hunted through and thinned out. There was nothing about Orfia that Croff hadn't told me.

I thought about the problem while I got Bandit into shape, rode his fat off, stuffed him with vitamins until faint dapples showed on his glowing coat, filed his feet and rubbed his legs with liniment. Even Googs lost weight and seemed to feel better.

Maverick had another litter of kittens which inspired Olger to lecture me on the evils of overpopulation so I told her to go ahead and get the spaying done after weaning time.

Gorwyn seemed thoroughly disgusted with me, even went so far as to hint he might send the law after me if I didn't call a halt to my truancy.

"I admit I'm no genius but don't I pass all my exams and hand in most of my assignments?" I said.

"Irrelevant. There are rules in every organization and things operate better where there is obedience."

"I'm not a thing. Besides, you sold Groppo so there's nobody interesting around here anymore."

"The ape was raised for selling as are all my animals. How else do you think we manage to live so comfortably here? The government is very stingy these days. And please don't refer to the beast as if he were a person."

"About the truancy, you don't really care whether I'm here or not."

"Indeed?" he said in his fussiest manner though he gave me a flickering, odd glance.

"It's just as well because I'm the restless type and can't tolerate being tied down. I'm staying out of mischief so there'll be no repercussions. You have nothing to worry about."

This time he snapped at me. "I'll be the judge of that. Don't ever let me catch you ring traveling inside my building or I'll have you confined to your quarters."

I visited a little town in Maine where Croff said he believed Orfia had mentioned she lived as a child. Only an ancient schoolteacher who somehow managed to survive on her Social Security was able to tell me anything.

Her name was Flava and she rocked in her wooden chair as if she knew both of them would soon stop for good. Also, I think that was the way she got her daily exercise. The way she sent the rocker all over the high porch made me pay attention. Dust from the road had settled on her so I wondered how long she had been sitting there.

"The reason nobody remembers Orfia is because she moved out of here as a young girl," she said. "Being the eldest citizen in town, I can cast my mind back the farthest." She reached out and tried to grasp my hand. After a few times, I gave in and let her hold it.

There had been some trouble and Orfia's parents took her and her older brother and moved away. What kind of trouble?

"Those days or these, what's the difference?" said Flava, blinking her faded eyes. "There's so much distress, who can keep track? But the fact is I don't really know. Orfia was a good little student, sharp as a whip and eager to learn. I seem to recall it had something to do with her injuring another student, supposedly beat him up pretty badly though I saw him the day after they said it happened and I can swear he hadn't a mark on him. Orfia and her family moved right after that. Of course it's possible the two incidents weren't connected. My memory isn't all that trustworthy."

She went on to tell me about how the town had gone through a period of change before reverting back to its original condition. "The so-called good life of the late last century didn't get up to these parts until a few decades ago but all it did was spoil most of the people in this town. Used to be we fished for a living when the water was fit and we had all the lamps and coal we needed. The new energy took most of our life away because it made us fat, lazy and good for nothing. Instead of wondering how to get supper we wondered how to pass away the minutes and hours of every day."

"Is it better now?" I asked.

She squeezed my arm, invited me to come closer and didn't seem offended when I declined. "If human beings are happy it doesn't matter about energy and comforts. This town is a tottering derelict because the people in it think they can't live their lives without the government telling them how. They're all waiting for the lights to come back on."

"They'll have a long wait."

"Won't they, though? The whole idea is to get something to eat and a place to sleep. There are modern ways to do that and there are the old simple ways."

Before I left, I leaned down and let her kiss me on the cheek. Her lips were paper-thin and delicate. Like the town, they threatened to blow away with the first brisk wind.

At least I learned the name of the boy Orfia had supposedly

tried to kill. Carston. Neither he nor his family lived there anymore but I found an old librarian who told me Carston had
moved to Stillwell which wasn't far away. So I went to Stillwell
and was told Carston had moved north. Where? I might try his
cousin who lived in the yellow house at the end of town except
that she was in California and wouldn't be back for a month or
more. Where in California? Nobody seemed to have the address.

Back at Mutat, I invited Tedwar to visit my farm in New Jersey. Instead of turning me down with words he threw a twenty-
pound dictionary at me. Limping down the hall to my room I
considered the virtues and advantages of never again inviting
him to go anywhere or of even being in his vicinity.

Browsing through the newspaper ads a day or so later I came
across one that made me sit up straight: URGENT MEET ME
PEORIA NOON TUESDAY. It was then Monday so I hoped I
had only missed seeing the ad the past week. I jumped out of a
school window into Waterworld the next day and went directly
to the cornfield. Croff didn't show. Not that day or the next
Tuesday.

By the time I decided to go to Atlanta to try and track him
down he was already buried. No one was safe from robbers, according to one of his neighbors, and of course that was how
Croff had died, by a nasty specimen who liked to break people's
bones. Whoever did it had worked quietly and gained entry into
the apartment by removing an entire window after which they
beat the owner to death and made off with the valuables. Would
I like to visit the grave? No, if the victim had left any messages
for anyone the neighbor knew nothing about that. All the old
man's personal belongings had been gathered up by a niece who
lived in Virginia. Wasn't it tragic how some brilliant and famous
people lost their sanity and became common dregs? It was a fact
the old man had money in the bank. Several banks, in fact, and
under different names. The niece had been quite surprised about
it.

I went to my farm in Jersey, took Bandit and Googs and escaped into the peace of the woods, remained there until I ran
out of tins of dog food and the old hound began trying to run
down rabbits. She couldn't have run down a turtle so I took her
back to Olger.

Why had they killed Croff? He had been doing exactly what they wanted, stayed out of sight and existed as a nonentity.

"I've decided to be firm with you," Gorwyn said to me. "What are you, fifteen now? A long way from your majority which means you have no rights."

"That doesn't sound very democratic or Christian."

"I was speaking from an abstract viewpoint. I've received reports about your running across the grounds, leaping into rings and scaring people half to death."

"What people?" I said. "Nobody comes near this place. Have you noticed how orphanages have an abandoned look about them? It's because the inmates are the public's responsibility and we all know what the public does with its responsibility."

"If this were an orphanage I'd have you transferred to a detention center. From now on you can't leave the premises without permission. Do so and my best runners will be after you pronto."

"Like who?"

"Padarenka and Mikala."

My mouth must have been hanging open because he told me to close it.

I went to hunt up my old friends. "You were already killed once because of something that had to do with me," I said. "Don't you ever learn?"

"Stop flattering yourself," one of them said. "That didn't really have anything to do with you, and besides, what we do is none of your business." They looked to be in fine health, had obviously eaten well during their absence, wore new clothes, moved with confident airs. I smelled bribery.

"You sold out," I said.

"To whom?"

"That's what I want to know."

"We work for nobody but Gorwyn. If you have any more questions, direct them at him because we find you boorish and a brat. We're glad you helped us once and we'll pay you back sooner or later. Meanwhile don't run or we'll chase your tail off."

"You spilled your guts to Gorwyn about me, didn't you?"

"You keep harping on that. Who cares what a freak you are?"

The fact was they were too dumb to make a living at a real job. Dumb and lazy. And ungrateful.

Gorwyn told me later he had rehired them because they were good runners and because their looks were an asset to the place. Sometimes agents from government or industry came to interview a prospect and it didn't hurt to have handsome people on the staff.

"Why am I never interviewed?" I asked.

"You're underage."

"All prospects start out that way. I get older every day."

"The fact is I've been forbidden to offer you to anybody."

"By whom?"

"The juvenile courts. You're a pauper, you're physically incapacitated because of your amnesia, and furthermore—"

"Never mind."

Sometimes he let me help him with his pointless experiments. At least most of them seemed pointless to me. He was such a dry stick of a man with no sense of humor and no tolerance for error. What made this a luckless attribute for him was that he made more mistakes than anyone I knew. He was clumsy, impulsive, impatient, unimaginative, gullible and even sadistic in a way, propelling terrified experimental subjects into rings when they didn't perform to suit him, cuffing others, depriving them of rewards. Usually, though, he was just ludicrous.

He had a small lab close to a ring channel at the edge of the property, nestled in high shrubbery so that he was nearly always able to work in solitude. Except when I barged in. The small concrete building wasn't situated so close to the channel that the primary stream of rings penetrated its area but there were enough circles drifting away from the main course and coming through the walls to us. They were mostly small and slow moving which was what Gorwyn wanted.

"Did you know animals are like us?" he said. "Only some of them can see rings."

"What's the ratio?"

"I think about fifteen percent of humans can see them compared to about sixty percent for animals. That isn't limited just to warm bloods. I've known snakes to have a good eye, also fish, frogs, even insects. It's a matter of physiology and has little to do with intelligence. The fact that a brain and pair of eyes perceive a ring automatically sets up all the other stages of the muting process. For instance, you see a ring because your body and your mind are capable of melding with the ring in the mutating process. If you can't see one it's because the two of you aren't attuned to one another, having nothing in common, aren't mutually attracted, or whatever. That's why rings constantly move through non-perceptive organisms without affecting them. There's no kinship."

He didn't break the law too much, retrieved most of the creatures he sent to other dimensions. It was illegal to enforce travel on anything, the idea being that reality was precarious enough without adding more unknowns. No one knew what might happen to interdimensional equilibrium if experimenters were permitted to shove just anything through. It was assumed that human travelers did no harm since they returned to D-1 and thereby reestablished the status quo. Anyway, Gorwyn was good at making harnesses that didn't mutate into something too different from the originals to do the job, even had a bug net that brought them back alive and well.

He had a workable monitoring system consisting of sensitive cells that registered changes in the atmosphere of the room. The rings themselves were too alien or tenuous to detect but their color was something that could be perceived by instruments. The first row of cells on a squat black machine registered color and size, the second row read and reported both so that Gorwyn pretty much knew at all times what was in the room and where it was.

"I'll tell you something I'll bet you don't know," he said. "My readers show there are more than just green, blue and yellow rings. There are also blacks, browns, reds, grays and whites. The only problem is, people and animals can't see them."

"Is that so?" I said, remembering another time when a dead man named Deron called me a liar because I said I saw other rings. "What about all this non-organic junk you send through? It doesn't have eyes to see."

"The rules are different in that area. Some junk in the company of living organisms goes on through while some can actually go through by itself. For instance, my instruments tell me there's a small blue ring in the corner of this room. If you carried this insect net with you and went through it, your clothes would disappear and reappear only when you returned but the net would become a clay sphere that could hold any number of flying creatures. If you simply tossed it in by itself, it would become a piece of shale."

"What happens to my clothes?"

"Theoretically they're in limbo or a dead area that exists between dimensions. Clothes don't mutate so they only go part way in. I assume, of course, you're accepting my explanations knowing they're only opinion. There are others who've done more research than I. Go up north and you'll find a slew of people who spend most of their lives studying the subject. I just dabble at it. It's my hobby."

Having had enough learning for one day, I skipped the rest of my classes and went to Waterworld, tucked myself inside an empty shell and went to sleep.

A clanging in my head awakened me. My shell was washing against a steel girder. By accident I had found the metal monstrosity again, or subconsciously I had chosen the correct-colored ring.

Following the girder's contours was difficult because I was so small but by frequently stopping to rest I managed to cover considerable territory in the next several hours. Here and there landing platforms stuck out from the metal and I could see nets floating free. They were empty so I didn't stop but continued onward in what seemed to be an upward course. In Waterworld I never really knew north from south, east from west.

On through water that grew murky I went until eventually I came to what seemed to be the ceiling of the green dimension. And all along I had assumed the place was boundless. It felt like such a hard and metallic ceiling, so cold and impersonal and I didn't know what to make of it when the vibrating started. Beneath me maelstroms were created.

The concussions on the other side of the wall or within it were regular like a vehicle running over evenly spaced ruts in a road and generating rhythmic bumping sounds. In fact I thought I could hear the thumps when I pressed my forehead to the cold surface.

So intent was I on the sounds that I failed to perceive the band of swimmers until they were too close for comfort. They were approximately five meters below me, too near for me to try and run for it. Flattening my back against the hardness of Waterworld's ceiling, I maintained my position without drifting which wasn't easy to do since the steady thuds above me tended to propel me away.

Had I been of normal size they would have been on me in an instant. Or so I thought. Their failure to see me might have had something to do with the fact that a big shadow suddenly fell over me. There were five of them swimming leisurely as if out for an afternoon constitutional but I knew they were scouts on the hunt for snoops like myself. It was also my suspicion that they worked for a bone-breaking psychotic by the name of Erma.

All five were big and strong and could have swum rings around me but, since they didn't expect any danger from tiny intruders, they were conducting their sweep well below the wall they were supposed to protect. Their eyes were directed downward and I counted myself fortunate as they swam under me and moved on out of sight. After a long while I decided it was safe to move. They really ought to have seen me. I couldn't see how they missed.

Continuing my investigation, I snooped and pried for what seemed hours before finally discovering it was a huge, round pipe above me and not a flat wall or ceiling.

I didn't learn it all in one day. It took me three weeks of coming to Waterworld in the afternoon and swimming for several hours before I found out where the pipe went. It was the same old one I had found in Gothland, except that this was the beginning of it. Propped on floating girders, it plunged through a big blue ring.

It was a letdown for me to realize Erma was like every other criminal. She wanted the pot at the end of the rainbow. She was like any alchemist who dreamed of mutating muck into gold. The fluid in Waterworld was piped into Gothland where it changed into a thick, acidic substance that hurtled on into Earth as an entirely different combine. It didn't take me long to realize what that combination of elements was. Black, thick and rare, it seemed to mean the difference between civilization and the Stone Age. Erma was up to her neck in oil.

Pat and Mike came to pester me every time I showed up at Mutat.

"I can't help it if I see rings better than you," I said.

"Baloney on that," said one of them. I think it was Mike. She had a tiny mole right in the center of her forehead. "Luck is the only reason you take off so fast without our seeing you. We're supposed to keep you in your classes. Don't you care about our jobs?"

"Not particularly."

For that remark they put the leather harness on me and made me walk around the grounds like a dog. Occasionally they booted my tail.

"Cogitate upon that," said Pat. "How do you appreciate it? Our livelihood is more important than your pride. Why don't you say that over and over again until it sinks into that thick skull of yours?"

# 11

I CAN TRUTHFULLY SAY that in all the time I knew Gorwyn I never really liked him. He was clever, intelligent, prissy, chilly, pedantic, dictatorial, cranky and an odd bird. He was, however, the only man in town, or in other words I had nobody else to talk to. The twins were dum dums, Tedwar always threw something at me whenever I went near him, the other students my age were all male and not inclined to notice me as anything but an outsider. At first they made crude remarks whenever I passed them in the halls, until I began devising things to dump on them such as ink balls, balloons of honey, stink bombs and such. I became known as that skinny wretch who took everything seriously.

I talked to Gorwyn who listened with a contemptuous air and continually made condescending responses. Practically everyone I knew agreed he was off his shelf. He hadn't been director of the school very long. He sometimes leased practically every student in the place to industries, other schools or individuals in need of muters. He kept close tabs on them by sending runners to make sure they weren't being neglected or abused and he made certain they were returned on time but I didn't think his heart was in it. If we had all dropped dead he would have gone right on experimenting in his lab.

He sent me into D to gather drees and worm shells so he could test their normal counterparts to see if and how their stay in another dimension had affected them. Of all the transmutations I witnessed or heard of, the process of a turtle becoming a worm in a shell once it entered D was the most cut and dried. That animal simply never became anything but a worm in a shell whether it went into Gothland or Waterworld and the differences between the two alterations were miniscule. One had a tough exterior capable of withstanding high temperatures and corrosive elements while the other had the same tough outside capable of absorbing and using water. The worm part looked exactly the same though their internal workings had to be poles apart.

Gorwyn said he had heard a horse did the same thing, changed into a winged organism like Pegasus no matter which dimension it entered. There weren't too many opportunities to check it out since horses were expensive and scarce and the extra-large rings seldom touched down on the ground.

The experiments seemed pointless to me though I kept my opinion to myself. My randomly gathering drees couldn't tell him what he wanted to know since he hadn't examined them before they changed but he seemed to think he was gaining considerable information from the rabbits, squirrels, skunks, turtles and what not that I brought back. When I kept asking him if they showed any abnormal characteristics he ran me off the premises, banished me to the main building and had Pat and Mike escort me to and from classes. He really was off his shelf.

He relented when I agreed to let him hook me up to his mechanical contraption and monitor my brain waves. The thing reminded me of the execution chairs of olden times, was cold and metallic and smelled of battery acid. Gorwyn frowned and scowled as he performed the necessaries.

"I know exactly what I'm doing, just as I always do," he said, strapping my arms and legs.

"You're going to kill me," I said. "I know you don't like me."

"Have you changed your mind? Say so and it's back to the main building with you."

"The straps are too tight. What's that thing?"

"A crown of wires. It won't hurt."

"Is all this exactly legal?"

"Not exactly. Want to quit?"

"Yes."

"Too late."

There was no use my asking him later what he had learned from the experiment or if he had learned anything at all. I think he lied nearly all the time.

"It was interesting because that's the second time I've used the crown but your brain activity is no different than that of a non-muter. I could have gotten the same results with a regular monitor."

"It made my head buzz. Things knocked and slid around in there."

It was about a week later that I took it upon myself to visit a police station in New Mexico. It seemed to be far enough away from my usual stomping grounds so that if I wasn't graciously received it wouldn't be easy for them to trace me.

Lieutenant Solvo was bored and sleepy and looked as if he thought I was a crackpot. It was difficult for me to believe that someone as immobile as he could be a crook. He was a burly, gum-chewing Indian with eyes so big and dark they were frightening. They were fathomless, told me nothing about the mind behind them. On second thought I didn't think Solvo was slow at much of anything.

First he wanted to know my name and address, scowled when I stumbled over both, sat back in his chair and yawned while I told him about oil. Not a shadow flickered in his eyes, not a muscle in his face twitched which assured me I had wasted my time coming here. Either he was corrupt or didn't believe a word I said.

"I suppose locating you later won't be a problem," he said, proceeding to shatter my illusions about anonymity. "Your story tells me you're a muter, you're an adolescent so if I need to talk to you I'll contact Mutat. You're either a resident there or they'll have an idea where you can be reached. Have you seen any of this oil coming out of the pipe?"

"Don't need to. I can add one and one."

"Those huge structures in the other dimensions must have been seen by many travelers."

"Not necessarily," I said. "I've never found any boundaries in

D. No matter how big an object you stick into infinity, it's still a drop in the bucket, right? The few who wander too close in Waterworld are captured in nets and killed. Sloks take care of intruders in Gothland."

"You know so much for one so young and so small. Maybe you're thinking to fool an old fool, maybe you're telling me a bunch of dreams, maybe everything you say is fact. When you placed your head against the pipe in Waterworld, how regular were the pulsations? How many times a minute would you estimate?"

The speed with which he shifted from low to high gear made me blink. "I don't remember. They were slow. The slower, the more oil, right? And the bigger the earthquakes for the rest of us."

"I'd like the names of all the police officers your friend contacted."

I gave him two or three names Croff had mentioned, where they worked and whatever else about them I could recall.

No sooner was I out the door of the building than someone silently fell into place behind me. Without missing more than a step or two I turned and retraced my route to Solvo's office. "That's all I need," I said. "A tail. If everything I said to you is true, I can't afford to attract any more attention than I already have. Those people I told you about are dangerous."

He waved a hand, smiled a smile. Really, it was nothing. "A thought on my part to see that you returned to your home in safety. But since you object, consider him nonexistent."

He was, but that was only because somebody else took up the chase which wasn't a merry one since it took more cunning than I knew I had to lose her. I believed Solvo was trying to tell me something by insisting upon keeping tabs on me but I didn't know whether to feel reassured about him or doubly worried.

Pat and Mike weren't half as good as my new tail. I walked into the lobby of a skyscraper, took an el to the twentieth floor and horrified some onlookers by opening a window and diving out. Hopefully, whoever was following me would immediately be dissuaded. Landing in D-2, I loped up a smoking hill and barely tipped its crest as I gained the distinct impression that a goth had left the very same ring behind and was even now imitating my movements.

I didn't believe it but I flashed on down my hill and crouched behind some rocks. Though I waited with more than normal patience nobody came. No goth broke the horizon, no employee of Solvo's showed to enlighten me. Thinking she might be hiding, I crawled to the hilltop and looked around. There wasn't a soul in sight.

Now I knew a little bit about what Croff must have felt when he had no one to go to. He had wanted to unload the responsibility of his knowledge and so did I. For all his efforts he was six feet under and I seemed to be following hot in his footsteps. What I had done was probably sic another enemy onto my trail.

I stood on the slope in Gothland and wondered if my eyes had played tricks on me. Had a girl really come after me through the ring and was she skulking in goth form in one of the myriad cracks and crevices below?

Eventually I grew angry. I tried to be subtle about it, carefully concealed myself before calling a green ring to me, went through in a hurry and grabbed the nearest cluster of weeds as a shield before whirling to watch the entrance into the dimension. I wasn't certain but there seemed to be a slight blurring of color after which there came an impression of movement close to me and then some seven meters away a swimmer materialized.

She was about a meter and three-quarters long, fifty kilos in weight, tan of skin, black of hair with fine features and eyes like Solvo's. When she didn't find what she was looking for she stopped short and floated while I and the clump of seaweed drifted unnoticed past her. She swam some twenty meters in all four directions before coming back to her original position, all the while seeking, searching, looking for an adversary who had apparently disappeared. There was something about her stance and the way she peered through the water that made me think she was not only puzzled but excited and pleased as well. She was good at muting and maybe she didn't often meet someone she couldn't catch.

It didn't take her long to show me just how good she was. After prowling around and not finding me, she called a blue ring to her that had been meandering just off to her left, and not only was I amazed to see someone besides myself have command over dimensional doorways but there was also the fact that she did it so rapidly. I had never made it a practice to send rings zooming through space but this spawn of Solvo bossed them as if they were made of smoke. She flitted out of Waterworld faster than I could blink, left me hanging onto the seaweed and wondering if perhaps now wasn't the best time to make my getaway.

I hesitated just long enough for her to play out her waiting game. She popped back into the water close enough to my hiding place to make me flinch. I and the seaweed drifted with more enthusiasm, but she must have thought her sudden appearance accounted for the movement so she didn't investigate.

Spying a familiar blue ring, I called it to me, swam through into Gothland, leaped up an escarpment that was low enough for me but too high for a normal sized animal and crouched down with about a split second to spare. The Indian came through the misty doorway like a wraith, landed like an oiled spring and stopped dead still. I was confident she hadn't actually seen me leave Waterworld but had probably only noticed the slight warping of the area as I traveled. Anyhow, she was a speedy demon and like no other muter I had ever met. She was also short of temper, paced the hot ground below, glared first in one direction and then another, growled low in her throat and generally made like someone who didn't appreciate what was happening.

She was too sharp to fool around with and I had other business to attend to so I raced along the mountain ridge until I found a yellow ring that took me to Mutat.

Someone had blitzed my room, spattered ink on the walls, threw mud on my clothes, filled the tub and dumped in my shoes and books, put bugs in my bed, etcetera. Not wasting a moment's time, I stomped down the hall and kicked in Tedwar's door, found him in the bathroom and hauled him out into the living room where I proceeded to kick him around.

He got away from me and ran behind the couch. "You make me sick!" he screamed. His red hair was askew, his eyes were wild. While he yelled he grabbed up books from a shelf behind him and threw them at me. "You stinking hog! You have to have everything, don't you?"

Like a rabbit I leaped up over the couch and clamped my legs around his neck. We both fell to the floor with him on the bottom and he hit his head hard. He began to sob but I didn't pause, punched him, gouged him, elbowed him, kneed his ribs.

"I don't care what you do!" he shrieked. "Stay away from him! He isn't yours, he's mine!"

What he said was a little bit interesting so I stopped pounding him, intending to continue with added zest in a second or two, right after I found out why he was so bilious.

He was far gone by then. His face purple and his eyes bulging, he drooled and cried his heart out and after a while I discovered why he hated me and had given my room the business.

"You ruined it!" he said, glaring up at me as if I had horns. "We were beginning to get along! You're a filthy slob! I'll kill you if you don't stay away from him. He doesn't need you for his experiments and you have no right! I can do them as good as you! He isn't your father, he's mine!"

I had a headache all the rest of the day. One thing I couldn't stand was someone else's emotional traumas. It was enough just handling my own. A couple of nurses had showed up and carried Tedwar, kicking and shouting, to the infirmary and I went to pack my gear. I was stunned over the whole thing. I'd had no idea he was Gorwyn's son.

That evening I tossed my suitcase out a window and then muted down onto the campus. Pat and Mike were behind me but I didn't care. When the time came to lose them I would do it. There was a note on Tedwar's bureau telling him how sorry I was and that I hadn't tried to steal his father's affections.

I was almost at the end of the drive when I heard a scream and looked over toward the ring channel where something unusual was happening to one of the circles. Too far away to tell what it was, I walked closer and then dropped my suitcase and stared in horror. A large brown ring had left the channel and was dancing across the grass. Tedwar was inside it, helplessly tumbling within some kind of vortex.

Close enough to grasp him, I reached out to do so when the ring darted away. I called to it and was surprised when it kept on going. Tedwar's screams grew shrill. I don't think he saw or heard me or was aware of anything but the horror enveloping him. The ring was drawing him in and though he couldn't see it he was going even deeper. In another moment he would be all the way into the brown dimension.

There was nothing I could do. Pat and Mike ran with me, oblivious of what was going on and probably thinking I was playing a strange trick. They couldn't see brown rings. This one wouldn't do as I commanded but left the ground to soar high in the sky, hovered directly above me just long enough for me to see it when Tedwar was suddenly sucked all the way in. At a sedate pace it left the area.

Gorwyn reportedly was so upset by the occurrence that he locked himself in his upper story apartment and refused to see anyone. Police swarmed over the grounds looking for clues. Suicide was illegal and they were after information to dispel the rumor that Tedwar had been trying to do away with himself when he fiddled with the equipment in his father's lab.

They didn't understand that equipment, neither did anyone and Gorwyn wasn't about to come out of seclusion for more than a cursory interview, so they snooped and speculated and gave their private version to the press. The boy was playing a prank, had manipulated some highly sophisticated machinery that hadn't a thing to do with his disappearance. There were searchers in both Gothland and Waterworld but of course they were in the fringe areas near entrances to the campus. They didn't expect to find Tedwar. Like other runaways, he would come home when he was ready.

I heard his screams again when I went into the brown dimension. Getting there wasn't easy and I didn't love the idea, but no one else was doing anything. Tedwar hadn't come home and who would go and bring him back? They said muters traveled at their own risk. How true and how helpful to Tedwar.

I couldn't get Gorwyn to come out of his rooms, he wouldn't talk on the phone, nobody seemed willing to pursue the matter and after the weekend had passed I finally accepted the inevitable and went to do what I could.

My good eye functioned as keenly as ever so that as I stood beside the ring channel on campus and hunted for the right color I saw one almost immediately, a madcap kind of sphere that behaved crazily. It was a muddy brown shade, two meters in diameter with a skinny corona and a core as black as the pit. There wasn't a thing about it that looked good. It didn't flow evenly like the other rings but bumped and dragged along, gave feeble little lurches, swerved or sometimes sagged and lost its roundness. It occurred to me that the dimension might be closing up shop and going out of business, shutting down, turning in on itself and automatically rejecting all travelers. It wasn't a pleasant thought. Supposing I mutated into a fat organism while the dimension turned out to be a pair of walls closing together? Supposing?

My entrance wasn't a matter of simply barging on through, for the ring skipped away from me like a shadow, turned its opening in another direction, was obviously telling me to trek anywhere but into its bosom. Since I couldn't see off-colors straight on anyhow, it was all right with me when the thing showed me the side of its rim. Behind me, Pat and Mike called in tones growing puzzled and anxious.

"What do you think you're doing, brat?"

"She's off her shelf. Always has been. Hey, you, quit moving around like you're on eggs. What's the matter with you?"

I turned my back to the brown rim, reached behind me, touched it, felt an awesome coldness. Possibly I was about to become a penguin. "You guys are okay but you're blind," I said. "Don't you see this ring? It's exactly like the one Tedwar took a ride in."

"Come away from the channel," said Pat. "Your brains are baked. Believe me, no matter which ring you take we'll be on your tail. You can't get away from us when we're this close."

Feeling, touching, investigating, I moved closer to the throbbing rim which was relatively placid now, scarcely bobbing, and the thought came to me that it wasn't worried because it believed I had gone away. Never before had I ascribed any intelligence or awareness to rings but I gave the idea serious consideration as I prepared to slip around the side. Always from the corner of my eye I kept a bit of it in sight. It grew colder and I grinned more widely at the twins.

"Now you see me, now you—" I said and traveled quickly, not to shock them with my sudden disappearance but to penetrate the ring's interior before it could skip out on me. In I went with a gasp followed by a groan because though the world around me changed a great deal I remained the same thin skinned human who liked warm weather.

The planet was dying. It had been around for a long time and its substance had decayed. Its shape changed, its mass shrank in some places while bloating in others, it lost command over itself so that it bulged out of position in space. Eventually the more solid parts began to collapse so that over the eons it became two jutting escarpments approximately three hundred meters apart. In between was simply and utterly nothing. The dimension had split and would soon go hurtling into vacuum.

The last faint glow of heat or energy was too deep inside the separated escarpments to keep the air warm and the loss of power might also account for the fact that I didn't mutate into another life form. The world was too old and worn out to do its job. In a flash I appeared on top of an endless finger of brittle rock with brown air all around me and a cold breeze whipping through my hair. Sinking to my knees, I hugged my chest and stared around. All about me was sadness. I could feel it everywhere like a heavy hand. The ring hadn't wanted me, couldn't fully accommodate me but here I was and my coming had almost drained whatever energy was being generated in its heart.

I thought all those things as I knelt on what little there was left of the planet. Its reserves were so dangerously low that it might not be able to sustain both me and the boy caught between the escarpments. While I had sneaked in just far enough to land on one of the two rocks, Tedwar had been caught in the vortex and must have hurtled through so that his momentum carried him into the empty space between. Now another force had him in its grasp and wouldn't let go of him until the world was totally without power.

The planet used its flagging strength to hold him in place and prevent his falling away. There he was, suspended, while beneath him and all around him spun a dark maelstrom that might have been the very soul of the dimension. He screamed and kept on screaming because he knew who and where he was.

As quietly and as carefully as I had ever done anything in my life I backed through the yellow circle behind me, found my old familiar Earth pretty much as I had left it. What an incredible thing it was to realize that a few arm lengths away, Tedwar hung between two halves of an expiring world which was millions of light years away in the sky.

My impulse was to immediately bolt but I knew better, raised my hand in a wave and grinned at Pat and Mike who were still staring in amazement at the blank space where I had gone in and come out again. Nonchalantly I walked away with them following, went inside Mutat, took an el to the thirtieth floor, entered my apartment and gently shut the door in their faces. They knew I was going out a window. I could hear them racing down the hall to try to head me off but I slipped back out the door and ran the other way. Easing open a window at the far side of the building, I called a blue ring to me and dropped into Gothland.

# 12

BANDIT WOULDN'T GO through the ring. I knew by the way he shied that he could see it. Whether he became a winged creature or a slithering horror in D, I had to try and get him to Tedwar, but he had always been a balky beast and now he dumped me every time I galloped him toward the big brown circle.

"That's a diseased looking object and I'd never go near it," Olger said of the ring. She had never traveled in her life and didn't plan to because dimensional doorways refused to allow her to penetrate them. "Like a brick wall," she had told me. "At first they feel as if they're ready to let me in but then all of a sudden that wall is there. I think it's because I have something wrong with my head. They don't know how to handle me."

"As if they know so much," I said.

"One thing they're bound to know is a human being since they have to contend with them all the time. I have a feeling about them and me and I can't be convinced otherwise. I was dropped as a child and a part of my brain died. That part is necessary for the rings to do their job, so they won't let me in."

"I have to get this horse through."

"You aren't perfect. When will you learn your limitations?"

"You didn't see Tedwar stuck up in the air like I did."

"It wouldn't have mattered if I had since I couldn't do anything for him. You're like a doctor trying to breathe life into a corpse. How long has he been there? Four days? He's probably starved or dead of thirst."

"Help me," I said.

"Put some stained glasses on that animal so he can't tell one color from another and flip them off his eyes just as you jump for the ring. What do you want me to do with your property when you don't come back?"

"My will is in my bureau. I left everything to you."

It took me all day to buy the material, fashion dark glasses and get Bandit accustomed enough to them to run with them looped across his eyes. He hated every second that he wore them and so did I. We ate up the fields racing back and forth, with him dumping me every so often and me getting up more slowly each time, but finally I had him where I wanted him and away we went after a crumpled brown ring a quarter of a kilometer away. Partially sideways to us, the thing limped along like a deflated tire, made practically no headway as a nearly blind horse and a girl scared half to death bore down on it.

It was just as well that I couldn't see the ring too clearly. In fact I don't think the mission could have been accomplished any more successfully had all the circumstances been perfect.

At the last moment I reined Bandit onto a parallel course with the ring, kept edging him into a slight angle more directly toward it and just about the time he began to get mad and dropped his head in order to dump me, I gave him a heel order to leap sideways. At the same time I yanked on the cord that hauled the glasses off him. His head went up as the brown color flashed before his eyes. He immediately made ready to flop flat on his belly and to Hades with the rider on his back. His reaction came too late and we quickly went into D.

Why I had bothered to put a strong bit on him I didn't know but I must have figured it couldn't hurt to consider every possibility. There was always the chance it wouldn't mutate. I wasn't in the habit of guessing right most of the time and that instance was no exception, a situation I readily acknowledged as the bit and bridle fell away into the wide-open abyss between the two shards of rock that made up the brown dimension.

My anxiety wasn't for Tedwar as I crossed over from home to the alien land. If he was still alive he was alive and that would be fine, but what about my horse? During those few moments I realized how reckless I had been to accept Gorwyn's mutterings as fact. Who besides that eccentric had ever told me D turned horses into flying steeds?

I was fortunate and the incredible occurred. Bandit didn't change his size much which made me wonder how much extra effort the doorway had been forced to expend in order to help him survive. It didn't alter me at all just as Tedwar remained unchanged both in form, position and physical condition. However I wasn't considering his mental state then and in fact wouldn't have thought it significant if I had. My horse was what commanded my attention.

He had always been a handsome dark bay, round of rump, long of body and straight of legs and all those parts remained the same, but my knees were shunted farther back on him as two fat, feathery wings appeared low on his withers. They were great silken appendages that allowed him to zoom through space like a trapeze artist. His head was slightly different, looked longer and narrower while his eyes grew smaller. Other than this he was the same Bandit with an obvious delight in his new self and his new surroundings. I wondered what would happen to me if he dumped me now.

Up and up we flew with me hanging onto his mane and feeling the power of his wings against my legs, wondering if he realized all that had happened and also hoping he would eventually obey my commands.

For a while he did exactly as he pleased and simply soared through space of which there was plenty in the dying world while at the same time I vainly tried to guide him back to Tedwar.

The atmosphere thinned, the light became fainter, space about us seemed to wobble yet we cavorted and spun and eternity waited for my brute companion to begin thinking intelligently. I believe he did toward the end when the planet about us gave notice that it was about to expire. Whatever energy source enabled us to exist had to have a relationship with the yellow ring whose counterpart on Earth already sagged in exhaustion.

Reality grew darker around us and I began yelling and kicking harder. My eyes never left the yellow ring and I sensed before I

actually saw its shape drastically alter. It withered like a vine in
the sun, started to shrink inward upon itself, warned me that the
same thing was happening to the dimension. An explosion or an
implosion was about to take place and there was no more time
left.

Tedwar suddenly fell as the energy holding him in place faltered. He plummeted between the escarpments, dropped like a
stone just as Bandit heeded my urgings and went after him. A
slight flutter of wings was sufficient to drive us below the hurtling body and we gauged it just right so that he landed solidly
in my lap. Intense heat was generated as the foundations of the
mountains split and began their endless journey through the
infinity of outer space. Bandit's great wings flapped, faltered,
flapped again as he gave a panicked whinny. Up, up against
heavy pressure he flew while broken rock pitched, heaved and
exploded around and below us. Through a narrow passageway
of clear space he clawed his way with wing and hoof battling
the invisible adversary of inertia.

There suddenly wasn't enough air to breathe. Leaning across
Tedwar's limp body, I hugged my horse's neck and asked him to
do the impossible. With a shuddering gasp he let loose with a
rapid flapping of his wings that lifted us past tumbling debris
and carried us to the raw yellow wound that was rapidly closing.

I don't know how we got through that miserable hole. It
seemed too low and not nearly wide enough while the four
corners tried to fall in on each other until there was nothing but
an irregular gash leading to safety. We saved ourselves with
hope and the stamina of desperation. Like a diver going into a
wave, Bandit gave a final thrust with his wings and then
stiffened out with his front legs pointed forward, his head down
and his body and back legs as straight and sleek as he could possibly make them. Meanwhile I had my own head ducked and my
right leg clasped over Tedwar's legs to make him fit tightly
against Bandit's side.

The cold of outer space touched us as we skinned through that
shrinking hole. It reached for us and sought to claim us while
our impetus shoved us across the last and final meter. We
pitched onto the field of my farm, two damaged human beings
and a horse who was enraged because he had lost something of

beauty and power. Bandit dumped his double burden and galloped away.

I sat up and rolled Tedwar over, expecting him to be his normal, repulsive self, perhaps a little the worse for wear and possibly in a grim mood, but no sooner did I touch him than he leaped into a crouching stance to face me. He was totally gone in insanity. His mouth was slack, his skin was a dirty gray and his normally sparkling eyes were like gunmetal, opaque and unyielding. Perching on his heels and glaring at me for a couple of seconds, he let out a screech and fell on me. He outweighed me by too much so I couldn't get away from him, particularly after he got me around the throat with his crazy hands.

I couldn't believe it because I didn't want to believe it. There was no one around to help me. Olger was the only person for miles around but she couldn't be alerted to come out of the house and help me unless I was able to make some sounds, which I wasn't. The evening sky was beginning to open up over me as a more intense blackness descended upon my head. It was like going under a needle, like being beaned with a loaded sock. One moment I was alive and well and rather pleased with myself and in the next my soul prepared to follow my lost memory into the limbo of extinction.

A redskin named Lamana saved me by lassoing Tedwar about the neck with a length of garden hose and hauling him off. Later she told me he was practically foaming at the mouth, especially after she anchored him to the water tub in the paddock. She wrote her name on a pad and when I squeaked it out she shook her head and said the accent was on the first syllable and the first "a" was long.

While I languished in bed and refused Olger's cooking, Lamana performed a few services for me such as standing by while the law slipped a white jacket onto Tedwar and took him away, such as trying to get in touch with Gorwyn and such as taking over my care as if she had received a personal request. "He's gone," she said, meaning Gorwyn. "Some say he was kidnaped, others that he fled willingly, but the woman now in charge of the school informs everyone he went on extended leave."

She went to Stillwell, Maine, to see if the cousin of Orfia's childhood acquaintance, Carston, had come back from vacationing in California. Not yet.

Why did Solvo insert her into my life? I suspected it was because he either didn't trust me or didn't know exactly where I fit into the picture, not that he was familiar with all the picture. I couldn't slight him for ignorance since it was one of my own flaws. Whether I liked it or not, Lamana was going to do her job which seemed to be to hang around me and see what I did. She had a thick skin so that when I suggested she get lost she merely smiled in mocking fashion and pretended to be absorbed in some task or project. Who was Solvo? Only a policeman?

"He knew about the pipe before I ever walked into his office," I said when I was able. "And don't cloud the issue by asking me how I know he knew. That's why he sent you after me. I'm probably the only good lead he has. He just sits in that cop station as a decoration. He's a government man too, isn't he?"

"Too?" she said.

"I know a couple of others. Or I used to."

# 13

THE INDIAN LED ME through D. She didn't even bother to look back at me so the outlandish shapes I assumed remained my secret. We moved so fast toward the end of our journey that I couldn't say what color rings we penetrated or what dimension we finally landed in.

Eventually I came to the conclusion that the place was Earth but what was the difference when it looked more alien than any place I had ever been? We were on a red butte that looked down on flat prairie so far away nothing moved or stirred on its surface. The boiling sun peered over the morning horizon like a sore eye while the wind snored like a drunk as it worked its way through trees and scorched brush. In every direction the world was burned and awesome, scarlet and fierce, drugged with loneliness and neglect.

"Who needs D with this around?" said Lamana as she stood on the edge of a cliff and grinned at the sun. "When I was little I wouldn't ring travel and screamed at the top of my lungs every time somebody tried to get me near one. My mother brought me up here on my eighth birthday. In her opinion the first and best ring travelers were Indians. She left me here and told me not to come home unless I did it by stepping out of D directly in front of our house. I was up here six months."

Lamana showed me where to find water, what roots, herbs

and fruits were edible and then she startled me by waving good-
bye and walking away. All that night I waited for her to return
but she didn't and by morning I realized I had become the subject of some Indian experimenting or something.

The sun almost became a person to me during those days, a
domineering parent who never let me out of sight except at night
when his companion, the gurgling wind, took over. There was a
therapeutic feature on the butte which I never positively
identified other than to suspect that it might be the total isola-
tion of the place. I had food, water, sun, wind, my thoughts and
a disinclination to do anything but loiter on unbelievably high
ledges and stare at the scenery.

It took me a week to climb down to the second line of bluffs
where I found more of the same emptiness. It was a spot where
only the past existed, the present not really being used yet.
Nothing so hollow could be real.

I woke up one night when the wind was unusually feeble, disturbed by rustling sounds and a smell that was bad enough to
gag me, but sleep quickly captured me again and subdued the
memory until the next afternoon. Going back to the place where
I had made my bed, I inspected rocks and ledges for marks or
prints and found a few spots where outflung brush seemed to
have been broken by the passage of something.

Not until I saw the lummox did I actually believe she existed.
The time I had spent on the mountain seemed to have wiped
away nearly all of reality but myself. I alone had inherited the
earth. The only thing that threatened to burst my dream bubble
was the plane diving out of the blue one day, a small, fancy machine that buzzed the mountain once and then tore away over
the prairie to disappear. It didn't return.

I was walking one evening down a rocky path hitherto
untested by my bare feet except that I knew that one of the few
patches of woods happened to be situated somewhere ahead and
slightly below me. I was downwind at the time so the smell of
the intruder reached me well before my first glimpse of her.

Rounding a bend in the path I came to a shocked halt and
stood riveted for a moment before shying to the left and con-
cealing myself behind a boulder. After my breathing slowed I
cautiously climbed upward to a point from which I could look

down on a ledge almost directly ahead while the woods loomed to my right.

She must have been three and a half meters in height, weighing about two hundred kilos with a dark, furry hide and a shape somewhat like a bear though she walked erect and was obviously intelligent. When she finally stood and turned to give me a view of her face I saw it was covered with hair. Her two mammaries were large and round. She had hands and feet that were like my own except for their size.

She sat watching the setting sun, an alien out of place and out of time for I instantly realized she didn't belong in my world. Once my initial shock passed, my attention was drawn to the woods and the sickly greenish-yellow light emanating from it. There was a large, ill-colored ring just inside the entrance of trees and I guessed the creature on the ledge had traveled from the forbidden world within its perimeter.

The stench coming from the alien was powerful and almost strong enough to drive me away but my curiosity held me fast in the rocks where I waited until the sun plunged out of sight like a falling star. I heard what sounded like a sigh coming from the creature whereupon she slowly climbed erect, turned and walked toward me. My heart froze as the thought came to me that she had smelled me and was coming to dispose of me. In that I was wrong because nobody who smelled as badly as she could sniff anything but the most overwhelming of odors. Lumbering past my place of concealment, she picked her way along the path to the right, entered the woods and walked through the ill-shaded, ill-shaped ring.

Gradually I became engrossed in the lummox, as I called her, and just as gradually she became engrossed in me. I would awaken at night with the full moon splashing light on her hairy face as she stood over me and watched me sleep. I could have sworn she knew how much her smell offended me for she always hurried away when she saw me looking at her. In the evenings she sat on that same ledge below and watched the sun go down.

There was no way off the mountain except by climbing down to the sterile wasteland or by traveling through the world of the lummox. Many times I stood before the round opening and considered at least taking a glance into it but turned away at the thought of a planet that had spawned the huge, shy, ugly, stinking lummox. Sometimes the ring moved off or went completely away but six days out of seven it could be found somewhere near the same spot.

Every day the sky was a blazing furnace with not a single ring to be seen anywhere which seemed to me an odd situation since Earth had plenty of dimensional doorways floating on the wind like pollen. Still, there weren't any near enough to my mountain for me to see let alone to call to me so I languished in indecision while time passed. My neuroses and my anxieties faded into obscurity as my interest in the lummox came into being, and of course that was why Lamana had brought me there in the first place. She herself had been stranded on the mountain and she certainly had also become acquainted with the creature from the other world. Just as certainly she had traveled home via that alien dimension which meant she possessed more courage at the age of eight than I at fifteen, sixteen or whatever I was.

It was curiosity that finally led me through the ring in the woods. I had to know why the lummox came onto the mountain to watch my sunset, for it was mine just as was everything else there. The intruder was just that, and she surely realized it for why else did she remain remote and unobtrusive? She took nothing from my dimension, ate no food as far as I could tell, left no debris but merely came to see the sun go down.

It should have been easy for me to guess why. Once I went through the ring it was all clear. Her world was as objectionable as she, a place where ghosts would have been delirious, where vampires could have flitted with joy, a dank and dark swamp so bereft of light and cheer that not even an alligator would have been proud to call it home. There was nothing in lummoxland but a few creatures, swamps, rotting vegetation and a stench strong enough to knock the nose off an elephant. The first time I went in I took one look around before stumbling backward, gagging and retching.

Over a dinner of berries I considered that getting home was going to be a tougher proposition than I had anticipated. The lummox found her world so dismal that she came over into mine to experience its sky, sun, wind, flora and occasional human castaway. If she couldn't tolerate the place, how could I? It was true there had been a number of rings in the swamp area. I would have to give the matter much thought.

The fact was, my dilemma was no dilemma at all. There were a few things I had to do with my life, some people I needed to reckon with, and there were one or two situations that had to be handled by persons who were better equipped for it than I. Compared to the lummox I had no problems. She came to my world, an offensive and beastlike thing, and remained so without transmutating into something else. Though intelligent, she hadn't wanted to experiment with all those other rings I had seen, otherwise she wouldn't need to come onto this mountain to find a little beauty.

Putting off responsibility was as easy for me to do as anyone, meaning I procrastinated the day of my return to civilization by loafing in my out-of-the-way Eden until my flaccid conscience finally singled me out. I had to go back. The problem of what to do about the lummox was one I had already solved in my mind, so I bestirred myself toward making a slingshot out of a large twig and the elastic in my underwear.

Lummox didn't like it when I began blitzing her with hard nuts and stones and she particularly wasn't fond of it when she got beaned while watching old Sol doing his fancy disappearing act. Knots on her head or no, she endured my sadism well beyond expected limits until at last one evening she gave a scream of pure rancor and came after me.

Through the ring in the woods I traveled into beastland, after which I slogged through a few dozen meters of smelly swamp toward a quantity of varied colored rings that turned skittish and started to scatter as I approached. My slingshot vanished upon my entry into the dimension so I fished for stones in the muck to hurl at lummox who had already gotten the message and understood she must follow until she caught me.

Allowing her to get close to me, I called a pinkish ring into my vicinity and dived through, not caring what it turned out to be like but only needing to get away from the stink filling my nostrils. As far as I can recall, that was the first and only time a plan of mine turned out completely right. The pink dimension was more green than anything else, a fine and fertile planet with a blue sky and a big sun that startled the lummox so much she for-

got about her determination to tear me to pieces. The last I saw
of her that day she was sitting on a hill munching flowers.

A few years later, after my problems of that period had been
taken care of by time and circumstance, I went back through
the pink ring to see how things had developed. The place was
full of lummoxes who every so often went back to the swamp to
remind themselves of how bad it really was. There were no people in the green world to bother the new inhabitants or to be
bothered by the ferocious odor they carried with them, nor was
there anything to mar their idyllic existence. Feeling as if I had
nailed down a corner of the lid on Pandora's box, I waved good-
bye to all the hairy folk and left them forever.

# 14

TEDWAR'S DOCTOR ASSURED ME that since the boy's family couldn't
be located he was better off remaining in the hospital. Drugs
would keep his mania in check. Without them he was capable of
much savagery. It was too bad, but the doctor saw no real hope
for recovery. It was that type of malady.

The spy, mayhem and murder business seemed to have shut
down, but not permanently in my opinion. Ectri wasn't at his
farm in Jersey nor was he teaching in Boston or pushing papers
or needles in Washington. I didn't know where he was. Lamana
mentioned seeing two blonde twins loitering on the fringes of
my property so I went on the hunt for Padarenka and Mikala,
without success.

"Nobody's home," said Lamana. We sat on a fence on my
farm and watched Bandit graze.

"Except you," I said. "What does Solvo expect to learn by
your keeping watch on me?"

"He never tells me anything but only orders me around and
hands me a paycheck twice a month."

"You work for . . ."

"The state of New Mexico, what else?"

"You work for Solvo and he works for Washington. The state
of New Mexico just happens to be growing around him. Why
don't you want to go see the pipes and oil?"

"It wouldn't be intelligent," she said.

"I knew a man who said he had heard of others besides myself who could call rings. I don't suppose he could have been talking about you? His name was Croff and he used to be a big man in research."

"I personally know of three people like us. They're members of my family. Tell me again about the lummox. Did she really try to catch you?"

"I'd rather talk about the plane. I don't know exactly what day it was, the ninth after you left me I think, but I watched it closely and in my opinion the pilot didn't mean to buzz the mountain. I believe he was looking for something or someone in particular in the area and was surprised to find it on that rock. He left in a big hurry."

"How could anybody know you were out there?"

"They couldn't unless you told them."

"I didn't."

"By the way," I said, "if you ever get the time, look up a man named Bud Jupiter. He used to work with rings."

"What about him? Has he got anything to do with the pipe?"

"I don't know. At this point I'm just idly curious about him."

She soon made the excuse of going into the house for a drink but I guessed she was on her way to tell Solvo about the plane, which suited me fine because I was ready for D myself except that I didn't head in her direction as I dived into Gothland.

Across a big rock flush with the ground I laboriously carved one of my supposedly interesting and therapeutic messages: CONCENTRATE ON BEING SMALL. WON'T IT BE NICE TO GO HOME?

On the wall of the broadest labyrinth I could find I carved: DON'T SPREAD OUT. THINK TINY. THINK HOME.

My impression was that during Kisko's more lucid moments he was a normal sized goth, but whenever he slipped into dementia his mass expanded until he was like a great cloud. I had often heard him scream when that happened, an eerie, shattering cry that was broadcast wherever I went. He kept drifting in and out of rings, not all of him or he might have been back home by now, but just parts of him penetrated into other dimensions so that he trailed through reality like gas, a bit here and a bit there.

It was as if he tried to go home through everywhere.

I didn't know if he saw my messages or whether he perceived anything in a rational light, except that he ate the drees I deposited on the ground or left dangling from ledges or secreted in labyrinthine crevices or even dropped beside a rare ring channel.

I went on the hunt for Gorwyn. Heading for Mutat, I picked up Pat and Mike somewhere along the way, which disturbed me. They shouldn't be trailing me. They weren't that good.

Hopping into Peoria, I hid in the corn, watched and crouched for several minutes until they appeared on a flat piece of ground a good distance away. They turned directly toward my hiding place and fell down behind a slight rise where they tried to wait me out. I moved and so did they, across the cornfield and road into waist-high hay, and I was certain they still hadn't seen me though they seemed to know exactly where I was. Something new had been added to their repertoire of tricks. Overnight they had become infallible runners.

Once in a while I was capable of having a good idea and I had one then, called a blue ring to me and disappeared into D long enough to find a yellow entrance onto the street in Kentucky where Croff used to have his apartment. I went into a diner, ordered a soft drink and sat down to wait. The twins were clumsy and not very bright and I wondered how I ever could have thought they were good at the business. Like a pimple and its mirror image they popped onto the street in full view of the diner while at the same time I went out the back door into Waterworld.

They didn't follow me there nor did they show up in Gothland when I visited that dimension, but every time I poked my head into normal space on Earth they were Johnnies on the spot with their yellow curls, big blue eyes and the radio somewhere in their pockets. That had to be it and of course I had an instrument in my body that gave off the signal they were following.

On the bureau in my room at the farm I left messages for Olger and Lamana after which I faded into Gothland with the intention of not coming out until I solved at least some of my problems. Down labyrinths I prowled with a big weight on my mind and a conscience that wouldn't quit. Kisko should have been taken to a hospital where they might have done something for him but instead I had shoved him into D where he didn't belong, and now he was worse off than the Flying Dutchman who at least had known what was happening to him.

Grieving didn't help but I did it anyway, meanwhile visiting all my old haunts to see if they harbored any cheer. Occasionally I saw Kisko drifting like a cloud that wanted to go partly here and partly there until it was strung out over the landscape in a web shape. I saw him, black and tenuous, trying to gather his forces to stay out of a yawning green ring above an escarpment, but a trailing skirt of fog seemed to be sucked in, or he swooped in, and then the dimensions vied for him by rocking and swaying. It was getting so that he created maelstroms of water and wind almost as powerful as those caused by the pipe propped up by dimensional openings.

It seemed to me that somehow I picked up a little bit of his shadow, a cloying portion that dogged my footsteps. If I popped into my normal world of Earth, there the shadow lay behind me, or if I swam in Waterworld a dark tag drifted along with me. It was larger in Gothland and more persistent, resting upon me when I paused, swooping beside me as I fled. I recalled that day in Waterworld when the enemy swimming crew nearly caught me by the pipe and surprised me by not seeing me. Maybe Kisko was laying more on me than a shadow.

DON'T BOTHER TRYING TO PROTECT ME, SAVE YOURSELF, I wrote on the wall of a big labyrinth. Not that I believed he was doing anything other than wildly stabbing in the dark, reaching out to clutch something of substance, but at least it meant he wasn't dead yet. Of course, he might rupture something within the dimensions if he kept wandering so I would have to do something drastic if the situation didn't change. What, I didn't know.

Nothing was happening in the big pit in Gothland. It appeared the enemy had been security conscious no longer than it took them to build the junction on the pipes and now they didn't care who looked at it. I could see there were two junctions, the first constructed against the second, and I assumed the instruments and weapons had been moved into the latter. The day I tried to get into the old one and became adrift in the flow of liquid, I had simply undershot the mark. Now I couldn't get into the section holding the instruments because the doors were welded shut.

Reasoning that the machines regulated flow and possibly even consistency at this point in the pipe, I gauged my distance and ring color, called one of the spheres drifting along empty passages and gingerly tried stepping into the second junction.

They were way ahead of me and had set up some kind of reflecting material so that as I traveled through the blue ring I didn't focus on it long enough but rather glimpsed the yellow side of its inner rim which placed me right back where I started. At first I didn't realize what happened and tried getting into the housing through several different rings of similar shade. It was like running up against a brick wall. The housing itself, or the metal elbow or junction, possibly was painted with something special though it looked ordinary enough as I crouched in the pit and looked it over. I considered that the inner wall of the cylinder might have received the treatment, whatever it was. No matter, I couldn't get in. Thinking I might get stuck inside the wall if I persisted in trying to penetrate the mirror-like structure, I gave off and went elsewhere to see if the enemy had made anything else off limits.

There were kilometers of pipe which meant my investigation would require considerable time so I went home to see how Lamana was doing. Arriving in my room about midnight, I made no noise but went straight to bed.

"We picked the twins up with no trouble," she said to me at the breakfast table.

I marveled at how easily she had inserted herself into the family, as if she'd been asked or as if she'd given a logical explanation or account of her eternal presence. There wasn't a doubt in my mind that if I stepped out of line she would hogtie me and carry me off to Solvo. The problem with that was that I didn't know where the line was or anything else about it. For all I knew she just liked my company.

"They aren't too proficient at dodging tails," she added.

"And?" I said.

"As you anticipated, one of them was in possession of a receiver that picked up a signal coming from you. Very sophisticated."

"Where is it now?"

"In the hands of the law."

"Or its pockets. I intended for you to hand it over to me, seeing as how it's pretty personal."

"Unfortunately Solvo didn't view the situation that way."

"So he's a fascist at heart. What's his G-man rank?"

"I could have told you I didn't even find the twins," she said.

"Where are they?"

"We let them go."

"Track me if that's how you get your entertainment," I said. "As far as I'm concerned, you're as crooked as the rest."

Blinking her big black eyes, she said, "Is this the end of a fine friendship?"

"I wasn't aware that one had begun, and do you mind leaving one of those pancakes?"

Not caring who knew where I was going, I made it as tedious as possible for any tails by taking a train to Mutat, getting off in town and walking. It occurred to me that anyone following me wouldn't necessarily suffer as much as I because as soon as they realized where I was headed they could simply ring travel on to the school. But they couldn't be sure that wasn't exactly what I wanted them to do.

It wasn't important. Upon my arrival at Mutat I went about the business of locating Gorwyn. Sorry, no forwarding address. Maybe Tedwar's hospital could tell me something. I knew they couldn't because I had already inquired there. As for Gorwyn's equipment in the lab, the new director said she stored it for a while and later gave it to those attractive twins to dispose of at auction. Then they ran off with the money and she was left with practically nobody to go after truants, which reminded her that I belonged on the thirtieth floor and not loose on the economy.

I didn't think much of the security in the school, especially after I was snatched out of one of the hallways in broad daylight. I was busy making plans in my head about how I could track down Gorwyn and see if he was in any trouble, visit Tedwar, even see if I could locate Wheaty, find out where Ectri was holed up, take a stab at trying to determine whether or not Solvo and Lamana were honest law or corrupt—there were a dozen things I intended to do after I picked up the few odds and ends left in my room.

They weren't waiting for me in my quarters which was just as well for I wouldn't have entered on a bet once I saw how the doorknob had been plucked from its hole like a bottle top twisted off. One look and I was promptly pessimistic because I could recollect but one acquaintance who handled objects so carelessly.

Her favorite frock was red-flowered, sleeveless, knee-length and thin, blossoming around her tree trunk legs as she came down the hall after me. She had little brown eyes, a small nose and mouth, short brown hair and enough muscles to handle anyone thoughtless enough to disagree with her, and though she sounded like a tank as she ran, she covered space quickly so that she had me backed into a dead-end corner before I could think to try one of the nearby doors.

Obviously not just Padarenka and Mikala had owned a radio set that tuned in on my whereabouts, or else my question about Solvo's honesty was now being answered. Of all the people who might want me for no good purpose, I would have preferred any but the cow who bounded toward me and picked me up by the neck.

"Stinking flea," she said. Her physical exertion had caused her to work up a lather and she stank like a goat. One of her problems was that she didn't know her own strength so that I nearly strangled as she slammed me against the wall and held me there while she told me what a pain I was and how if she had her rathers she wouldn't lay an eye on me let alone a hand.

From the corner of my eye I saw two men coming down the hall and wasted time hoping they were friends of mine, but they were with Erma and it looked as if I was going to be kidnaped. She didn't bother gagging me, just jammed my face against her bosom and held me that way while we took an el to the ground floor. If there were guards on duty, it remained a mystery to me. My guess was that they had been bribed or bruised, but either way didn't help me.

It didn't seem too big a misfortune to me that I was finally dumped all by myself onto a piece of terrain somewhere in the Pacific. It was better than getting killed. Erma didn't say anything as she sat beside me in the expensive little jet that looked like the one I'd seen from Lummox mountain. The two men went into the pilot's compartment and that was the last I saw of them. A few hours after our takeoff, collapsible blades came out of the plane's roof; it converted into a copter that landed on a sandy knoll and I was literally tossed through the doorway.

"Let's see you hop around now," said Erma. "You'll stay here until I'm good and ready for you. Don't bother looking for rings. If one has set foot in this territory in the last fifty years, it's invisible."

Coconuts, papayas and brackish water from a pond were served up to me daily by the island while the sun tried to boil me alive. My nose peeled ten times before the skin toughened and tanned. Meanwhile I looked for a way out and wondered how long it would take Solvo and Lamana to come and see why I was out here. Unless they already knew. And besides, maybe they wouldn't anyhow. They might be glad I was stationary for a while.

I was too angry and disgusted to build a hut, not that I could have anyway since the vines were six inches thick with not a single sharp rock showing up anywhere. Every day at about the same time the rain battered me bruised and soggy and always I scanned the sky for a rescue ship in the form of a ring. All I saw were faint reflections of something far off, not actual circles but little flashes of partial disks that were like the images I created when I rubbed my eyes hard.

Sun and peeling nose, clothing so abused that I ended up with only the briefest part of my shorts left, I became a castaway in every sense of the word. Every day I trudged to the top of the knoll to see if anything broke the monotonous horizon of water, every afternoon I crawled under a rock and slept away the worst of the heat, in the evening I lay on the quiet shore and brooded over the fact that I was without kin or friend, and each night I dreamed of Kisko lost and mad in D.

It took me too long to realize how wrong Erma had been and that the partial disks I sometimes saw in the sky were good old-fashioned rings. The reason I couldn't see them most of the time was that they were the color of clear water, or to use Erma's own word, practically invisible. That I could see bits of their rims was only due to my special kind of sight and I wasn't too convinced it was all that much of a blessing right then. Going into weird dimensions was hazardous no matter how desperate the situation.

Ring detectors couldn't pick up the clear orbs because they had no color. Somehow knowing Erma and her ilk were less than perfect heartened me so that I summoned enough courage to at least try to examine the things in the sky. I lay on the sand and stared upward. Little faint curved lines showed here and there like ultra-thin sides of the rims of lenses. Similar to fast-spinning coins of water, they were visible for a moment and then gone, there above me and then way off toward the horizon or backward over my head into oblivion. At times they ducked to earth where they became impossible to see against sand and grass.

As it turned out, they weren't rings and they didn't open into dimensions but rather they were all a single corridor that might have been the core of reality from which everything began its journey. They were no different from ordinary rings in that I could call them to me but I couldn't manipulate their motion and had to sidestep into one as it flipped in my direction.

It was like stepping into a hallway of glass or into a diamond the facets of which mocked and cast my image everywhere. My physical makeup didn't change. Haggard, sunburned Daryl walked into a place of silence and glittering walls where motion never ceased and where I seemed to hurtle through infinity. The surface beneath my feet was hot so that I spent the trip gawking and hopping, not that I actually went anywhere but the things I saw were concerned both with time and space and so it appeared as if I were present where it all happened.

I stood on a platform that sped through the universe and revealed to me a statistic: a vast number multiplied by forever represented more worlds and space than my mind could envision. The millions and billions of rings within my view were but a miniscule sample of the legions I couldn't see. The slightest difference in the shade of rings meant worlds of a different nature, one single added molecule of pigment meant a doorway into a planet whose only relationship with any other might be its orbital path around the same star. The variations within the color spectrum were significant and I saw them all as I took my strange trip through the hall of glass.

It was fitting that the way out of such an astonishing place was simply a matter of stepping backward. Like a piece of debris on a spinning coin I flipped out of the dimension and dropped onto the sand of my island prison where I lay staring up at the sky as if it were a painted mural superimposed upon the real one. There were things going on out there in space that we mortals didn't dream about.

It didn't take me much time to discover that no matter which clear ring I skinned through, the view on the other side was exactly the same. A fast trip through outer reality was fine and dandy and I liked looking at all those rings but the repetitive entertainment wasn't getting me off the island and back into human action.

Naturally I had already considered tripping out through one of the spheres hurtling past the platform and in fact had tried to call some to me, but they either didn't hear me or couldn't respond. Conceivably space was distorted while I stood on the platform or I myself might have been spatially out of position. Maybe millions of light years of distance separated my physical body from the rings, thereby making communication between us impossible.

Whatever the reason, it didn't help my situation which was growing worse as I sickened of my diet. In the end my boredom with the same fare every day of the week served to get me off and away, so in retrospect the food seemed good. Before I escaped, though, it was only bad. I would find myself gagging as I swilled coconut juice or I felt as if one more bite of papaya would rot every tooth in my head. My jaws ached from lack of conflict, my tongue rebelled for want of titillation, the whole world could have ended for all I cared if I soon didn't get something interesting to eat.

# 15

THERE WAS A SMALL COVE on the western side of the island where I usually spent my mornings, in a little rock-shaded nook beside a pool surrounded by a miniature beach. The ocean beyond some high boulders was noisy and violent while the pool was quiet, tranquil and clear. One day the water was unusually transparent and I thought I saw what looked like a large clam or oyster in its depths. Immediately I plunged in, swam down about five meters and then retreated to the surface. Sucking air in and out of my lungs for a few moments, I went back in and down approximately eight meters before calling it quits and heading upward.

The water had been clear during my time of submersion but there was no way for me to estimate how deep the pool was, so I lay on the sand and hyperventilated for several minutes before sliding in and swimming toward the bottom. Approximately twelve meters down, I stopped abruptly for two reasons. My maximum had been reached and there was a startling object below me. What had looked like a clam from the height of the beach was a blue ring. I had no more time to stay there and inspect it, and pulling with my arms and kicking my legs, I flashed up through the pool and emerged just as my lungs expelled the last of their air.

I had a problem, an enigma, a puzzle, a challenge and a possi-

ble way off the island. Lying on the sand and listening to the
surf, I tried to draw it on a mental diagram. Twelve meters
down and then up to the surface was my limit, I knew, no matter
how long I hyperventilated. The ring seemed to hover some five
meters farther down and to reach it I would have to swim below
the depth where nitrogen automatically started building in my
blood which meant that once I passed say, thirteen or fourteen
meters, I would be committed and beyond the point of return.
No way could I safely surface after that. Pleasant thought, especially when I considered how way off the mark had been my
original estimation of the so-called clam's depth. What if water
distortion made me think the ring was seventeen meters down
when it was actually fifty? Or what if I passed sixteen meters
and the ring moved?

Fear was a hitchhiker that didn't harass me until I was well
beyond help, and maybe I subconsciously planned it that way,
but it didn't matter since the idea of living and dying on the island was repugnant enough to make me reckless. The water was
cool and clear, I had what felt like a week's supply of air in my
lungs, I had bidden good-bye to the beautiful but sterile rings in
the sky but more particularly I'd said farewell to the coconuts
and papayas. No tramp steamer or flashy jet was going to come
along and pluck me from my station, and the fact was if I stayed
there long enough Erma would visit me one day and knock my
head off.

The only thing I left up there on the beach was my life as it
had been and now I forged toward China with every ounce of
strength I owned. As the meters passed me by with fleet fingers,
silence increased, as did the pressure in my ears. Not depth
happy, I nevertheless felt like humming because I was on my
own again and in charge of what happened to me. Besides, opti-
mism warded off that old hitchhiker who stood in the wings and
grinned with wicked good will, waiting for me to start thinking
seriously about the madness of what I was doing.

Never having heard of underwater mirages, I began specu-
lating upon them as I continued downward. Anything to ward
off fear, except that this concept wasn't a wise one since it could
be blown out of proportion by imagination. The pain in my chest
became so deep it hurt my spine. My feet grew numb, my thighs

burned, my nose pained as it strove to perform its natural function. I thought it unfortunate that my brain was clear and aware of everything occurring within and without. My estimation of my depth was twenty-four meters, increasing ever more slowly as my body rebelled against the orders given it.

The point of no return had me now, and its grip was merciless, cutting off my hope and confidence with impenetrable walls of water that hovered just a breath away. One of my last energetic thoughts was curious: too bad I wasn't my mother, tall and strong and far more skilled, because then I could have gone on for at least another forty meters; she had lungs like a porpoise.

I was done and I reached for the ring knowing it was too far away, a tiny brilliance that had looked so large thirty meters or more topside. Reaching couldn't hurt and moving like a slippery snake couldn't do any damage and I figured I might as well go out active so I gave one last and final kick before getting ready to let all that water have its way.

Again I reached out and slithered sideways as though I had already arrived at the shiny little circle. It worked and the ring was really there and I groaned as I transferred from the pool into Gothland. At the last moment I had the impression that a dark piece of friendly fog gave me a needed little shove.

In retrospect I think I expected to land on my head but I didn't land at all, merely floated through brimstone and black cloud like an inflated balloon which was as good a description of me as any. Not that I cared since the pressure of anticipating death in deep water was gone but my new physical self still amazed me. I was an oversized goth but there was little weight to my mass. Coming in with a bloodstream full of nitrogen had changed the normal course of things so that the transmutation was accomplished differently. I was a blob of a goth who floated through space and never touched down, a light and lonely entity sailing above lava pits, tar rivers, mountain ridges and scampering drees.

Red rain sent me earthward, belching gas tossed me toward the sky, even the scant wind coursing along the ground scattered me like dust. I was blown about by every whim of the elements and once I was thrown beneath a waterfall where I bounced up and down for the longest time before being hurled clear. A breeze slammed me flush against an escarpment, sent me scraping all the way to the top where another flurry made me careen into another hard wall.

Finally I learned how to use my slight weight as ballast and sail and pretty soon I was dodging obstacles with no trouble, utilizing windflaws to my benefit, avoiding mountain ridges and hard rain areas.

I sported for a while, manipulated my peculiar self and even enjoyed the sensations but eventually I recalled my plans for the future, searched out an appropriate ring in the area, invited it to visit me and vacated the premises.

The first thing I did was rent another homestead in Jersey. I intended to stay away from my farm until something could be done about Erma. My new house was old, decrepit and crowded after Lamana moved in. For the first few days she camped in the back field, refusing to answer any questions and cooking over an open fire until I gave her permission to eat in the kitchen and sleep on the couch.

"We're busy sometimes, you know, which is why we didn't come and look for you," she said, which obviously was an untruth since she had scarcely let me out of her sight during the past weeks.

"The fact was you knew exactly where I was, out of everybody's hair and you decided you liked it that way."

With a shrug, she said, "The fact was I accidentally dropped the receiver and broke it into fifty pieces. My father wanted to do the same to me. It's a highly specialized instrument and it took our experts all this time to repair it. Where were you?"

"No place. Incidentally, what do you think you're doing in that getup?"

She adjusted her headband, ran two fingers along the feather attached to it. "Did I ever tell you I was a good scout and tracker?"

"And the suede shorts, top and leggings ward off marauding white eyes?"

"I smoke a pipe and burn goat ears to do that."

"You're more educated than I am. Why do you do this stuff?"

"Because my mother loves being an Indian. Because all my uncles carry their little sacks of corn and their stinking pipes.

And they're educated, too. It's my business, you know. Mind yours."

"Okay."

"What would one of your enemies think if they saw me coming at them with a tomahawk?"

"It would scare them worse than a goth."

"I agree. Incidentally, my father conferred with an expert regarding the electronic object in your body. It isn't in your head."

"Who says?"

"X-rays would clearly define it. The thing in your head belongs there."

"What does that mean?"

"It isn't a machine and a blood clot would change over a period of time."

"Then what is it?"

"The expert is willing to take a picture," she said.

"My brain will fry if I get anymore pictures taken. In the meantime, where's the radio and who put it there?"

"It's probably in a place you can't easily reach. Shoulder blade, most likely."

My back began to itch. "How do you know so much?" I said. I was angry at the thought of someone having made a walking footprint out of me. What did it matter whether it was a bloodhound or a person with a machine following me? The whole idea scuttled my attempt at independence and privacy. "That can't be right," I said suddenly. "I have amnesia. I can't remember anything."

"You don't read enough. Amnesia doesn't hang around as long as you've had it. Somebody put the whammy on you. They looked deep into your eyes, squeezed your tiny intellect until it was no bigger than a pea and then they plucked out your memory. It'll come back when it's supposed to."

"You mean I was hypnotized?"

"By someone who really knew the business."

That afternoon we went to Pittsburgh to see the big earthquake which turned out to be a deep valley of smoke and fire. It would be quite a while before it was known whether anything still lived in that vast crater.

The quake outside Topeka was similar except it had taken

place in open farmland and not a life was lost. The awesome hole reminded me of the brown dimension where everything was in the process of collapsing and dropping inward.

"What if this is happening all over the universe?" I said to Lamana as we stood with a crowd near the lip of the great depression and looked at the broken earth. Overhead a pair of police planes cruised and waited. Were they interested in me in particular? I didn't wait to find out but encouraged Lamana to walk with me back toward the highway where a variety of rings were ready to be used.

"Is Solvo going to do anything about anything?" I said. "If those rings aren't freed from those pipes . . ."

"Progress is slow, especially when you don't know who your enemies are. Be patient."

"At least I agree with part of that. I can't understand how I was so lucky to pick a police station at random and find your gang."

"We aren't a gang and maybe your choice wasn't so random. Someone cleaned out your past memories. Possibly they also left some suggestions, such as New Mexico if things got rough."

"More manipulation! I don't know if that makes sense or not. If you aren't part of a gang, what are you?"

"A member of a family that's been in the law enforcement business for a long time. We were already investigating the source of the earthquakes and when you came in with your story about oil we knew it was the right lead."

A little while later we sat in Gothland beside a bubbling tar pit with Lamana gawking at me as if I were more of a freak than I actually was. She didn't need to talk for me to know what she was thinking. It was the first time she had ever really seen me in D. Grinning in grisly fashion, I led her a merry chase through labyrinths and amphitheaters until we reached a wide-open park-like area where Kisko sometimes came. The place was dotted with rectangular stones that looked like picnic tables while in the ground around each were four shallow holes. Resting in one of the furrows, I showed Lamana how comfortable it was and how easy it was to rise up slightly and rest my front paws on the table.

It was a disturbing experience as I imagined a time in the past when the park was full of goths lounging around the tables while they had their feasts and celebrations.

We went back home, lay on a hill of Earth and admired the stars.

"I wonder what those double rings are?" she said.

I thought she was kidding, so I ignored the question. "Do you think it's true rings open into those solar systems up there?" I said.

"Everybody seems to think so."

"That doesn't make it true."

"It'll have to do for an explanation until something better comes along. Galaxies drift through one another and that suggests a lot of possibilities, especially if some are constructed of matter that isn't quite like ours."

"Yeah, in a billion years the world won't be the same," I said.

"The entire galaxy will be different because by then we'll be passing through other star masses. What's the use of worrying about it? Unless our brains develop we'll never have all the answers. We need to be more intelligent."

"About everything. For instance, how do I get Kisko out of D?"

"Anyone who gives you an answer to that will only be guessing. His realities aren't normal because his mind is abnormal."

"I see a leg or paw in D-2 sometimes, but that's all," I said. "Once in a while his head appears, or his back, but there's nothing attached to them but his cloud. I know it's him because I can sense him all through it, but he's either screaming or moaning so I don't know if he's aware I'm there."

Thinking about it made it seem worse so I tried not to but my mind kept slipping away from new subjects and returning to the old. How much of his memory had he retained, and did he know what the pipes and flowing oil were doing to the worlds? Some of the highest escarpments in Gothland were collapsing or sinking while in Waterworld floating mountains, rocks and collections of seaweed were on a fast journey nowhere. Maelstroms were being created everywhere so that there was no such thing as a calm swim. People complained to the government and were advised to stay home.

"Ectri does nothing suspicious, by the way," said Lamana.

"We checked all the places he works in or out of, we put a one-week watch on his home, and all we learned is that he's quiet and keeps his trail clean."

"Nothing works out of me," I said. "My enemies act like angels while my friends give me a big stall."

"I'm telling you what I know. Solvo wants you to confer with his medical acquaintances."

"I can't go running around making everybody nervous if I'm locked in a hospital room?"

"You're in a good mood," she said. "I might as well make it worse. Olger told me Bandit won't stay out of the rings. He's flying all over the universe."

"He's an idiot!" I said and left her there while I went away to brood alone. I had no family, there was no one I could fully trust and now my horse had given up waiting for me and was entertaining himself by doing exactly what I had forbidden him to do.

It didn't take me long to reach the decision to turn myself over to Solvo and his medics. After all, what was there for me to do as long as Erma was free to pop in on me whenever she felt the notion? That she hadn't come after me yet was enough to make me worry. At least for a few days I wouldn't have that on my mind.

The hospital Solvo put me in was staffed by Indians who got a big kick out of never allowing any human emotion to enter their expressions. "You don't fool me," I said to the tiny mite who was in charge of seeing that I didn't remain out of her view for so much as a minute. About a hundred years old, she watched me so intently that I found myself doing the same thing to her. "You plan to scalp me when I'm asleep," I said.

Her name was Chameleon and she was incredible. "I have the idea you don't speak English, Spanish, Redskin or anything human," I said. "If you want my opinion, you sneaked out of a wrinkled, gray ring. Anytime you like, you can go back through it."

She spent her time scurrying across the room to peer from the twentieth-story window after which she darted to my bed to secure the blanket around my shoulders and then she looked in the bathroom to see if any strangers had appeared there since her last search.

"You're nuts," I said. "Sit down. Don't move. Stay still for twenty seconds." Doctor Oregon came in and I said, "Why do I have to stay in bed when I'm not sick?"

He was an old stoneface from way back. "This is a hospital, isn't it? Where else would you be but in a bed?"

I accused my ancient overseer of being kin to a lizard. Once I grabbed her hands as she fussed with my bedding and was surprised to find she had strong muscles beneath her thin skin. "You like me, don't you?" I said, but she only looked at me with her blackberry eyes and showed me some of her capped teeth that were so white and even they made me think of a shark.

The room was large with just the one bed and a great deal of electronic equipment in a corner. According to Doctor Oregon, the machines prevented my signals from going any farther than the building. No matter how tough Chameleon thought she was, I had no intention of staying in bed, so I got up one evening to look out the window. Right away she didn't like it and complained without saying a word when I made motions for her to bring me a chair. She was good at humming, moaning, whistling, grunting, even growling and by then I had learned that the only time she was totally quiet was when I was in bed with my eyes closed.

They used a strange kind of machine on me that reminded me of Gorwyn's crown of wires in that it made me dizzy, but there the similarity ended. I stood in metal shoes in front of what looked like two tall sheets of glass, one of which bore a red diagram of my body. A sonarlike signal came from the diagram, penetrated a part of me and reproduced what it found onto the second sheet of glass. When the two didn't match, the reproduction was in purple. It wasn't a slow process. The figure representing me on the blank pane grew from appendages to pelvis to torso and head in a matter of minutes, and all the time I stood in the metal shoes and tried to overcome my vertigo.

"The diagram on the left is of a normal person of your size and body weight," said the doctor. "The one on the right shows us divergences from that norm. As you can see, there are a couple of irregularities."

He told me later that the duplicator was a handy thing to use in diagnosing injury and disease since it pin-pointed problem areas. As for me, I had a series of electronic instruments inside me that couldn't be excised because they were in the form of a tape a centimeter long and extremely narrow. He said they had probably been introduced into my bloodstream by injection where they traveled for a while before lodging in the wall of the left ventricle of my heart. They weren't hurting anything and they were already in a state of decay which meant they would eventually be inactive and harmless. As for my head, I had a little extra bit of matter in an untouchable spot and it wasn't mechanical or the result of trauma. It belonged there, was something I had been born with.

"It's nothing to be concerned about," said Doctor Oregon. "This sort of thing crops up once in a while. It's nature's way of trying out something new, like when people first started seeing rings. We're sure it's the reason you transmutate into such unusual shapes. Probably it's a survival mechanism."

The surprises kept coming all the while I was in the clinic, but the one that startled me the most was when their leading psychiatrist tried to break my memory block. She turned out to be the little bit of wrinkled leather who daily kept the eagle eye on me.

When I laughed as she approached me in the comfortable chair they had provided for me, Chameleon turned her berry eyes full on me and showed me how she could change their color from black to crystal. Maybe she enjoyed stunning people to distraction, maybe not, but I sat still after that first attempt at levity and didn't crack another smile. I might have gaped somewhat but I considered the situation dead serious. Never in my life had I ever seen anyone change the color of their eyes. Later I thought about how impossible it seemed and decided she must have hypnotized me. I never did find out.

Chameleon's touch was feather light on my face, fond and possessive, as if she had a stake in the thinking property behind it.

"I'm not going to remember," I said.

Staring at me, she hummed a tune of mockery and derision. Again and again she stroked my forehead and gradually I relaxed and let her play witch doctor to her heart's content. I could tell by her humming how she felt, first impertinent and then solemn, dedicated, disbelieving, annoyed, persistent and at last resigned to failure. Her crystal-colored eyes worked like twin diamond drills that pressed against my psyche and tried to break through.

It would have been agreeable with me had she succeeded. I wasn't holding out or resisting but there was that hard wall somewhere between the back of my head and my eyes and it wasn't going down that day nor was it willing to be penetrated. It was present, it was strong and Chameleon couldn't champion it although somewhere through the session I sensed a slight shifting. I knew it when she realized and accepted her defeat, watched as her incredible eyes darkened and became as of old, was aware of her mood though not a flicker of expression touched her face. She was sad and the final caress she gave me was full of regret.

"I can take care of myself," I said, trying to reassure her. "I get along fine, really."

I was grateful to them for not trying to keep me there once they found out what they wanted to know about me. After inviting me to return sometime for further tests in regard to my special talent, they literally showed me the front door, sans advice, and I took to the path eagerly and anxiously.

"Want to go catch a slok and drag it into home D to see what it really is?" I said to Lamana who had probably never blanched in her life and didn't then. "I don't suppose you can explain to me why it's possible to haul something dead from D and revive it?" I said as we went down the road. I knew already that if she didn't know the answer to the question she could at least make an intelligent guess. Like Deider's children, she had a whopping mind.

"As far as yellow rings are concerned, the carcasses are all part of each other and are changed to their original forms, the same as usual. Don't ask me why something dead or blind in One can't go through any ring at all. I have an idea, though, that it's because One is a truer dimension for us. I think if you found a native in Two or Three, brought them here, killed them and shoved them back into D, they'd resurrect. Of course I've never met any natives of D."

Thinking of shell worms, I said, "How come?"

"Chance. I've muted to maybe six or seven different worlds

but that's a drop in the bucket. I could travel to a million without finding an inhabited one. There are so many."

"But we're closer to Two and Three which is why the majority of rings here are a certain shade of green and blue," I said.

We walked, talked and watched the sky for planes while we prepared ourselves for the hunt. Like Daniel Boone who had nothing better to do, we were off to do battle with a grizzly.

# 16

HE WAS A BIG SPECIMEN who was obviously annoyed by our intrusion into his territory and broadcast his displeasure in a blasting screech that could be heard throughout the labyrinth. As I anticipated, Lamana was immobilized by the sight and sound of our target so I quickly climbed some high rocks piled along the tunnel's side, thereby gaining the slok's full attention.

He had been filing his teeth on a broken stalagmite directly across from the stones I climbed and now we were both above Lamana. Casually I took to a narrow tunnel leading upward into the mountain, planning to whip about and attack if the slok decided to go for my smaller companion, but he had probably received orders regarding the giant goth and promptly took to my trail.

As soon as I was assured that he was after me, I lengthened my stride to get him away from Lamana who fell in well behind us. At the end of the tunnel was a six meter drop into a frothing pool. Above and to the left and right were sloping paths leading around to the right to an amphitheater one or two meters above the level of dark froth.

It took me several minutes to get through the tunnel after which I exited at top speed along the path to the left. The slok followed me while Lamana chose the path to the right and headed down into the amphitheater. In the meantime I slowed long enough for the chattering monster to draw close behind me. When it felt just right, I came to an abrupt halt and gave him both rear feet in the mouth. He bounced against the side of the mountain and dropped into the pool. Somewhat slowly he attempted to climb out into the amphitheater where Lamana waited to kick him back in. By the time he was ready to try to get out again, I was there at the pool's edge. My companion and I used him for a football until he was so exhausted he was barely conscious.

The normal thing to do when a ring happened along that one didn't wish to enter was to blink, demur and close one's eyes until it went by. After Lamana and I hauled the slok out of the labyrinths and up to the surface, we found the air so full of rings we had to pause while a group of them passed us. We selected a big yellow one with enough pigment in it to satisfy us that it would exit somewhere decent on Earth and just as we were preparing to go through with our prisoner, an earthquake or a maelstrom struck. The yellow sphere bobbed upward and away while the ground beneath us opened wide. Lamana cried out at exactly the same moment that I saw the other ring. There was no avoiding it, at least not as far as she and I were concerned. The slok fell into the abyss where it disappeared into a harmless river of bubbling lava but my companion and I pitched headlong through the forbidden gray circle.

The first thing I noticed was that I had wings. My second flash of inspiration was a desire to go home. My body was much the same except that it was approximately one-tenth its original mass, meaning I weighed twenty-two kilos and was four centimeters long. I was more like an insect than a human. So was Lamana, and so were all the fliers in the green valley below us. That fact alone should have been enough to occupy my mind but it was shunted into obscurity when I saw the gigantic, toady creature squatting in the center of the action like a stone Buddha.

"Let's get out of here," I said to Lamana as we collided in the air.

"I can't fly," she said, her eyes wide. "I don't even like heights. What am I doing up here?"

Whatever we might have decided to do had we been left

alone remained a matter for speculation because a businesslike
pair of winged citizens left the valley floor and came up to see
us.

"Get back on the job," one of them said. He was a young male
dressed in gossamer shorts, boots and a wrap that went around
his ribs. "Why are you naked?" he asked, frowning. "What do
you think you're doing?" A miniature man, he was handsome and
fierce of expression with wings growing from his shoulder
blades. They were skin colored and webbed with ligaments. Like
flags rippling in the wind, they spread and held him aloft.

"They were torn from us in our work," I said, wondering if
that would do.

"Come with me," said the female. "I'll see that you're issued
new ones."

I didn't want to go anywhere near the toad and I noticed that
our escort stayed well to its rear as we flew to what she called
the supply depot. It was a mound of what looked like hollow
green glass. Either the fliers spoke my language or my brain had
been altered so that I could speak theirs. A few other things
seemed familiar to me. For instance, when our escort brought us
clothing from the green mound, I knew that boots always went
on first and then the rib wrap followed by the shorts. That was
the way miters were supposed to dress.

"You both look strange," said the woman, staring at us. "I
don't believe I've ever seen a person with yellow hair. And what
country does this companion of yours come from? She has outlandish bone structure."

"That's because we're from the outlands," said Lamana. "Wild
country. Unusual."

"Why do you stand gawking about? Go back to miting."

I still wasn't certain she wasn't speaking something very close
to English. I supposed we all looked like normal women as we
stood there with our wings folded and out of sight. They were so
thin and flexible that, when in repose, they formed only slight
bulges on the back. But the woman with us was like none born
of Earth. Her ancestry simply wasn't mine and Lamana's. Her
ears didn't stick out enough, her nose was too long and narrow,
her teeth were too small, her eyes were too round. Hair, long,
dark and wavy, hung down across her chest. No wonder she

stared at us. As we stood there, a blue scarab climbed out of the
soil and waved its feelers at us. Big enough to relieve us of our
toes with its pincers, it scattered into a dozen parts as the alien
hauled a weapon from her waistband and let loose with three
rounds of fast flame.

Plainly almost anything that crawled might be a problem to
the fliers. Around the depot dozens of gardeners pushed little
mowers that demolished the high grass and anything skulking in
it. In the distance a big, green, glittering lump reared into the
sky. It was the city. It was home.

Since Lamana and I seemed to have a disinclination to move,
the supply officer called a flier to accompany us to our work
area. Though the tips of my wings seemed to stir first, the initial
movement was made right at my shoulder blades so that the pair
of webbed appendages unfolded like accordions. Up as high as I
could I stretched them, followed by a couple of vigorous flaps
and then I rose with grace and no enthusiasm.

The distant city, the supply depot and the valley were beneath
me now and all were dwarfed by Dinglo the glot who was the
biggest thing on the planet. Rank and loathsome, his was a
pacific species and the fliers were fortunate to have him except
when they accidentally flew in front of him. Hundreds of winged
people labored over his exterior to keep him healthy. Lamana
and I took our places on an empty scaffold at the back of his
neck, a perilous position but not so much so as those on his face
and head.

The ropes supporting our scaffold hung from bumps on
knobby protrusions dotting the glot's hide. The knobs were big
as boulders and provided us with plenty of smaller warts from
which to hang our quivers. We also used them for climbing or
we could cling to them between shots. Bags of antiseptic and
wound packing hung within reach.

The area in which we worked was approximately one hundred
and fifty square meters. Score was kept by a system of electronic
signals. Somewhere in each working area on the glot's carcass
were embedded instruments that gave off beeps whenever a mite
struck home. The first beep was followed by a second that
sounded after the wound was treated and packed. The signals
were recorded on a screen in the supply building. So many de-

merits were given depending upon how much time was required to take care of the damage. A sharp team of miters drew lavish praise. That was their payment.

"We should be looking for a yellow ring instead of playing this game!" Lamana yelled.

"Who says it's a game?" I yelled back, jerking my head toward two o'clock.

She grabbed an arrow from a quiver hanging nearby, fitted it onto the bow which she scooped up from the scaffold, whirled and let fly just as an enemy sailed in for lunch. The missile caught the parasite in the distended portion of its abdomen which caused it to explode. From our position all the way to the ground we could hear the shouts of fellow fliers as they expressed their opinion of our having blessed them with an unwanted shower.

"They'll get us for that," said Lamana, giving an almost imperceptible nod toward eleven o'clock. It was my turn to fill my hands with weapons, my turn to fire, and I found out I was sufficiently skilled with the strange bow. Of course I hit the mite in the belly and again everyone got wet.

Mites were several varieties of winged parasites that forever lived within the aura exuded by glots. A gray mist rose from the warted behemoth, foul smelling to fliers but attractive to the mites who dipped, hovered, dived and dodged all through their waking hours. Most of them were pale yellow in color and approximately thirteen centimeters long with filmy wings, black head, bulging eyes, long sucker and many legs. They weren't intelligent which was the reason why they didn't give up glots and form an attachment for some other host.

One got through and squatted on Dinglo long enough to take a sizeable chunk out of his neck. After Lamana filled it full of arrows, I flew upward with a bucket and swab, shoved it off and doused the wound with antiseptic. Knowing how to do my job was no problem since there were miters everywhere whom I could imitate. Quickly I packed the hole with wadding that would fall out when a scab formed and then I returned to the scaffold and the battle.

Someone who was perched on Dinglo's crown made a bad shot and hit a fatso in the belly. Junk rained all over us. Lamana's wings took a direct hit and I had to do some fast scrambling to catch her before she fell. I used a swab to clean her off after which we both wasted time yelling at the bad shot above.

I was in the act of dispatching a fatty when the general alarm went off, a blast that knocked my bow out of my hands. Everyone on, around or about Dinglo who was capable of doing so dropped whatever they were doing and took to the air. An electronic probe embedded in the glot's scalp had scanned his brain and signaled that he was preparing to leap.

The signal was always unexpected and I wasn't ready for it but even so I managed to leap up and outward at the same time that I spread my wings. Not so far above me another flier did the same thing, but his spring was too energetic and carried him forward into Dinglo's view. He screamed as the big red sucker flicked out and gathered him to destruction.

Watching the glot take his first hop of the day was as awe-inspiring a sight as I ever saw and I nearly forgot to keep my wings working. He could have turned around and licked up enough fliers to last him all afternoon but he was stupid and only took a couple of graceless, gigantic jumps across the field before settling down again. Most of the scaffolds fell off him along with buckets, swabs and quivers full of arrows. He sat on a few hundred items, unblinking, grossly unintelligent and essential for the world's tranquillity, at least the part of it inhabited by fliers.

People retrieved their equipment and went back to the job, either climbing or winging to the proper warts, knobs and bumps. The work load was heavier after a hop because all the mites seemed to think their host was leaving the area and swarmed down for a free ride and a final munch.

Lamana and I settled ourselves in our old spot and began firing arrows one after another. According to the number of beeps given out by our signal, we were just barely going to be able to hold our heads up in front of people at the end of the day.

As if we hadn't enough to do, a troop of sphex attacked about an hour before quitting time. By then it was beginning to grow cool so we knew the invaders weren't overly serious but were simply trying to harass us, which they did. Since they weren't exactly brilliant it was coincidental that they came from the wrong direction. They charged us from Dinglo's rear.

Spotters sounded a new alarm and we fliers prepared for a move on the glot's part. He didn't wear a horse's bit but a jolt to one of the electronic anchors in his cheeks would encourage him to turn away from pain. He turned now, scattering fliers, equipment and mites. As soon as he saw the sphex, his sucker flicked out and in at lightning speed as he gathered the creatures in by droves. When it finally dawned on the enemy that their numbers were being drastically diminished, they broke ranks and aimed for individual conquests.

A sphex stabbed the flier nearest to me in the back with its stinger, paralyzed her and then flew away to find a suitable place to deposit her and lay its eggs on her. Another came at me, buzzing frenziedly and with good will, sucking heartily as it made plans for my body. It was twice my size, long and red of skin, gray winged, a head like a giant fly, eyes bulging, mouth scarlet and drooling. Its stinger was short but adequate. Backing up in mid-air, I sucked in my stomach as it lunged. An arrow pierced one of its eyes and drove on through to protrude from the other. The creature died and fell out of sight. Lamana hovered just above me, her bow and arrow ready to take care of anything else that flew near us. For the first time in my life I fully retreated, darted behind my friend and maintained a vigil in that quarter of the battlefield while she dispatched sphex as fast as they attacked.

It was actually Dinglo who finally routed the enemy and that was as it should have been since he was in the field for just that purpose. There was a mature glot in each of the six fields surrounding the city, serving as aggressive sentinels who kept away sphex and anything else hostile that happened along.

A squadron was sent to find the maverick who had paralyzed and kidnaped the female flier. It wasn't too long before they brought her back unconscious but otherwise unharmed. By morning the effects of the venom would be gone.

I couldn't recall having worked so long and hard in one day but after the sun went down I discovered that a flier's real labor was just beginning. At that time glots, mites, sphex and other insects went to sleep and then the fliers opened their city and lived a human existence.

Nearly staggering with exhaustion, Lamana and I dropped our equipment in a pile outside Supply and followed the other fliers to the city.

"There are no rings that I can see," said Lamana. We flew close together and stayed away from our associates.

"I feel strange," I said. "All this feels so homey and familiar."

"Which ought to teach you something about how strong is the pull of the body. But the mind should be stronger. In other words, let's get out of here."

"In the dark? With no rings in sight?"

The city was a jewel of a mound dotted with openings that sloped upward and then wound in, through and around the interior. There was no such thing as individual property. Even the living quarters were occupied each morning by new tenants, the old ones having settled down elsewhere. A guard came by and informed Lamana and I that we were scheduled for sleep during the first six hours of the night, for which fact I was grateful as I didn't think I could have stayed awake much longer.

In my cubicle was a bunk, bureau and bathroom. The bunk was made of spongy material that peeled off in thin layers. I peeled off the top thereby giving myself a fresh, clean bed. A worker stopped in the doorway and aimed a fanlike machine at the ceiling that freshened my air. Another machine came on and sucked up the dust. The bureau was a shelf built into the wall. It had a single garment lying on it. By picking it up, I activated a motor inside the wall which caused the shelf to roll upward and disappear while a second shelf bearing another article of clothing rolled into view. There was also a small library that operated on the same principle: read or scan a book and then send it on its way while another presented itself to you.

Sleep wouldn't come so I scanned a few books. They were amply illustrated which was fortunate for me since the written words of the fliers were practically indecipherable. Their photography, on the other hand, was clear and comprehensible so that I learned a bit about my environment and its inhabitants.

It would have been just as easy for the fliers to build an underground city but that would have been impractical because they were claustrophobic. Even now the mound's off-duty personnel stirred fitfully. Specters haunted their dreams while sinister sounds reverberated against the walls of their subconscious. Only a small part of the city was occupied because fliers always built on too large a scale. Thousands of cubicles in the center were vacant. In fact my own was close to the empty area and I could have sworn there was activity in the abandoned quarters. Consulting another book or two, I finally decided the sounds were my imagination.

There were factories of all kinds in the city, food processing units, complex machinery and no price tags on anything. Fliers were comfortable and satisfied with just enough to get by on— food, shelter and working companions. They were a rich, kindly, industrious people.

The walls in the sleeping quarters lost their glow as fliers settled down. Vividly green at first, they dimmed perceptibly and continued losing their potency until at last it was possible for me to just barely make out the far wall of the corridor outside my quarters. The arched opening seemed smaller now and my active imagination threatened to keep me awake.

My wings began to ache so I lay on my right side. My eyes were glued to the doorway as I imagined armies of sphex marching from the empty core. All around me noises grew louder and more sinister, so significant that I forgot everything else and concentrated on them. It was true that my fellow boarders hadn't very keen hearing while mine seemed to be much the same as when I was human. I wondered if Lamana was lying in the next cubicle listening to those sounds.

I lay on my other side but still my wings ached. Eventually I discovered that the best sleeping position was on the stomach so I rested that way with my head toward the hallway. After a while I could stand my curiosity and growing suspicions no longer and walked out of the cubicle. I wasn't too surprised to discover that Lamana was already there and staring with interest at a tunnel leading straight to the center of the city.

"I swear they're all deaf," she said to me. "How else could they ignore that racket?"

Of course that was why the sphex managed to infiltrate the unpopulated parts of the city. Nobody could hear them. One at a

time they had sneaked past Dinglo, found an abandoned entrance at the top of the mound and worked their way into the
core. It was quite comfortable there and food could be taken
from the granaries and warehouses after the work forces went to
sleep. When their numbers were sufficient, they would simply
march forth, stab the fliers into insensibility, lay a full load of
eggs and turn the mound into a sphex nursery.

Lamana and I crept down the passageway which seemed
never to end and which suddenly looked as black as the pit.
Somewhere ahead of us something ponderous shifted its weight, a
dry and rasping sound that was ominous because we knew it
hadn't been made by any person. It came again followed by a
low keening whine as antennae touched.

Even before we saw the humped, lumpy-headed shadow on
the wall we knew the enemy was near. Quietly we trailed the
single specimen as it clumsily walked away from an open gran-
ary. It had room to fly but it didn't dare because the sound of its
wings might have alerted restless sleepers.

For what seemed like kilometers Lamana and I tracked the
thing until it came to a high wall dotted with many archways.
On the other side was a large recreation area and the sounds
coming out of the openings were deafening. The sphex didn't
much care by then how much noise they made because they
were preparing for their invasion. There were thousands of them
in the park, crawling on top of one another, six deep in some
places, all making half-hearted attempts to be quiet but obviously excited by thoughts of the coming battle. No doubt they
expected to lose a few fliers who were awake and working near
the mound's exits for they would escape once the alarm sounded,
but the sphex plainly had hopes of capturing the majority of the
city.

Lamana and I beat them by about ten minutes. They had long
ago reached their complement necessary for an attack but they
were stupid and didn't acknowledge the fact until they were so
numerous they couldn't find crawling space. Then when they did
decide there were enough of them to conquer the opposition,
their leaders quarreled about the exact moment of invasion.
They were still trying to make up their minds as Lamana and I
took wing and headed for the nearest alarm.

It was such a loud squawking noise that fliers were literally knocked from their bunks and working places. Hosts of winged people fled into the halls and hurried toward the openings leading to the outside. Not everyone abandoned the city.

Many armed themselves and marched on the enemy. There were bows and arrows on shelves in the corridor for distance fighting while for close combat there were the fire guns. I helped myself to everything I could carry and took a stand in a corridor not far from my cubicle. A sphex zoomed on the wing straight at me, so unexpected I barely ducked his stabbing weapon as he went above me. I heard him crash as someone else brought him down.

My rules became uncomplex: if they crawled they were burned, if they flew they earned an arrow. It didn't take long to stop them in that corridor as they quickly piled up and made it impossible for the live ones to get through. Slowly we retreated and found another hallway where we dug in and killed so many it became almost automatic. Burning and letting fly with arrows, we were adamant while the sphex came in hordes that never seemed to end, clogging hallways until they couldn't move. It would take them a while to clear passages to freedom.

In just a matter of a few hours the city was abandoned by its builders who formed a swarm in the sky and began flying south. The sphex were still trying to get out. Their bodies blocked the exits so that the majority would still be inside when the sun came up and shone into the eyes of the six sleeping glots.

At dawn there would be no one to activate the paingivers in the glots' jaws. The beasts would be drawn toward the bright green dome they were supposed to guard. With gigantic hops they would travel to the glittering object, squat around it and literally lick it into nonexistence. It wasn't really glass and even if it had been, the corrugated tongues would have worn it away in a short time. Then the giants would wander in the fields until some other fliers came along and decided it would be a good place to build a city.

"There! See!"

I had been flying along reliving the battle in my mind and anticipating more when Lamana's words dented my consciousness. With savage disappointment I saw the cluster of yellow rings bobbing through a cumulus cloud. With raw dismay I remembered who and what I was.

"Now!" she said, as if she knew my thoughts. "Don't hesitate and don't think but one thing. You want to go back to Earth!"

But I didn't, not even when I broke from the squadron and followed her toward the cloud. My comrades, my work, my weapons, my future world—what were they if I couldn't enjoy them?

I felt a distinct dislike for the Indian beside me as I let my wings carry me to the nearest yellow ring. At that moment she was unwanted and unnecessary, much like my conscience when it butted, unbidden, into a dangerous situation. I could have remained a flier and probably I would have enjoyed my existence as long as it lasted, partly because fitting into this society was so easy and partly because here in this world I could forget the other, more complex one.

Had I told Lamana I needed a vacation and would stay in this land a while longer, she would have seen through my rationalizing and given me a lecture. The conscience was full of thorns and I think I bled a little as I left that dimension of green mounds and winged entities.

My problems too often came in bunches and this was one of those days. I transmutated with my mind full of regret at having left an interesting existence and right away I was doubly troubled when the process didn't take place as it should have. I was supposed to drop beside Lamana onto an innocuous plot of Earth somewhere on the west coast of the U.S., for that was the kind of ring it was. Neither Lamana nor I was prepared for the warping of space and mind—for all of twenty or thirty seconds while we hovered between realities—that occurred around and within us. For a brief period of time we were on some strange kind of carousel that careened between worlds and gave us the impression it was about to spin out of control. Then we settled down to a merely dizzy universe.

I could have sworn we touched a piece of Earth after which we were bodily snatched up and deposited elsewhere.

# 17

GORWYN SEEMED A LITTLE surprised to see us and not too pleased which was normal for him. "Now that you're both here you might as well come in," he said.

I took a last disbelieving look behind me. We had just left the land of the glots. The fields here were so dry and parched that it appeared as if the area was swiftly becoming a desert. The mountains in the distance were bleak and shrouded in fog. It seemed a strange place to live, but here the building was, sitting on a hill, an old-fashioned stucco mansion with a rusty iron gate and a knocker shaped like a gargoyle.

"Is this Earth?" Lamana said to me in a whisper, ignoring Gorwyn. "Are we in D-1?"

He wouldn't have been Gorwyn if he hadn't had a lab and eventually he led us into it. The place was big enough to put the cubbyhole at Mutat to shame, and not only that, it had more equipment than I had ever seen in one room before.

"Let's make a break for it," Lamana said out of the side of her mouth.

Wondering what her problem was, I walked past machines, pulled open cabinets, noted a few odd items here and there. The things supposedly sold at auction from the old lab at the school sat on a shelf above a computer, even the crown of wires, except that it had been remodeled and looked more complicated.

"Of course I've seen Tedwar," Gorwyn said to my question. "He isn't actually my son, you know. Not by blood. His mother was my second wife. She died when he was small."

"Where are we?" said Lamana. "Which state?"

"Nevada. It's quite unexpected that you landed in my back yard." Gorwyn looked at me. "I'm through with Mutat. It was only a temporary assignment, anyhow. These days I pick and choose what I do and right now I'm deep into experimenting. Want to help me?"

I thought of Tedwar and for some unaccountable reason I shivered. So Lamana and I had landed here on Gorwyn's property, and it was surprising but coincidences always were, weren't they? There wasn't much difference between landing in California from a ring and landing in Nevada. Both were in the same general vicinity, especially when one thought in terms of infinity.

There was a servant named Lavac and that constituted the complement of the household. For two people it seemed a huge place but it was a pleasure for me to take a tour of it in spite of the fact that Lavac sneered when he spoke and muttered under his breath when he was supposed to be silent. He carried a brown bottle the tip of which stuck out of his jacket pocket.

In the basement was a swimming pool which I planned to use later, but what was really interesting was the fine construction of the rooms upstairs, the genuine wood paneling, two-centimeters-thick doors, heavy staircases, high ceilings and marbled or wooden floors. There were great fireplaces in almost every room with ornate hearths and solid mantels. On the walls were the busts of bears, deer and tigers while stuffed birds sat on perches with enough reality to them to make me give them wide berth.

As I walked through that magnificent house I thought of my farm in Jersey which had been made of heavy cardboard and then sprayed with a tough mixture of mortar and plastic. Not only my house but everybody's was made like a crackerbox the walls of which wouldn't support a framed picture. Here on the walls of Gorwyn's mansion were thick tapestries seven meters long and as wide, large portraits with frames made of solid maple and huge hooks that held up voluminous drapes.

Other marvels were electric lights, electrically powered

freezers, washers, dryers, food and drink dispensers. Gorwyn explained that he had his own generators.

He had an armory too, full of modern heat guns, old six-shooters, ancient tridents, even a small cannon.

"As a matter of fact I have a kit that makes tiny instant atom bombs," he said, as I held up an out-of-date twenty-two and pretended to shoot Lavac in the brown bottle. "The disadvantage of owning weapons is that they're pointless. There are no enemies to be brought down anymore. The world is civilized."

For lunch we had steak that I hated to chew because it was so beautiful. Lamana had no such compunction, stuffed her face and kept her eyes on our host. She never glanced at Lavac who served us, just watched Gorwyn and never let him out of her sight. For the first time since I had met her she was behaving like an outlander and I hoped Gorwyn wasn't embarrassed by her rude attentiveness.

He was in fact neither embarrassed, amused nor even concerned, seemingly, but talked about politics, doom and the tawdry items in the department stores in town. Lamana broke her silence to ask where town was.

"A few miles west," he said.

Thinking what a marvelous place the mansion would be to live in, I excused myself and went into the hallway to look for a bathroom. Lamana started to follow but Gorwyn took her by the arm and led her to a clover-shaped aquarium inhabited by goldfish. He was speaking to her in low tones while she was casually pulling away.

The bathroom was more like a lounge, wall-to-wall mirrors that showed me a scroungy, dirty person with a tired face, decorated wall paneling, elaborate cornices, thick carpet. I was somewhat disappointed to discover the utilities were no different from those to which I was accustomed.

"How did you get that old crown of wires and the other stuff back?" I said to Gorwyn when I returned. "Some woman took your place at the school and had everything auctioned off."

"There aren't many people interested in that kind of equipment. I heard about it and managed to retrieve it."

We sat in the living room like three members of a happy family. Lavac disappeared into the upper regions and I didn't see him again. Since it was August we didn't need artificial heat but I imagined the enormous fireplace was loaded with burning wood.

"I'm working on a new phase of the ring business," said Gorwyn. "Why do muters who come back into Dimension One land with their clothes on?"

"Why do they?" said Lamana.

There wasn't anything particularly wrong with her tone yet I sensed a keen frigidity. Inwardly I sighed. One day she would have to learn that not every harmless or productive person was ordinary or even sane.

"All the openings are like one opening," he said. "All the doors are like the same door."

"That makes a lot of sense," I said. Lamana gave me a glance only I would have been able to interpret as scornful.

Gorwyn sat back in an upholstered, blue velvet monstrosity of a chair, crossed his legs and beamed at us as if we were a pair of little children or idiots. "Imagine a corridor with many doors opening onto it from both sides. The space of Dimension One or Earth moves along the corridor. It's not only the dimension, it's also a single opening or doorway into which all the others exit. No matter which one you come through, you end up coming through the same one."

"We don't exit in the same time period, though," said Lamana.

"We're talking about space, not time."

"Is that why the dead revive when they're brought back?"

"No, of course not. Resurrection has to do with the rings themselves. They return you to your natural condition. They're survival mechanisms, remember. You were once a living human and that's what you are when you emerge from other dimensions."

"It sounds as if it has a whole lot to do with time," she said.

"What about dead drees?" I said. "I've brought them back but sometimes they're still dead."

"A creature has to be of a certain size and state of intellect or it won't always revive. The smallest I've been able to work with and have complete success is a forty-kilo dog. Cats, rodents and the like just don't make it every time. In fact they don't more often than otherwise."

Lamana stood up. "Thanks for your hospitality but we'd better be going."

Open-mouthed I stared at her.

"Daryl and I are old acquaintances," said Gorwyn. "I've found her to be a very satisfactory assistant. I'd hate for her to walk out now. However, if you yourself are in a hurry . . ."

It was like water off a duck's back. "We have so many pressing items on our schedule," said Lamana. "For instance, her horse is sick and in need of treatment. He thinks he's an eagle."

"Well, I guess my work can wait. Go if you must."

"I'm not going anywhere until I try that swimming pool downstairs," I said. "Is it all right with you?"

"Certainly."

A few minutes later I was yelling at Lamana. "You're acting like a rude idiot! You'd think he was Bluebeard!"

We were alone in the pool, or at least I assumed Lavac wasn't skulking behind the pillars holding up the ceiling.

She put her hands over her ears. "Don't shout."

"I won't even talk to you. I'm going to do what I came to do." I dived into the warm, clean water and swam. It was pleasant and even enjoyable but I couldn't help comparing it to Waterworld.

"Be reasonable," Lamana said when I hauled myself up onto the tiled walk to rest. "This bird is too strange to be true. Think how coincidental it was that we landed right outside his house."

"Do you have another explanation for how we got here?"

"No, but I still don't like it. I don't like him or his rummy servant or his lab or this whole place. Where did he get those generators and all those machines? How did he get permission to own them and all that computer junk? You know the government doesn't allow people to waste energy."

"He does ring research. He's an eccentric and he's rich."

"And noncommunicative, like a glot. Your perception is so cloudy I can't believe it."

I went back into the water to put distance between myself and her one-track logic. She was getting possessive as if she had taken upon herself the task of being my overseer or older sister. I had no family and didn't plan to adopt anybody at this late date.

At dinner she angered me by announcing that she couldn't

stay because of pressing business. She would leave when the meal was over and she was grateful to Gorwyn for his hospitality. I had been enjoying the beef roast as if it were a delicacy that had gone out of style long ago, which it was. I also gained comfort from looking at the glittering dinnerware, the low-hanging chandeliers, the stained glass on an entire wall, the lace tablecloth and the fat legs of the table. The richness and beauty of my surroundings faded in exact proportion to the pace at which Lamana explained her need to be off and away. No doubt she expected me to accompany her when she left. She was in for a disappointment.

She didn't behave as if she expected anything from me or anyone, waved farewell, smiled, dutifully walked to the front door and let herself out.

"She didn't like me," said Gorwyn. "Probably it's just as well she's gone. We won't miss her too much, will we, when we're doing all those fascinating experiments? Who is she, by the way? Where did you pick her up?"

"She's a friend." Watching out a small window beside the door, I said, "She's fallen down."

"She has bad feelings for me. I definitely picked up gray vibrations in her vicinity."

"You think she fell on purpose?"

"The thought occurs to me," he said.

"She's holding her ankle. She's trying to get up."

"No doubt the pain is more than she can bear."

"She's honest. I've never known her to play tricks."

"It looks as if I still have two house guests."

I ran to the gate, swung it open and went on through. The sky was gray, beginning to fog over, ominous looking and without real color except for a couple of rings bobbing eastward. Her face twisted in agony, Lamana held a hand out to me.

"What a swell time for you to get clumsy," I said, starting to take hold of her.

"Look out behind you!" she cried.

I whirled just in time to see a green ring dart from behind a stone statue and, before I could react, Lamana raised her feet and did what she must have been longing to do all along. She gave me a swift kick in the seat of the pants and sent me out of the world.

Enraged at what she had done, I swam in Waterworld until I found a ring the same shade as the one we used to exit from the planet of the glots. To my surprise I landed in the middle of Yellowstone, not in Gorwyn's yard. I tried again and again but each time I took the bright yellow ring I ended up in the park.

Something was out of kilter. Where colors were concerned, my memory was infallible. The ring Lamana and I used to get away from the alien planet should have led me right back to Gorwyn. Somehow Lamana had known it wouldn't or she suspected it, otherwise she wouldn't have bothered booting me in the rear and sending me elsewhere.

Since I couldn't solve that particular puzzle while wandering among the redwoods, I sneaked home to consult maps of Nevada. I didn't expect Gorwyn's house to be marked on them but they carried descriptions of items of interest and might possibly mention that remarkable structure. They didn't, not that I had much of a chance to find out. Olger had barricaded herself in the farmhouse and refused to come out because Bandit had brought a friend back from one of his vacation spots.

The creature was as big as he but there the resemblance ended. It looked like a Komodo dragon replete with leathery hide, enormous tail, reptilian head and wicked face. Lumbering around in the paddock in the wake of my steed, it seemed content and not at all discommoded at finding itself in an unfamiliar dimension in an unfamiliar form. All it wanted to do was tag after Bandit, drink astonishing quantities of water and eat hay a bale at a time.

"That horse has been in the paddock and through rings and that's about all," Olger said to me. "Every time I behave as if I'm going to put him in the stable, he gallops off to another planet. Now he's brought that monster to keep him company so I can't even go out of the house. It jumps over fences like a frog, eats everything in my flower gardens, has even started on the small trees."

A passerby had already called the police who came the next day, took one look at Komo and ran for their nets and ropes. It did them no good. As soon as they showed they were in earnest

about capturing the outlander, Bandit trotted toward a fat blue
ring and led his friend into parts unknown.

The days passed and Lamana didn't show up. Neither did
Erma or anyone else I knew. I went to see Tedwar. The place
where they kept him was neat and clean and surprisingly modern. The energy shortage precluded the use of fans to combat
the late August heat but the building wasn't a highrise and had
an extraordinary number of windows. Brooks and shade trees
dotted the landscape while a shield on the roof of the building
prevented the sun from baking the insides.

"What are you doing here?" he said, much subdued from the
last time I had seen him. "I don't mean anything to you."

"I'm the reason you're in here, aren't I?"

"As usual you're being stupid. I've always been this way. The
older I get the more difficult it is for me to control my condition."

"You look good," I said, and it was true. He was the picture of
health. When he talked, though, or made a quick movement, he
gave me the impression that he was concentrating, deliberately
cautioning himself. He was too much in command. There was no
such thing as a relaxed moment for him. He was a spring held
coiled and tight.

"What kind of medicine do they give you?" I said when he
remained silent.

"What do I care as long as it keeps me going so that I don't
have to be wrapped in wet sheets or locked in a rubber room?
Don't ask me if I'm ever going to be normal again. I've never
been normal in my life. I'll stay here until they're sure I understand how to treat myself with the medication and then they'll
transfer me someplace where they can keep an eye on me.
Probably an orphanage."

I couldn't ask him if he had any family other than Gorwyn.
The words wouldn't pass my lips.

His eyes glittered with what seemed like amusement as he
said, "My father won't come to see me. You know why, don't
you?"

I managed to mutter a negative answer.

"You're an idiot," he said. "Really sickening."

"Is your real father alive? Maybe I can get in touch with him."

"What's that supposed to mean? Gorwyn is my real father. He put me in that ring because I made you decide to leave Mutat."

The agony on his face was too much and I glanced away. The room was small and full of two-way mirrors. We sat at a table where we could easily be seen by whoever monitored our conversation. I looked back at Tedwar and decided he didn't really look unusual except for his eyes. Was that shiny flickering the result of the new paint on the walls that glowed like yellow light or was it caused by the workings of a mad mind? I remembered him trying to bowl me over in the gymnasium, laboring overtime to do me some kind of damage.

"Why me?" I said without thinking, but he seemed to be reading my mind and grinned as of old, with malice and ill will.

"You're so easy to detest, always so helpful and so full of conscience. The world isn't really what you think it is. It's rotten and the sooner everything stops the better."

"Is there something you'd like me to bring you, some candy, soda, anything at all?"

"The key to the front door."

"You shouldn't be so down."

He showed his teeth in a distorted smile. "You sound like the stuffed shirt who came to see you at the school. He said practically the same thing to me when I told him Mutat was a house of freaks."

"When was that?"

"A few weeks ago."

"He had gray hair, light eyes and an educated air but there was a bit of a tramp about him?"

"That's him."

"What did he want?" I said.

"You. I told him to try the North Pole."

"He didn't say why he wanted to see me?"

"No. Stop asking me questions."

He didn't want to talk about anything anymore so I left him and went outside to see if the rings in the sky were as prolific as when I came in. I didn't intend to be caught unprepared when or if Erma, Solvo or anybody else came after me. These days it seemed I was being pursued by everyone. I thought of Croff coming to the school to see me. Whatever it was he had wanted to tell me, he must have thought it was important.

Thinking and strolling across the grounds in front of the building, I passed some benches beside a stream. A muscled orderly sat under a shade tree and I stopped beside him.

"Do you know Tedwar?" I said.

"You a relative?"

"A friend."

"I'm surprised he has one. Yes, I know him. He's the closest thing to a monster I've ever seen. His brain is literally corroded. Half the time he can't remember he's human."

"Prognosis?"

"Sorry, but I haven't an optimistic thing to tell you. He has the idea we're going to transfer him to an orphanage but it's only a dream in his own mind. He isn't fit to be anywhere but here. But I expect he'll be let out when he's grown since that's the way society does things."

"He lies a lot, doesn't he?"

"All the time."

From there I went to see Croff's niece. He had dabbled in antiques, left a fortune's worth besides which he also dealt in coins, stamps, fossils and odds and ends that were all worth money. His niece spoke kindly of him and hovered near while I looked through the objects in the room. It was jammed with Croff's leftovers.

"I stored it in here because there are some other nieces and nephews I'm trying to locate," said the woman. She was Croff's blood relative but looked nothing like him, being short and tough with a steel smile and gentle eyes. "I guess we'll divide the spoils," she continued. "My uncle had a good reputation among us." She fell silent and gave me a curious stare.

"I was in trouble once and he helped me out," I said.

She didn't object so I wandered through the room, picked up one or two things, frankly snooped. What did she care? I was just a kid. I even emptied a carton, took everything out and put it all back in a piece at a time. Why someone in Vermont would want to mail such stuff to Croff was a mystery, but the postal mark showed it had been delivered just a day or two before he came to Mutat to see me. There was a bottle of eyewash, a frayed paperback, a roll of tape, a pair of motorcycle goggles, a scarf, a cup, a tieclasp and some safety pins. A small parcel of worthless junk.

"He was very generous," said the woman behind me. "I didn't know him very well but he was reputedly kind. All these valuable things really surprised me because I assumed he spent his money on ring research.

"The government paid for that."

"I expect so. Isn't it foolish how the world runs after those silly circles, investing all that money and energy?"

I guessed she couldn't see the silly things. "Yes, it's foolish."

"I'm sorry you think there was something even worse about my uncle's death," she said as she showed me outside. "I mean, I can tell you don't think it was a burglary and killing by strangers."

"No cryptic messages with my name on them, nothing in his will, no scrap of paper?"

"No."

I said good-bye and went away. I could always find Erma, kidnap her, beat the daylights out of her and make her tell me who and where Appy was. Also, I could fly to the moon and declare my genealogy for twenty generations.

# 18

BUD JUPITER. He was just a crazy old man, like thousands of other crazy old men wandering around institutions, but there was something alarmingly familiar about him, alarming because it was so wrong and out of place and impossible. As I stared down at his shrunken face, I was relieved that my memory failed me. He reminded me of somebody but I didn't know who and for some reason I was glad of it.

Solvo had put me onto him, responded to my written request by sending a letter of his own. He didn't mention Lamana and didn't seem to be interested in what I might be doing.

Bud Jupiter must have been close to ninety, weighed about two hundred and eighty kilos, talked to himself and, according to the nurse with us, wandered away from the place and went downtown every chance he got.

"He's bad," she said. "Always was. Been here thirty years and can't be relied on for anything. Isn't that right, Bud?"

"Shut your mouth." Jupiter had no teeth. He was skinny, not because they didn't feed him but because he couldn't stay still. He was like a racehorse in a stall. A dozen times he went to the window and looked out. Sometimes he stopped behind another tenant to peer over his shoulder at the drawing table. "That stinks," he said once and the man placed his hands over his work and closed his eyes until the critic moved away. "Everyone in this place is trying to kill me," Jupiter said to me. "Do you believe that?"

"No," I said, but he had already forgotten his question.

"You can't talk to him," said the nurse. "He's so senile it's pitiful. If I didn't spoon feed him he'd starve."

"Where did he come from?"

"That's no secret. He's university educated and made a big name for himself in transmutating. He was the first person to come up with logical explanations for how it worked. I guess you could call him a pioneer. Any library has all kinds of information on him, except he lost his mind in his fifties and that was the end of his usefulness. Went downhill ever since."

Wondering why I had wasted my time going there, I left the institution and went to chase down other leads to my mystery. Ectri, for instance.

He wasn't in Jersey, Boston or Washington. From a memo on his secretary's desk in Boston I gained the information that he was at a Veterinarians' convention in Tulsa. From there he went to a small experimental clinic in Trenton. I knew because I followed him.

He, another man and a woman were doing work on immunology and had cage after cage filled with mice, rats, hamsters and guinea pigs. At least that was the kind of work the signs outside the clinic claimed they were doing. I scouted the area for rings, saw none and settled down in a patch of woods to watch the place. Once in a while I sneaked across the grass to look in a window. The thick shrubs and trees growing all around the building prevented them from seeing me while I had the advantage of spying at leisure.

The disadvantage was that they didn't do anything with rings, didn't even come out to look at the sky. There was absolutely nothing interesting going on and I was about to give up in disgust when Ectri came out in the middle of the afternoon and headed straight toward my hiding place in the woods. He was carrying twin suitcases. Making like a certain Indian acquaintance, I tiptoed away and hid in a pile of leaves, making so much noise it was a marvel he didn't hear me.

There was a ring channel in a clearing in the woods. Ectri stopped short of it and waited patiently, and before I knew it the woods were full of human derelicts. They must have come from drunk tanks, gutters, abandoned buildings, charity houses, old folks' homes, etcetera. All were middle aged or past. Some were ancient and tottered between trees as if they were on their last legs. From a shed hidden in a grove, they brought out folding chairs and then everybody sat down and waited for their turn with Ectri. He played the opthalmology bit, retrieved instruments from his suitcases and examined their eyes, occasionally applied drops, said things by way of encouragement and comfort. He wasn't sinister enough to suit me.

I was close enough to hear him and he was asking them if they saw the rings. Any rings. His fifth patient, an old man, croaked that he could see something blue from the corner of his eye. Ectri gave him another drop or two from a bottle and the old man said he could see the ring more plainly than before. It was big and round, he said, wide enough for a man to walk through. He shrank in his chair when Ectri invited him to do just that.

"Behind me," said Ectri. "Come on, follow me."

The crowd gaped and gasped as the two seemingly vanished into thin air. No one talked or got up and left though Ectri and his companion were gone a good twenty minutes.

"That's a danged sight better body I had in there!" said the old man to the seated spectators upon his return. "I tell you, I was powerful and I felt young. I think I had maybe a couple or three gray hairs is all. I want to go back."

A woman dispatched herself from the group, stepped up to him and laid a hand on his arm. "I'll teach you but you have to mind me, otherwise you'll do something dumb and maybe get yourself lost or killed."

"I expect I can get just as expert at muting as you."

"But not all at once," she said. "You need to learn colors. Tell me right now if you're a good listener, or just sit down and don't waste my time."

"I'll listen!"

She led him to another blue ring and the crowd enjoyed the spectacle of seeing them march off into nothing at all.

"I see shadows but nothing solid," said Ectri's new patient, a tall, middle aged woman.

"It's necessary for you to see the colors."

"Gray won't do?"

"Not a bit. They're either green or blue. Take your seat with the others and concentrate. Focus on one shadow at a time and see if they don't clear up into something."

Practically everyone could pick out some part of a ring before the session was over. Some saw shadows like the tall woman while others saw bits, pieces, streaks, momentary flashes, and all seemed to improve after eyedrops and concentration. It was my guess that before long they would all be independent travelers.

For these people, seeing rings was like making visual contact with something totally outside their comprehension. Crammed with mind blocks of self defeatism, their blindness might be curable with logic and eyewash.

Would a human body saturated with alcohol or drugs or both mutate into a slok once it went through a ring? I didn't know but I tried to find out. The majority of the rings in the channel were of four or five shades of blue and green which meant that Ectri's students were muting to the same four or five places in Gothland and Waterworld. Circling through the woods, I moved to where the channel flowed out of sight, chose a blue ring that was infinitesimally darker than most and stepped through. The difference in color was slight yet I landed several kilometers from my desired destination.

I found one of the right spots by simply running a zigzag course on the hot surface of the planet. Eventually I came to an escarpment overlooking flat ground where three whimpering goths crawled about and watched while their leader showed them what to do. Obviously these people hadn't been saturated with much of anything but determination before they came through. There wasn't a slok in sight. For a while I lay on the cliff and observed as the teacher showed her students the lava pits, tar pools, brimstone rain and finally the labyrinths.

By the time I got back to the woods outside Trenton, Ectri was gone. Most of his audience were now in other dimensions. The chairs had been put back in the shed which was then locked after which the stragglers walked through the trees to a crumbling road leading to a crumbling city. They were the dregs, the outcasts, the drop outs who didn't work, pay taxes or vote. Their homes were as hopeless as they, gutted rooms in dead buildings, damp cellars beneath ancient wooden frames, mausoleums musty with the smell of long forgotten dead. Anything with a roof and a floor would do; a place to sleep, a cubbyhole in which to hide from the occasional marauder whose burned out brain sent him or her on a rampage through the derelict city.

There were food dispensers on two or three corners offering cheap, unsaleable items such as boiled cabbage, beans, bread, fruit. The machines required energy but the government said it was worth it to keep the dregs of the world alive. The food dispensers were everywhere in the country. All over the country rotting cabbage, beans, bread and fruit lay in the streets.

I followed Ectri's dregs, or one in particular, into the city past the first broken signs, walks, streets and buildings. She slipped between some split concrete and disappeared. I followed, found the route leading down a clay tunnel into an old water pipe that ended in an earthen cave. Hastily I backed out and went to find someone else to follow. Anyone who lived in a wet cave couldn't be all sane and though I didn't demand much from dregs I wanted a minimum of logic.

No sooner had I stuck my head up out of the hole than an arm encircled it and hauled me on up into the dusky light.

"What you doing here?" rasped a voice. "Don't you know us dregs don't allow no brats in our fancy town?"

"Do you have to be dirty and stinking to be a dreg?" I managed to choke.

"No brats," said the voice but the arm loosened. This one was no embittered and disillusioned college professor or some other refugee from the elite of the world. Probably he had been a dreg long before he actually joined the ranks. Casually he picked my pockets of about ten dollars and change and then he booted my rear and set me on the road headed out.

It wasn't exactly a tent meeting a group of others were having in a concrete lot some distance away but it looked like one to me as I crept over and between blocks of stone to get closer. They built a fire in the center and sat around it while a member stood up to talk about the disadvantages of muting. One: they couldn't do any drinking or doping. Two: they couldn't remain dregs if they did anything so respectable. Three: muting was just another form of escape and bottles, pills and needles provided that.

Someone else got up and contended that ring travel wasn't anything like drugs, that it was a talent and everyone knew what you did with a talent; you at least tried it out.

The first speaker stood again and said Ectri probably worked for the government, that the whole bit was just another ploy to get them detoxed and into charity wards.

People began talking out of turn and by and by they were all talking at once. Then they were shouting. Before the brawl began in earnest I sneaked back the way I had come, located a ring zipping through the sky and used it to go to Waterworld.

I must have landed in Kisko's favorite territory or perhaps he was just feeling energetic but around me formed a surging maelstrom that alternated between being black and white, violent and mild, noisy and quiet. Sometimes when I tried to break through the wall of tumbling water into the calm I was sucked into black whirlpools and left to spin. Whether all the maelstroms or the dark shadows were Kisko's calling cards I couldn't be sure but I heard him raging and shrieking in the distance, still mad and lost and swinging in and out of dimensional doorways like a child in a playground. But he wasn't playing. By then I didn't know what he was doing, whether he had gained or lost ground in his attempts to save himself, whether he was aware of any part of reality.

There were many clues that made me believe he recognized me. His shadow followed me, he changed my environment in some way, such as maelstroms in Waterworld or dark, moving patches in Gothland. Even now he pursued me in the ocean and prevented me from having a peaceful swim. I climbed into an empty shell to see if the churning water might expel it, and it did. I drifted into a tranquil scene of floating mountains and seaweed for the span of five whole minutes before the aquatic storm located me again and began tossing me about.

Having had enough exercise, I found a blue ring and went to Gothland. On the broad face of the most obvious escarpment I could find I scratched a message: THAT WASN'T FUNNY!

An irritation with Gorwyn occupied my mind all the rest of that day. Lamana hadn't showed up and I could imagine how the experimenter might keep her prisoner for a while to explain to her how unthoughtful it had been of her to cross him up.

Disliking inactivity, I jumped on Bandit's back and went away with him and Komo to her natural habitat. It was such an astounding place that I climbed off my horse and stood on practically the only flat and substantial piece of ground anywhere around. I didn't change at all while my mount became a sleek, winged beauty. Komo muted into a lovely, long necked, gazelle-type creature with wings and tiny feet that just fit onto the sharp ridges and rocky spires that made up the planet. One after another the thin shards of turf ran for kilometers like endless racks beneath the pale sky. Whether there was flat ground somewhere I never found out. Several kilometers below the tips of the ridges was a heavy blue fog that didn't blow away or move, not that Komo or Bandit seemed to mind as they flitted through the sky or gracefully settled down on a narrow strip to graze, for all the world like great insects in an insane world.

It wasn't a place for people though I felt comfortable enough sitting beside the ring we had entered. Giving Bandit a last glance I went back home. He would follow whenever he felt like it.

Olger told me I had received a phone call from the Prospect Detective Agency. I called them back. After all this time they had an address for me. In a hovel in a dregtown in Memphis I could find Wheaty.

It was with mixed feelings that I went after him. It seemed paradoxical to me that traitors could remain human on the outside, like healthy looking gourds with nothing in them. Never having been to Memphis, I took a blue ring into Gothland and exited through a yellow one I knew would land me in southern Kentucky and then, with my best eye in operation, I chose another ring in Gothland that was slightly darker than the first. It put me in Columbus, away from my intended destination, so I knew the color I wanted lay in the lighter zones. A few minutes later I stepped onto a street forty miles from Memphis. Sick of rings by then, I caught a bus.

Wheaty had gone down in the world. With his hangdog eyes and his sagging cheeks, his hurt mouth and his wounded psyche that ran around in his skull like a cornered rat, he seemed surprised but glad to see me. "I should have given up the job before I cracked," he said. "But that's what cracking is. You do things you never stop paying for."

"Maybe you did some paying, but the man you owe hasn't collected," I said.

"What man? What are you talking about? Never mind, the world is on its way into oblivion. Don't you understand? Dark Ages, baloney, it's the living end. No lights or heat now and no food next. Kids going to the dogs. Crime everywhere. We should all refuse to get out of our beds in the morning."

"As usual you aren't making a lot of sense."

"You're not jaded yet. Just wait." A flicker of his old self showed in his direct look. "How did you manage to stay alive? How are the others? How come you haven't been crushed under the treadmill?"

"Let's go."

"Where to?"

"You already know."

"Outside?" he asked. "I never go there anymore. I can't take the threat. Everytime I see an outsider in clean clothes I get paranoid. He's about to kill me, or he's planning how to take something I value, or he's figuring out how to make my life unbearable."

I couldn't decide whether he had cracked in more ways than one.

"You think I pulled a Benedict Arnold on you?" he said. "I assume you're tickling me in the ribs, though that was never your way, as I recall. Speaking of the past, I have a great big recollection of a female elephant stomping the gonads out of me. I don't like to think about that, let alone talk of it. It wasn't that she was female because even though I like to be as chauvinistic as the next guy once in a while, I know there are women who become jocks at age six and grow muscles I'll never hope to have. It was because she enjoyed herself so much. You might say she dissuaded me from life. She showed me how bad the human race was. With every lump she taught me a severe lesson in ethics, most of which boiled down to the revelation that there aren't any except maybe in kids like you who don't know any better. I just walked away from everything and never went back.

I have a family somewhere that I never see so why should I worry about three people I used to do dirty work with?"

"I saw Deron's and Kisko's dead bodies after the female elephant got done with them," I said. "By some miracle Kisko was revived. That only leaves you."

"As a scapegoat, you mean? I don't care what you accuse me of. I'm so obviously a loser it would be asinine for me to try and deny it, which I wouldn't anyhow because I've given up everything that means anything to me. I didn't exactly do it on purpose but I found it provides a kind of safety and comfort I never had before. If I haven't got anything to lose then I can't suffer a loss."

He came willingly on the train with me, didn't seem to notice when other passengers stared at him. He was the worst looking dreg I'd ever seen. He told me he shaved once in a while to keep his face free of vermin; he didn't like to itch. I thought he must have lost fifty kilos and his rags stank. Not once did he look out the window.

"I don't care," he said now and then. "Who cares? What for?"

After I got him to the farm I bought him some clothes, handed him a razor and showed him the way to the tub.

I placed a chair in the middle of the pasture and had him sit on it.

"You're making a mistake," he said.

"About what?"

"Everything. You see the world through the wrong facet of the glass in front of you." He looked around, unafraid. "What's the idea? What am I supposed to be doing out there?"

"You're a target."

He kept looking around. "For what? I don't see anything."

"Not even all those rings?"

"Where?"

"Straight ahead of you."

"You know I can't see rings. I can pick out a couple of faint lines but that's all."

"That's more than I thought you could see. Anyhow, I'd appreciate it if you just sat there."

"Not that I'm overly curious, but tell me why."

"Kisko's in D somewhere. I want him to come out and get you."

"And you don't care what he does to me?"

"No."

It was disappointing in more ways than one. I didn't savor the thought of him suffering and perhaps being destroyed but the fact remained that he belonged to Kisko. That was the case as I saw it.

For three days he sat in the field. I thought his mind might have gone since he finally took to chuckling and chortling as if at some private joke. Every evening at sundown he came in to dinner, slept in the living room and then went back out to the chair at sunrise. He told me more than once that he aimed to please and hoped I succeeded in killing him because he was tired of living, if that was what one called it.

On the third evening Kisko came out of nowhere like the tail end of a ghost, wispy and languishing in seeming ennui. There was no hurry evinced as trails of fog filled the air around the chair where Wheaty sat bolt upright. His weak blue eyes stared and his teeth showed in a grimace of fear and disbelief but he didn't cry out or leave his seat.

"Why should I be punished for a guilty conscience?" he said in a loud voice to the blue-gray air enveloping him. "I don't even know why I feel guilty. It's just there. Like, my baby teeth came in and I grew a few inches and I grew some more hair and then I grew a guilty conscience. I swear, that's the worst thing I ever did in my life."

The clouds gathered more closely and more thickly around him. "I'm sorry you're sick, boss," he said. "I'm sorry either of us was ever born."

Something unusual happened to him as he sat talking in a rasping voice to the fog. His body lost its rigidity, his expression became puzzled and then he said, "If you say so." Then he was gone. Like a wink of an eye or the turning of a page of a book, reality was different all at once, had moved on a pace or a parsec and Wheaty no longer sat in the chair in the field that constituted part of my property. The ghost had taken him.

# 19

I WENT TO STILLWELL, Maine, to see if the cousin of Carston, Orfia's childhood acquaintance, had returned from California. She had and informed me that Carston lived in New York.

I wasn't expecting much of anything when I arrived at the address which was partly why his first words knocked me for an inward loop.

"How is your mother?"

Just like that I had a family.

It was an ordinary apartment in a highrise overlooking a congested city. The sky beyond the windows was gray with coaldust belching from a smokestack across the river. Carston and I sat in the living room on furniture made of cardboard, styrofoam and cheap fabric. Not that he was poor. He said he was an accountant for a growing business concern, so I knew he made a good salary. It was just that scarcely anything was well made. Someone in another room played a piano, softly and not too proficiently. Carston was broad and balding, friendly and at ease and not overly surprised that I should be there.

"The whole country is turning into a missing person. Everyone seems to be taking a walk. You're very much like her," he said as I carefully felt my way into the nearest chair. "I'd know that, you see, because I haven't seen Orfia since we were both about your age."

He remembered the trouble back in Maine since he had been so personally involved. After it happened, Orfia's parents packed up and left which had grieved Carston since he had a crush on Orfia.

"At least I did before that day we sneaked off into D," he said, smiling slightly and rather ruefully. "The world was different then. Ring travel wasn't something people did recklessly. That is, as far as we knew, Orfia and I and her brother were the only muters in town, and the fact was that we didn't mute. Not ever. Our parents and teachers used to lecture us against it like they did against drugs and porno. Most of the time they acted as if we were a little bit freaky. So we thought about it and read about it and looked at the rings but did nothing about it. Except Sonny, and I still think to this day he muted all the time and then lied about it even to us. Sonny was always doing something crazy. Anyhow, Orfia and I decided to go ahead and do it one day. We were so excited we couldn't make up our minds which ring to take. There was a big channel down by a creek we used to play in and on the day we did it we skipped school right after lunch and met at a spot where there were rings all over the place. It was like baptism, you know, except that we knew our parents and everybody else would be against what we were about to do, so that cut into our enthusiasm and made us a little edgy, but it didn't change our minds."

Carston paused, frowned and then smiled. "She didn't mean it, not any of it. She had no more idea of what to expect than I. Oh, we'd read books and knew we were going to transmutate into goths, and we'd seen pictures of them and Gothland but none of it was real. If we'd chosen any other ring our lives might have been entirely different. Orfia and her family probably wouldn't have moved away, we wouldn't have lost contact with one another and you might have been my daughter. We picked a ring that exited right on the tip of an escarpment and over the edge we went together, clawing and grabbing at one another in sheer terror, reaching out for some support and not thinking of the things we'd read about how it's almost impossible for a fall or slide to hurt a goth.

Again he paused. "Under normal circumstances we might have come out of that fall untouched but something went wrong when Orfia mutated and she turned out to be monstrously huge, much larger than normal, two hundred kilos and more, and while she grappled with me and I grappled with her, she literally nearly slashed me to pieces with her claws. By the time we got to the bottom of the escarpment I was convinced I was dying. Orfia had to drag me to a yellow ring and shove me through it. The most startling thing to me was that I was in agony and bleeding to death one moment and perfectly okay in the next. I simply got hysterical, blabbed everything and accused Orfia of doing it on purpose. My parents accused hers of having spawned a homicidal freak and the whole thing blew up."

He shook his head at me and his own thoughts. "That was it. They took her away and I never saw her again. I really think they were afraid she was abnormal and wanted to get her and themselves out of an embarrassing situation that could have become worse."

Her last name was Kint, he said, and she had blonde curly hair, blue eyes and features like mine.

"I was the cause of her trouble," he said. "That first transmutation must have been a fluke and I'll bet after that she muted into a normal sized goth like everybody else."

"You never went to Waterworld with her?" I said.

"I was terrified of water and couldn't believe I'd be safe there. To this day I've not been to that dimension." He shrugged and looked self critical. "The talent is wasted on me and always has been. I don't have the personality for it. I'm content with one world only."

Like too many other people, I thought, remembering an individual or two who would have traded an arm for the kind of vision it took to travel to other planets.

He didn't have any more information for me but I kept questioning him and he gave me what answers he could even after he grew tired of the conversation. Before I left he shook my hand and said he hoped I found Orfia. He obviously meant it, just as he obviously still suffered from an occasional pang of guilt about something that happened decades earlier.

Orfia and Miles (Sonny) Kint. There was no data about them at the county court house, not even in the census records. The deed books showed the purchase and sale of their property but nothing else. Since vital statistics, land and property information was recorded in a series of computers and eventually a microfilm copy was made for permanent storage, and since Orfia and Sonny couldn't be found in any of these, it was plain that some-one had gone to a great deal of trouble and money to wipe clean their traces.

I wasn't quite back where I had started. Now I might have a mother and an uncle. Of course I didn't really have them, not as long as Appy or someone kept them hidden, or as long as they voluntarily kept out of sight. Which was it?

The puzzles weren't over. The next morning I went out of the farmhouse to find Googs and take her for a walk and saw her playing with a pup who looked enough like her to be her exact miniature. It had the same pert ears, brown and black coat, stub tail and terrier face. It was about six months old.

"She went into a double blue ring down by the barn and when she came back out she had the other one with her," said Olger.

There it was again. "What do you mean, a double blue ring? There's no such thing."

"It's interesting to know you have a blind spot," she said. "The thing was there, all right, and the dog didn't want or intend to go in it but she ran around the corner after a squirrel and I heard her yelp just before she went through. Gone about a min-ute, I'd say, before she brought back the young one."

We walked down to the barn to the appropriate corner where there wasn't a ring anywhere to be seen. "Just as I thought," I said. "There aren't any rings in this spot. There never are."

"It's still there," said Olger. "Practically in front of you, cloudy blue and pink, like dying fire. Could be it's Hell. It sure looks like it."

"Take both dogs and push them through it."

"What? Why should I do such a thing?"

"Do it. Googs is mine and I care what happens to her."

Giving me an outraged look, Olger picked up both animals and seemed to scoot them through thin air. They suddenly disap-peared. We waited and by and by Googs came walking back into existence, wagging her tail.

"Now you've caused her to lose the little one," said Olger. "Tell me what you just proved."

"Nothing, obviously, except that the pup didn't belong here and isn't here."

"But it was her own. Flesh and blood never looked more alike."

"You know she didn't give birth to that pup."

"Then where did it come from?"

"I don't suppose you'd care to go in the ring and report back to me?"

That afternoon I went loping through some familiar territory in Gothland when I came across a message carved into a rock. It was large enough so that I couldn't miss it: GREEN DOUBLE RINGS. Frustrated, I sat on my haunches and stared at the words for five minutes. I had no doubt Kisko wrote them for me but I thought the least he could have done was to talk about something that made sense to me. I was tired of hearing about double rings. Olger kept chiding me about Googs and the pup, I had a strong recollection of Lamana mentioning the things and the more I heard of them the more I felt left out.

Why should Kisko write me about them? Why, for that matter, should he write coherently about anything? He hadn't come out of D after Wheaty but instead had drawn the other into wherever he himself was.

For the fiftieth time Olger remarked about it at dinner. "How can you sit there stuffing yourself while I talk of the demise of a human being?"

"That means dead, doesn't it? Well, I don't think Wheaty's dead. He was supposed to be something like it. I figured Kisko would feel his lure and come out of D to get him, and that way he might be well again."

"And now?"

"Now I don't know where either of them is or what's going on."

"Go ahead. Continue playing with people's lives."

"Somebody played with my life. In fact, they're still doing it."

I had a phone conversation with Solvo during which he politely inquired as to the whereabouts of his daughter. How did I know? Gorwyn was malicious but I didn't consider him dangerous. Yes, he might confuse Lamana or even lose her, but only temporarily. Yes, it was possible she was following a lead or clue. After all, he should know his offspring better than I. Yes, it was surprising to be told that Gorwyn's mansion wasn't to be found anywhere in the state of Nevada. Yes, Gorwyn lied now and then about a lot of things.

There were still no records concerning any of them. Tedwar, Gorwyn, Ectri, Orfia, Croff and the three or four others the latter had mentioned might never have been born for all the information there was to be found on them. Solvo didn't like it either.

"This happens all the time," he said, an obvious untruth. "The first thing a criminal does is clean up his tracks. Appy has erased everything that might lead to him."

"What about Erma?"

"The name and description ought to be enough to trace her but so far they haven't been, which means she's a background player. Forget her. Forget all of it. Go play games and leave murderers and crazy people to me. Or better still, come to the clinic and let my associates try once again to break your mind block."

That was on a Tuesday. By Thursday I was bored and restless and decided to take him up on his offer. I muted through an ordinary ring, expecting to land on the front walk of the building. Instead I found myself in Gorwyn's back yard for approximately three seconds, just long enough for me to recognize the place and start getting bewildered. There was the iron gate and the house beyond it and I thought I saw someone coming down the walk toward me. But then I went elsewhere, not of my own volition but at the whim of some unknown force. Pfft. One moment I was on Gorwyn's property, the next I sailed through blind space and stepped onto the concrete walk next to Solvo's building.

"Why don't you worry about Lamana and forget about me?" I said to him when I met him inside.

"My daughter is no cause for worry. She's on an errand for me."

That made me pause. "You found her? That's funny. She hasn't come to my place."

"Why should she do that?"

"I thought her job was to keep watch on me."

"Besides which, she's a good friend, eh?"

"What about the incident I related to you? Could somebody make a machine that picked me up when I was muting and set me down somewhere that I didn't want to go?"

He didn't answer that question or any of the others and neither did anyone else. Chameleon seemed satisfied that I was once more her prisoner and made all sorts of preparations that indicated she might be getting ready to offer me up as a sacrificial goat or something. She patted me, hugged and kissed me, threatened and cajoled, used her silver eyes to bedazzle me, but the wall in my mind slid around and then settled firmly back in place.

"Concentrate on double rings," said Doctor Oregon. "Try to see them in your mind. Talk about them to the old woman."

"It doesn't do me any good to think or talk about them. I can't see them no matter how I try."

"You only think you can't."

"Can you see them?" I said.

"I can't see any rings at all but Lamana and her family can and that includes the double kind."

"Have you seen her? Where is she?"

"On an assignment. Concentrate on the matter at hand. Let Chameleon help you."

First the wrinkled little old human tried knocking me out with a narcotic and asked me questions, and when that didn't work she used a series of televised images to try and put me into a hypnotic trance. The wall in my head shifted a bit but didn't seem to weaken at all so she stood in front of me and used her weird eyes to knock me out. I'll give her credit and say she was good enough to do almost anything to a human psyche that hadn't already been tampered with by whoever had tampered with mine.

In the end they all gave up and let me go, showed me the door once more and offered me their best wishes.

Disgruntled and feeling out of sorts, I went to the rest home to see Tedwar. For a while he talked just fine, told me a little bit about his schedule and what he was doing by way of therapy. Then the old black mood hit him and his spirits fell into the gutter.

"Gorwyn doesn't care about me," he said. "He told me so.

Every time I told him I loved him he laughed. He has no feelings for anyone."

"You're upsetting yourself," I said. "Try and calm down.
You'll make more sense if you take your time."

"How can I be calm? Don't you understand that I'm being
ripped apart by the agony of my existence? Help me. I don't
know what you can do, but help me."

Later the muscular orderly tried to reassure me. "How can we
help him when we don't know which part of his babble to take
seriously? He grows more unreasonable every day. Take my advice and stay away from him. He doesn't like you anyway. You
get his hackles up faster than anybody I know."

Thoughtfully I walked away. . . . Tedwar, unfortunately, was
nuts and he was likely to stay that way. Like old Bud Jupiter.
Which reminded me, what kind of name was that for a grown
man?

I'd been meaning to check it out and it was too bad I had put
it off so long. Or maybe it was just as well since what I found out
made no sense. At the library I consulted a familiar volume,
skimmed the bio alongside Bud's photograph, and then there it
was hitting me between the eyes. Naturally Bud was a nick-
name. Jupiter's real name was Apton. Once upon a time he had
been a big name in rings, had traveled the lecture route, had
bought homes in Japan, Egypt and Alaska and had gone completely haywire at age fifty-two. Now I knew that Croff had been
wrong about at least one thing. Practically everyone I knew was
somehow involved in my troubles.

The knowledge hit me in the wrong manner, weighed too
heavily on my soul, rocked me so that I grew even more confused. And dumb. I muted to Gothland in order to relax in a
safe place but then didn't check to make certain it was safe. I
didn't pay attention to where I landed, fooled around and was
careless, failed to look to my health and well being, strayed too
close to forbidden territory until I inadvertently happened upon
the enemy.

The slok was big and swift and I realized I would have to
work at it to get away from him but initially I wasn't worried because somewhere I had gotten the idea that I was the smartest
thing in all the worlds.

It was dumb of me to play with him and in the end I bitterly regretted having done so but that didn't help me as I raced down stone corridors in fear for my life. I knew he had seen me but it never occurred to me that he was waiting for me or anybody to come through those high arches. Anyway, I skidded through and out of the cave and then played games popping in and out of crevices and around or up over stalactites until I finally realized the slok hadn't gone on about other business but, in fact, had made me his business.

He wasn't giving up but remained as tenacious as lint, clung to my trail while I made genuine efforts toward losing him. Staying ahead of him was possible only as long as I had wide open labyrinths, but I lost ground when twists and turns became prevalent. He was better than I on short hops, more agile in skinning around corners, better even at low jumping so that it wasn't long before I could hear the chattering sounds of his teeth as he grew confident of catching me.

By the time it finally dawned on me that I might possibly fail to outrun him, I already felt the strain of the chase. I assumed the slok was also tiring but he didn't sound like it as he talked to himself about how much fun it was going to be to inflict damage upon my body. From the beginning I made mistakes. Instead of heading for large, familiar labyrinths I took those that merely seemed promising only to have them turn out to be too narrow or winding. Quick entrances into corridors and fast exits from them seemed to be the thing to do as my pursuer was forced to take time to decide which way I had gone.

The next labyrinth I chose grew more narrow instead of widening and I guessed it didn't empty into an amphitheater but came to a dead end somewhere ahead. Actually it opened into a crevice jam-packed with the bodies of two goths whose look-a-like features immediately attracted my attention. Both approximately fifty kilos in weight, they had the same head and body features, paws shaped the same, both tails curled at the tip, and the wounds in their throats were exactly alike. What I had here was a set of twins who had been made to bleed to death.

Now I knew what had become of Padarenka and Mikala, but the knowledge didn't help my situation. Backing from the crevice in a hurry, I snaked through a skinny opening through which the slok came much faster, and I legged it as rapidly as I could toward a generous looking archway.

On the other side was an escarpment too high and sheer to be climbed while to the left and right were solid walls of rock. Incredibly, I had boxed myself in. Not only that, the area wasn't spacious enough to allow me to maneuver freely which gave all the advantage to the slok who came clicking and clacking toward me like a maniacal caterpillar.

Strange, but I had a series of disorienting sensations or little shocks as the enemy emerged from the tunnel and made ready to attack. He traveled headfirst with his long body coiling and uncoiling behind him like a motorized spring, his teeth working, his dark hide glistening in the red light. Veering to the right as he spied me backed against the escarpment, he scooted up the wall with the obvious intent of getting above me and dropping down on me. At least that's what he seemed to have in mind until he too began being affected by the disorienting process that had me squatting on my haunches with my own jaws clicking. This mad creature who screamed and sped back and forth across the wall above me like a fly was familiar to me. I knew him. On the other hand, I didn't know him.

I had forgotten all about flight and fear but simply squatted and watched the thing move from side to side over my head until at last he gave a final screech and dropped onto the ground in front of me. For the first time in my life I saw a quiet, living slok. This giant perched on his bottom tip like a ballet dancer and weaved back and forth while his dark eyes regarded me with plain curiosity.

"Groppo?" I managed to croak. "Is that you, Groppo?"

He knew me as well as I knew him. There was no mistaking the aura surrounding him, not the aura of ape but one that conveyed his spirit to me. He might just as well have been standing before me in simian form.

He chattered unhappily for a moment and then before I could move he whipped about, fleetly sped down the tunnel and disappeared.

Trembling, exhausted, I staggered down the tunnel and headed toward the crevice where Pat and Mike lay dead, went around a corner and was brought up short. The area crawled with sloks. Quietly I backed into an empty corridor, sneaked topside and hunted for a ring that would take me to Solvo.

What happened in the next few seconds might have been even more frightening if I hadn't been so tired.

I no sooner walked through a yellow ring that should have put me on the sidewalk outside the clinic than I again felt a sensation of being leisurely pulled apart, and in the next moment I stepped onto a dirty patch of ground close to a cluster of noisy machines. There was black smoke everywhere and the strong stench of oil permeated the sky.

Somebody yelled, "Grab her!" but I was already flying down the hill, not that it did any good since the woman in the red dress was capable of doing some flying of her own. As big as she was, she moved like Mercury and caught up with me in a matter of seconds and grasped me by the neck, none too gently.

# 20

THEY HAD BUILT the barracks too hastily so that the corrugated steel walls didn't meet evenly at the corners. The windows were lopsided, pulling the thin, pliable screens awry. The living quarters consisted of cubicles spacious enough for one occupant, a toilet and a rock-hard bunk. I wore a leg iron that chafed as I moved. It wasn't long before the flesh around my ankle was raw. My chain permitted me to move from the bunk to the toilet but not through the doorway.

The smell of oil saturated the air, thick and heavy, menacing somehow. The stuff clung to the walls like adhesive, formed a slick coating on the floor, even made my bunk sticky and unfit. There were the sounds of machinery clanking and shrieking, the more muted tones of men and women cursing and grunting, and through it all could be heard the ponderous splashing of oil as it fell from a pipe into a tub.

Through the doorway of my cubicle I watched Erma. Her red dress was grimy with black smudges. She slouched on a stool, overwhelming it like a hen on a diminutive nest as she swilled soda and stared at the floor. I had learned right away that she wasn't wasting her time watching me. There were a dozen others to do that. Her duties included nothing so common. She ran the whole outfit.

Somewhere in the distance I heard the squeal of trains laboring up the mountain to loading platforms where workers made ready to transfer filled drums into boxcars.

From where I stood in my cubicle I could see another woman almost as big as Erma, wearing jeans and a checkered shirt. She lay prone on a table and breathed heavily. Her name was Bass.

"I'm tired," she said. "I'm beat."

"Shut up," said Erma.

"Why don't you do a little work out there and see how you feel?"

"Why don't I pound on you a little and see how you feel?"

"Nuts to you." Bass turned, lay on her side. "You're in a good mood. Did Appy holler at you? Is he upset because it's taking him so long to become the richest man in the world?"

"He's crazy," said Erma.

"What's the kid for?"

"I never asked him."

"What do you think?" said Bass.

"She knows where somebody is hiding. He wants them. That's all I know. Who cares?"

Nobody paid any attention to me, not even at mealtime though I detected the odor of food cooking over open fires or on grills. They had toast, meat and a variety of other items the smell of which blended to make an interesting atmosphere. It almost cancelled out the stench of oil. After grieving over my empty stomach for a while I lay down on the dirty bunk and fell asleep. Sometime in the middle of the night I was awakened by someone gripping my chin and shining a light in my face.

"It's a good thing you don't make many mistakes these days," said a man's voice.

"How could she get away?" said Erma.

"Tell me about the island."

"That was a fluke. I still don't see how she managed. But the grabbing machines are working perfectly now."

"This is important."

Erma snorted. "Yeah, I know. She's wearing a leg iron that stays on until I get orders to take it off."

They went away and left me in darkness and I lay thinking about the man's voice. It brought back memories of a ranch house, a scholar who couldn't ride a spirited horse and a body that had looked broken and dead.

At breakfast Erma brought me a chunk of hard bread and a bottle of soda. "Dumb knot," she said. "Why don't you tell them what they want to know and get it over with? Save yourself a lot of sorrow. You can order your amnesia to go away and it will."

"Just like that?"

She stepped on my foot. I was sitting on the edge of the bunk chewing the bread and wondering how I'd get the lid off the soda bottle when she eased forward and did it. It reminded me of the time Bandit accidentally got my toes under one hoof except that then I was standing in soft sand. Now my foot felt as if it were flattening out on the concrete floor.

"I get the idea you can't help sounding wise," said Erma. "It's your natural state. You were born wise. In my opinion you should cultivate a gentler and more lady-like manner."

"I'll make the attempt," I said, almost gasping with relief as she moved off my foot. "I didn't know you were Deron's pal."

She paused, grinning. "You remember when I gave him a licking in that cellar? He almost quit because he was so insulted when he heard that was part of the deal. Then after I knocked the stuff out of him he wanted to quit for more urgent reasons. Like bent bones. But he's a hog for money."

I couldn't say anything, merely gave her a sick look.

"That dreg who helped you and your nutty friend get away?" she said. "I pinched him in a couple of sensitive places and gave him a case of eighty proof. For that he made you believe Deron was dead and then he took you and the sap to town. I can't understand how that fellow lived. I worked him over good."

"So it was Deron who betrayed us?"

"Betrayed? What an old-fashioned way of putting it."

I saw him the next day. He was so much the same that I almost expected him to reach for a saddle and mount up. Perhaps he was a little thinner but that was all. His almond-shaped brown eyes went a little round when he saw me looking at him. It wasn't an act of surprise but more one of mockery.

"I forced Wheaty into D because I thought he did what you did," I said.

Deron looked interested. "Is that where he is? I've been hunting him and Kisko for quite a while. I thought you hid them away somewhere." He interrupted me when I started to speak. "Don't ask me how I could do what I'm doing or anything else foolish like it. Try to view the situation from a realistic perspective. This isn't something your fertile imagination can get you out of. It is, in plain fact, business and you know how people are where that's concerned. You're here because there's something you're going to do for us. If you don't we'll kill you."

"What do I have to do?"

"Hunt through double green rings until you find some people who don't want to be found. That's all."

"Who are they?"

"Some valuable acquaintances, let's say."

"Do you know Appy Jupiter?"

He didn't answer. He went away looking puzzled.

The next day I went to work. There was no getting free, even when they sent me into D because the alien dimensions couldn't sustain me and I couldn't seem to exit anywhere but back at the oil depot. I tried but it did no good. As soon as I exited D I experienced the familiar sensation of being caught in a maelstrom after which I always landed back beside the ring channel and whoever was conducting the experiment that day. Usually it was Deron.

"Don't fight it," he said. "It's like struggling against an ocean undercurrent. You'll only wear yourself out."

"What makes you think I'll tell you even if I do find something on one of those crazy worlds?"

"Not something. People. At least three. I figure you'll give everything away sooner or later when you start remembering."

"What specifically am I supposed to remember?"

"You'll know that when it happens."

I wondered if anybody wondered where I was or even cared. Was Solvo hunting for me? Was Lamana the least bit curious as to my whereabouts? Where was Orfia?

The way they propelled me into rings I couldn't see was only slightly interesting. They had a stack of monitors to tell them what kind of rings passed by and my chair was directly beside a large channel so that at any given time we were surrounded by circles of every shape, size and shade. They had a curved piece

SPACELING                    201

of transparent material set up in front of my chair that covered
me and prevented me from entering dimensions they weren't interested in. Somewhere on the property they must have had a
ton of machinery that manipulated me like a paper girl who
flapped into D at a moment's notice. Only in the exiting did I
have any say but not in my final destination which was, of
course, back to Deron.

It finally dawned on me, when the days passed and Solvo
didn't come for me, that one of the machines was either garbling
or blanking out the signal emitted from my built-in radio. I
couldn't be rescued if no one knew where I was.

Double green rings led to worlds that weren't ready for occu-
pancy. Since the transmutation process prepared a traveler for
survival on a planet and since none of the double greens could
support life, muting to them could be hazardous. The key to
safety lay in entering cautiously and pausing immediately. On
the other side of rings were narrow kinds of way stations, brief
areas of asylum, spots of territory where a muter could stand, sit
or even lie down and enjoy the atmospheric and ground conditions of their homeworld. It seemed that the dimensional doorways were in a more complete state of existence than the worlds
themselves, which made sense in a weird kind of way.

I stepped through a double green, for instance, and then
shrank back as a huge ball of boiling, sputtering matter shot past
me and hurtled through a blood-red sky. It was a world on fire,
perhaps newly detached from a sun, rocketing through space in
a frenzied attempt to cool and condense. Made of heat, speed
and chaos, it would remain so for eons, a bubble in the ocean of
reality, unfit for human habitation or any other kind, and so I
clung to my small oasis and stared about while at the same time
I felt behind me for the slight coolness that would tell me the
ring was still there.

Feeling like Noah, I once stood on a shard of safety as a world
of water floated by and sprayed me with its wild wetness. It was
dark green, almost black, and I saw large chunks of sod churning
in it. The horizon was ominous with the threat of rain while the
air gathered close and tried to smother me. As I stood beside the
ring and looked out at that ugly world, I wondered if I might not
have discovered another doorway into Waterworld. Was it pos-

sible that my beautiful hideaway of peace and tranquillity lay in those savage depths? I wouldn't find out. Not equipped with gills and other water breathing apparatus, I couldn't last five minutes in the dark water.

On another day I stepped through a green double ring and came upon a place that might have belonged at the core of creation. There was a swirling cone moving in the void and beckoning to me to enter it to my destruction, but I held fast to the oasis and merely looked the thing over. Its whirling motion seemed to suck in matter from beyond its narrowest point which was farthest from me. I could see how that portion kept growing darker and thicker, and yet the rotation of the entire cone was such that it obviously drew or pulled on the space nearest to me. A vortex or maw of gas and dust blew around the inner wall of the cone at such tremendous speed that it created a purple glow. Whatever exited from the far end of the cone was so consumed and tenuous that I had to squint to see it. There in the sky, so close I felt I could stretch out and touch it, was the suggestion of a fragile world, a planet of unearthly matter exuded by the vortex, growing from a tiny ball into something that expanded hourly. What kind of planet it would eventually become I couldn't imagine. Perhaps one day nearly weightless creatures like the fliers and the sphex would wing their way through that purple atmosphere. Perhaps nothing would ever live on it because each morning the horizon would catch fire from the infernal furnace roiling within its conical sun and burn whatever tried to form during the night.

Then there was the world of cool, flowing lava. I could tell it wasn't mud just as I knew it wasn't hot. Now and then a mass of it slid up the bank where I rested, hardened momentarily until more of the stuff washed over it and took it away. Curious, I reached down to touch a small flake that remained, cringed as my hand broke an invisible barrier and entered the atmosphere of the strange molten rock that flowed like a mud slide. A burning sensation made me snatch my hand back and I saw it was a bright red and beginning to blister.

Back through the ring I stumbled, bellowing at the top of my lungs. I continued to be noisy until someone brought a variety of things to pour over my throbbing appendage. For a while it was a hit and miss process until Deron tried vinegar which turned out to be the magical solution that stopped the burning and blistering.

"No more dumb experiments when you're in there!" said Erma.

"What kind of world has an atmosphere made of lye?" I said.

"Who cares?" she roared. "It could have been pure acid or marshmallow."

"But the whole place was like gray mud slipping and sliding all the time. There wasn't anything solid anywhere."

"Did you see any people?"

"No."

"Then we don't care what you saw. Shut up and do your job and no more poking your hands into those planets."

I knew they were concerned about my being injured only because then I wouldn't be able to continue working for them. "You could get any muter to do what I'm doing," I said. "Why does it have to be me?"

"Don't tell me lies," said Deron. "Nobody I've ever heard of can match you in D. We know you mute into a giant goth and a small swimmer, and you can see more rings than anyone. I remember once you told me you could see others besides blue and green and I didn't believe you. I know better now."

"But I can't see double greens. At least not consciously."

"The rings don't seem to care, do they? None of us can get through them but you can so you're the pigeon."

"How did you know I could do it?"

"I didn't know it but I was told you might be able to. Waiting around for you to regain your memory is taking too long."

"Who told you?" I was wasting my breath. He didn't answer.

Once in a while they let me rest and I began to notice a pattern. Every day about two hours before sundown we quit and I was put back in the leg iron. Each morning, an hour or two before noon, we stopped for about thirty minutes. They wouldn't let me go into D then and they never let me out of their sight. In fact, during that half-hour morning break, Erma or someone else practically sat on me.

"I think you made a mistake," I said to her one morning during the break. "You assume I can find one particular planet out of a few trillion. What makes you so optimistic? Or should I have said greedy?"

"Quiet."

I didn't like talking to her. She belonged in a rubber room, not free and untrammeled to roam the countryside. "Who are the people I'm looking for?" I said.

"Don't waste your breath trying to pump me. I don't know who they are and I care less. I just follow orders."

One day they got into an argument about what the monitors were registering. Deron said the readings meant a green double ring and Erma said they meant blue. Meanwhile I stood by, growing pensive. I thought Erma gave up too easily and of course it was because she didn't give a hang about me, but they sat me down in the chair and shoved me into what was supposed to have been a green double ring. It wasn't. It was one of the blue kind.

I had an impression of a cloudy blue color as I went forward into D after which I found myself walking across a sea of glass between panes so clear and unmarred they were almost invisible. I could make out their edges but that was all. Spread out everywhere around me were glittering cubicles with mirrors in them. All rendered reflections but some gave two, some three, some four and some more than that. I noticed that none gave a single reflection and I didn't know how I knew this without going into each cubicle, but I did.

The thought of not going into one never occurred to me. That was how strong the lure was. I walked into one that showed me a double image of myself. Upon all the mirror shards were two of me. An eerie feeling passed over me and I suddenly felt the necessity of getting out of there, of getting away from all the cubicles and escaping from that world as quickly as I could. How distinctly I recall racing across the sea of glass toward the yellow ring, my breath hot and hard in my throat.

My panic didn't cease or even lessen as I stepped onto Earth. I knew something was wrong. I felt the same but I was filled with a sense of foreboding. I saw Deron and Erma staring at me and then at something on the ground. Looking down, I saw a naked infant crawling beside me. She had silken yellow hair and big blue eyes. Suddenly she stopped crawling, sat up and began to sob.

She kept crying as I picked her up and went back through the ring. I didn't know where it was, couldn't see it, but I guessed it hadn't moved, and it turned out that I was correct. My actions were purely mechanical and if I'd taken the time to think about it I probably wouldn't have done it that way, to my further regret.

I took the baby and gave it back to the cubicle where it came from. As soon as I stepped between the glittering panes, the child disappeared from my arms and then I again sped across the glassy sea and leaped toward home, this time alone.

"How do I know what happened?" said Deron. "In the first place I'm no muter. In the second place I haven't a wild imagination. Maybe there's a bunch of babies in that world and one comes out with every traveler. Anyhow, we know the place is blue and we don't want anything to do with it. Green is our color."

"Maybe it was an hallucination," said Erma. "I don't see how that could have been a real kid. I mean, where'd it go?"

I told her and she sneered.

Bass was the only one who would actually carry on a conversation with me, which was unfortunate in a way since she had to be the most ignorant person in the camp. "I couldn't stay away from alcohol," she said to me as she recounted a little of her personal history. "I'd break out of the detox clinic, find a bar and go on a toot. My parents would send private hounds to sniff me out and back I'd land in the clinic only to wait for the best time to bust out. Then they both died and there was nobody to pick me up from the gutter, so that's where I stayed for too many years. If you want to know anything about dreg towns, just ask me."

She wasn't interested in muting or discussing babies that popped from nowhere. "Half the time I think it's all a joke and there aren't really rings all over the place," she said. "What good do they do me if I can't see them? Anyhow, I finally broke myself of the bottle and now I'm an upstanding citizen making her change by stealing from the tax collectors. Every time a barrel goes onto a boxcar it's a percentage taken from them since the stuff goes to companies through the back door. I like the work.

Keeps me from getting bored. The name of this state? Why, it's Pennsylvania. Don't you even know where you are?"

"Do you know if there are any other camps like this one?" I said.

"Oh, I doubt that. You know, the pipe is propped through a pair of those stinking rings, or at least that's what they tell me, and they don't want to do it again or maybe they don't know how. And you ask a lot of questions."

"Why are you so free about answering them?"

"Most likely they'll kill you when they're done with you, no matter what they promise to the contrary so what's the difference if I tell you stuff?"

"Will that bother you? Their killing me, I mean."

"Like water off a duck's back. This whole world is a slaughterhouse and everybody has to go sometime."

"I'd like to know why I'm here."

"You can blame that on Erma. She sniffed out the hiding place of a guy in Vermont named Trundle who had all the answers, only instead of bringing him in for questioning she broke his neck. She said it was an accident but I know different. She's an animal. So they went on the hunt for another solution to their problem, and you were it."

"How can I be it when I don't know anything?"

"They tell me you're better than nothing. Now shut up and quit bending my ear."

# 21

I REALLY TRIED to see the double rings they kept shoving me through. I squinted, crossed my eyes, blinked fast, gaped, tried peeking from angles but it did no good and I saw nothing. How a part of my brain could perceive something without my knowledge was a mystery that bewildered and agitated me.

"Don't think about it," said Deron. "What do you care whether you can see them or not?"

"You'll learn nothing from me. Suppose I find those people? I won't volunteer the information and you can't get it from me with drugs."

He took hold of my ear and made a good try at twisting it off. "Who says you won't volunteer anything and everything you know?"

"Maybe I found them already."

"You'd be surprised at some of the machinery we have. You're set up on a diagram like the blueprints of a building. You might call it an emotion reader."

"What am I supposed to register when I find the hidden people?"

"Something different. Erma will recognize it." He twisted my other ear. "How's that horse I loved so much? I figure one day I'll pleasure myself by putting a bullet in one of his big, brown eyes."

"He's gone," I said. "Took off into D after a female with wings. I expect he's raising a family and won't ever come back."

It was a chill, smoggy morning when Bass took charge of me during the thirty-minute break.

"Why do we knock off every day at this time?" I said. I had asked the same question more than once to the others but had received no answer.

"You're always asking me things, aren't you?" she said. "It has to do with solar cells on one of the machines. The energy runs out and this is the time we replenish it."

"Is it the machine that monitors rings or is it the one that regulates the transparent shield?"

"In fact I think it's the one that hauls you all over the place between D. You know, when you think you're coming out one place and you come here instead. What kind of feeling is that?"

"Like when you dive into a pool you think is full of water and suddenly you realize there's nothing in it."

"You're a funny kid. Sometimes you talk like you're older than me and then other times you sound about fifteen. Hey, what's the matter? What'd I say?"

"I'm scared," I said and started to sniffle. "You people all hate me. How much do you think I can take?"

"That isn't anything to do with me. I got no feelings one way or the other. Come on, close your trap. I hate blubbering. It never did me any good when I was hurting and I can tell you it won't do you any, either."

"Look how miserable I am," I said, spitting out the tears leaking into my mouth. "I don't get fed properly, every day my life is threatened, I have no mother or father. I might as well be a slave hauling blocks to build pyramids."

Eyeing me with an unrelenting expression, she said, "Let me give you a piece of advice. Nobody here cares whether you live or die or whether you got up on the right or left side of the bed. Do you get the picture? Quit whining and just squat in that chair for twenty minutes more and then you get to go into D."

"My behind has callouses from sitting here!" I yelled. "I don't want to go into D! I don't want to live!" Suddenly I shrieked and kept on shrieking. "Kill me now!" I shouted. "I'm not doing anything more for you or anybody!"

Bass took a few steps away from me and glanced toward the barracks. "Cut that out," she growled. "You'll make me look bad with Erma. She's liable to sack me."

"Kill me!" I howled. "Go ahead! Who cares!" Even as I bellowed and carried on I didn't think it would work. She had soused for so long her brain was damaged but she was a hound dog when it came to following simple orders, and her simple order for the day was not to let me get out of the chair. I bawled and screeched but all she did was chide me and watch the barracks to see if anyone was coming out to investigate the racket I made.

That an earthquake hit then was fortunate for me and not so unexpected or coincidental as the huge pipe protruding through the blue ring on the hill above camp caused almost constant tremors. Only once or twice, though, had the shaking been severe enough to knock things down. For instance, a tree had once crashed onto a generator and put it out of action for a full day and, only a few days before, the ground split under one of the troughs leading from the oil tub. But such damage was rare because the worst of the underground shocks created by the blue ring being held unnaturally stationary were released miles away.

Anyway, this particular shock was a strong one and seemed to cause the ground around my chair to tilt. Seldom one to entertain indecision, I was on my feet in a moment and taking advantage of the fact that Bass had lost a bit of her balance and was leaning away from me. I was wearing heavy boots and I gave her a kick in the belly that toppled her over backward.

She was slick as grease, agile as a rubber band, mad as a wolverine. One instant she was laid out awkward and sputtering, and in the next she completely changed her position and took a tight grip on my ankle.

Cringing as I did it, I kicked her hard on the jaw. Her head jerked back, her eyes slammed shut and just for a second she was out cold. Then she was wide awake, looking at me with murderous rage and grabbing at me. Workers poured out of the barracks led by Erma who never stopped howling as she raced across the treacherous ground like a winged leviathan. Her red skirt was held high so it wouldn't impede her progress, and it didn't, but that made no difference since I was in the act of doing what I sometimes did best—ring jumping. The circle was little and blue and I loved it as I went through it.

"Fancy meeting you here?" said Gorwyn.

In astonishment I looked around and realized the world had indeed gone mad if coincidences could happen this often for I sat smack in the middle of Gorwyn's front walk with a rope about my neck.

"What a relief!" I said and stood up and tried to hug him. "They're trying to kill me! How did you pull me here?" I followed him as he made little hops and skips to avoid my hands. He didn't move very far away and he didn't let go of the rope attached to my neck. "Oh, all right!" I said, giving up trying to climb into his arms. "At least I'm away from them. You don't know how grateful I am to be here."

"No more than I am to have you. Come along." He tugged on the rope and I felt pressure.

"Do I have to wear this collar?" I asked.

"Naturally. You don't think I want you to escape, do you?"

"Okay, I'll come peacefully. Where to?"

"How about Hades? Or how about my lab? Or the dungeon in the lower level of my house?"

"Any place but where I've just been."

The thing was, he wasn't kidding. After we went down a long, damp, winding, dark stairway made of stone and he locked me in a black cell, I still couldn't believe it. My hands on the bars, I tried to reason with him.

"I know you like me to do experiments with you, though I can't figure out why, and I'm willing to help you all I can. I feel as if I owe you plenty of favors. Why do you lock me up like a prisoner?"

"You're an idiot," he said, attaching some kind of flashlight to the wall outside my cell. In the eerie light he looked like a hollow-cheeked cadaver.

"Since when is that a crime?"

"Hardly ever, except in your case. You really should know better."

The sound of his voice must have traveled down a narrow corridor to my right and alerted someone in that vicinity. They began yelling and banging on the wall.

"Somebody's there!" I said.

"Yes, I have two other house guests."

"Who?"

"Your girl friend and Tedwar."

"Lamana?" I said, knowing how stupidly bewildered I sounded. "Tedwar? Why?"

"As long as you're all behind bars you can't get in my hair. The three of you are exasperating pests. Unfortunately for me, only one of you is of any use to me."

"Me?"

"True."

"Gorwyn?"

"What?"

"Are you crazy?"

"I've been called so once or twice."

Even as I asked I didn't consider that it might be true. Not at all did I consider it. "Did you ever know a man named Croff?"

He finished with the light and turned. Now his face was in darkness and all I had to read him by was his mild voice. "Oh, I forgot to tell you, he came to Mutat to see you. Instead, he saw me. Better yet, I saw him."

"I don't understand."

"Maybe he decided who you reminded him of. Or maybe he remembered something else. He only got a glimpse of me at the school and I really wanted to believe he hadn't recognized me, but then he left so quickly. What else could I do? Acting upon assumptions is the reason I got ahead in the world. I simply sent some people to stop my old colleague from opening the can of worms before I wanted it opened."

With my head feeling as if it were full of crashing cymbals, I said, "If I didn't know better I'd ask you if your name is Appy, but I've already met Appy and he's eighty years old and locked in an institution."

Quiet, eccentric Gorwyn had a fit. One of the raging, screaming, head banging kind. I couldn't see it but I heard it all.

He was in better form the next morning, seemed almost rational as he tried to pump me. Did I know anything about a pair of glasses? What kind? Very special ones. In fact they were more important than the oil which was merely a source of revenue. Not that money didn't come in handy.

The thing about Gorwyn was that he didn't care enough to be stingy with information. Erma had once called me a stinking flea. I wasn't even that significant to Gorwyn. As far as he was concerned I was a means to an end. That I also happened to be flesh and blood was just one of those things.

"We always took second jobs under false names," he said to me during one of our strange conversations. He was referring to his profession in legitimate ring research. "It was like a game, you understand. We ground away at our regular jobs until we couldn't stand it anymore and then we either loafed for a while in some hideaway or took a relaxing or amusing assignment where no one could find us. Gorwyn was my grandfather's name and I've used it once or twice before. I deliberately applied for work at Mutat in hopes of getting to you, and lo and behold, you dropped right into my lap. Oh, yes, I'm well acquainted with Orfia Kint. When I find her and her associates they'll regret having run off with the glasses. They were a group project and no one person was supposed to take charge of them or take credit for having developed them. Now the situation has changed. As soon as I locate the glasses they'll be my personal property and the others will be put out of the picture forcibly and permanently. It's the only way to live, really. I went along for years doing everything like a good little altruistic boy and where did it get me? Out, that's where. Since I've changed my philosophy I've probably become the richest man in the world. What do I care if the pipes are forcing those rings to stay still and are causing all those earthquakes? I'm a genius. What do I care if everything goes? Think of it. Many people have affected countries, nations, even the world, but whoever touched the universe?"

He was mad and mixed lies and truth like a chef. Sometimes he forgot to feed me. His manservant was no longer with him, having defected to his old dreg town, and there were many chores to do just to keep the house functioning. The government was so tight with energy that Gorwyn didn't have enough generators to power his machines twenty-four hours a day. The D-snatcher in particular needed much electricity so there was a large shield of solar cells on the roof to spark the machine during the times when the generators were too weak to power it. Gorwyn said he hoped this bit of information didn't give me any ideas about running because the D-snatcher in the oil camp in Pennsylvania would grab me if I tried to mute.

Whenever he made remarks like that, I looked about my cell and wondered how he expected me to do anything, let alone escape. If any rings ever penetrated into these dungeons, I had yet to see one or a part of one.

"It wouldn't be much of an inconvenience if you went back to the oil camp," he said. "I intended having you transferred here once I finished my preparations. I imagine you're curious. Relax. The crown of wires will eventually jog your memory block loose and in the meantime I'll use the old-fashioned method of simply shoving you through double green rings until you find my friends. I know that's where they are because I saw them go, but they had just knocked me in the head and my vision was so blurred I couldn't make out the exact color. So I'm forced to fish for them with you. Were you present during the scene I just described? Yes, you know everything. Why do you think I've kept you more or less within my sights ever since you showed up at Mutat? All I have to do is get your mind clear and the whole shebang will be mine. Funny, I never knew you existed until those last few days and now look how important you are."

"You told me you couldn't mute."

That amused him. "Don't believe everything you hear."

Sometimes he fed Lamana and Tedwar. My Indian friend had been kept captive because he checked her background and found she was a policeman's daughter and an active agent for the government and also because she had been suspicious of him right from the start. Just as obviously, her father and the people at the clinic had lied to me when they said they knew where she was.

"She's more sensitive than you," said Gorwyn. "And no doubt more intelligent. You're full of stupidities."

He didn't like talking about Tedwar and said only that the boy had known of the whereabouts of this house, had walked away from the hospital and had come here.

About the glasses, what did they do? Unlocked hidden resources in the mind. The wearer could see other doors to the worlds; there was no necessity for muting; just a step through one of those hitherto unseen rings allowed a traveler to visit another planet without changing his or her physical makeup, and they weren't affected by what they found. They could go and observe, and they could—oh, what difference did my knowing make since I wasn't going to live to tell the tale? But never mind the glasses, I knew all of it already and when my subconscious mind was ready to let it out, Gorwyn would be there to learn by it.

"They took turns with you," he said. "Before they turned you loose each one reinforced the other's hypnotic suggestions. How clever they were! I'm the one person they told you not to be afraid of. They thought that would be your best protection, and in a way I suppose it was."

My dungeon smelled of dust and mold, the floor was earthen and unbelievably cold. I didn't know when Gorwyn intended to take me out and try some experimenting but I almost wished he would do it right away. He behaved even more foolishly than before, as if his hold on reality was growing weaker. What would I do if he cracked and forgot I was down here?

As for Lamana and Tedwar, they knew I was here but so much distance separated us that although we could hear one another call, we couldn't make out words. Their voices came to me from different directions so I knew they weren't locked together, for which fact I was grateful, and so must Lamana have been since not too many days passed before Tedwar began raving. Gorwyn hadn't supplied him with medicine.

For two full days the three of us went without food or water. I lay listening to Tedwar shriek, wondering how a human voice box could create such sounds and remain so untiring. Some of the noise must have penetrated to the upper reaches of the mansion because Gorwyn finally came down and took him away. I called out as the two of them went by my cell but only Tedwar looked at me with a grimace so full of malice I turned away.

To my surprise he was calm when he came down to me late that night, or at least I thought it must be night. He had a flashlight and a handful of keys with which he experimented until he found the one that let me out.

"Lamana," I said as I stepped into the dim corridor.

"Forget her!"

"No, I can't go without her."

He argued for a few minutes while I persevered and waited for him to slip back into insanity, but he held on, finally relented and the both of us hurried down the hall to my friend.

He couldn't make up his mind whether he wanted me to kill his father or wreck the lab. He said he had taken Gorwyn's tranquilizers and flushed them away.

"You've never seen him without his drugs?" he said to me. "Then you haven't lived." Later he said, "Once he's asleep you can play war in his bedroom and never wake him up. Luckily for me he's getting worse, locked me in a room as if he believed that would hold me. He ought to have known better."

After we promised to help him he went on the hunt for some heavy furniture with which to barricade Gorwyn's bedroom door. He had decided not to commit the murder just yet. While he labored, Lamana and I backed off and did some plotting of our own.

"How did you get mixed up with such people?" she said to me from the side of her mouth.

"I had to work at it."

"Let's scram."

"You can go," I said. "I can't."

"What do you mean?" Her tone was grieved and bordering on anger.

"Unless I'm prepared to walk to civilization I have to stay. Any muting I do will land me right back here or at the oil camp where Erma's waiting to get her hands on me." There was another possibility. The D-snatcher at the oil camp would shut down at about eleven in the morning. According to what Gorwyn had told me, the machine in his lab ought to shut off about twenty-five minutes later which meant that for approximately five minutes neither would be operating. If I was lucky enough to hit the right time period, I could mute in eight hours.

When I finished explaining to Lamana, she nodded her head at Tedwar and said, "You want to hang around here for eight hours?"

She was right. Tedwar was functioning at the moment because he had helped himself to Gorwyn's pills but by his own admission they were now all gone. No more medicine was available for either of them.

Had I been able to get into the lab I might have wrecked Gorwyn's D-snatcher but Tedwar had changed his mind and wouldn't give me the key.

"Why should you have access to anything of my father's?" he shouted. "I'm his heir and all his property belongs to me. Shut up and stay away from me or I'll lock you in that cell again. I can't imagine why I let you out in the first place."

Believing he would eventually try to make good on his threat, I waited until his attention was focused elsewhere and then I motioned to Lamana. Together we slipped away, located a back door and let ourselves out into the night.

# 22

IT WAS PITCH BLACK outside Gorwyn's house with no stars showing. "There isn't a ring anywhere," said Lamana. "What kind of
place is this?"

"He couldn't conduct experiments with me without a ring
channel," I said. "Let's find it so you can get out of here."

We couldn't locate it. Though we stumbled all around the
mansion there were no rings to be seen which meant that the
channel had to be inside.

"How old do you think this building is?" I said.

"A hundred and fifty years?"

"Gorwyn must have spent a lot of time and money getting it.
It's built right around a channel. We were in the dungeon and
didn't see any rings so the flow must be upstairs. Maybe in one
of the rear bedrooms."

"I don't want to go back in there," she said.

"Nor do I. I can't mute anyway. The D-snatcher in the oil
camp will get me."

"Maybe if we muted holding onto each other?"

"We already were caught together once. No, that won't work."

"Then let's start walking."

Toward dawn Tedwar caught up with us. "You said you'd
help me!" he screamed at me. The rugged terrain had worn him
out. His clothes were ripped at the elbows and knees, he had

cuts and bruises and his eyes could only be described as wild. Still, he tried to hold on. "I couldn't stay back there alone," he said. "I hate him! I knew when he woke up and found you gone he'd be enraged."

"You know he doesn't want my company because he likes me," I said.

"Who cares about that? I don't any more. But you said you'd help me."

"How can I? You know very well you belong in the hospital."

"No! Gorwyn said you could help me. Once, when he was making fun of me, he said what I needed was a trip into D."

"What makes you think that has anything to do with me?"

"Because you're all he ever thinks about! You're the key to his success!"

He wasn't making sense, but then he seldom had. No matter how frustrated he felt, he didn't try to attack us, probably because he knew we would have tossed him into the nearest ditch and gone on without him. I imagined he was regretting that he hadn't brought one of Gorwyn's fancy weapons from the arsenal.

"Where are we going?" he said, sitting on a rock and blinking up at the sun.

Around us stretched as barren a patch of desert as I'd seen or imagined, with not a tree growing anywhere and with not even a mountain to mar the horizon.

"It looks like Death Valley," he said.

"All deserts look the same," said Lamana. "Just don't expect me to sniff out a water hole when you get thirsty."

"I already am!" he said.

"Notice how the ground slopes in the direction in which we're traveling?" I said. "It seemed only natural to come this way, didn't it?"

"For me it did," said Tedwar. "I wanted to find you and this was the easiest and most logical way to run."

"Gorwyn will think so too when he wakes up."

"He always gets up at the crack of dawn." Tedwar stood up and looked back the way we had come. "I know I'm crazy but he makes me look good. When he gets quiet and absent-minded, that's the time to stay out of his way."

"He was very quiet and absent-minded the last time I saw him," said Lamana.

We ran until we couldn't run any more after which we walked. The desert remained sterile and inhospitable but at least we were leaving the dead area where no rings abided. I saw some in the sky a good distance away and we stopped for a few minutes to discuss our strategy. By then the sun was high and suffocating.

I wanted Lamana and Tedwar to head for the rings while I veered in another direction.

"If Gorwyn's after us, what makes you think he'll travel toward the rings?" said Lamana. "He knows you won't mute."

"He can't be sure. He might think I panicked."

"How stupid," said Tedwar. "Have you forgotten he always knows where you are out of D? He told me he has a direction finder that follows a signal inside you. Some woman who works for him injected it into you. He said there isn't anywhere on Earth you can go that he doesn't know it."

Would that instrument in me never deteriorate? "What'll we do, what'll we do?" I said, and no sooner were the words out of my mouth than we heard the loud buzzing of a buggy coming at us. "It's still a long way off but it won't take him more than fifteen or twenty minutes to catch up with us," I said. "Is there any intelligent point in your being with me when he does?"

"How can I go away and leave you?" said Lamana, angry. "I'm responsible for you!"

"Says who? Besides, do you think you might be of more help to me free than locked in a cell beside me?"

Tedwar didn't say a word and hadn't since we first heard the buggy. Now he stared across the desert as if a ghost and not a man was out there in the machine. We still couldn't see it but the noise of its motor grew louder. Suddenly he broke away from us and began running toward the rings. Reluctantly Lamana backed away from me and headed in the same direction.

"I'll bring my father!" she said. "I'll bring them all!" She raced after Tedwar.

I hurried toward uneven ground, hoping to lose myself in the low slopes and rocky dunes. Gorwyn had to see me before he could catch me, not that I expected it to be all that much of a task for him but I saw no reason to march up to him and deliver myself into his hands.

The ground turned more to my liking, rippled like a washboard that served me better than it did the man in the buggy. I could hear it laboring behind me as it plowed up a ridge and plunged down the other side only to meet another hill, and I heard Gorwyn curse in a slow, steady monotone. He was thrown out once and had to clamber back into the machine as it climbed at a bad angle and threatened to tip over. Meanwhile I forgot how tired and thirsty I was and ran for my life. I knew if he ever got me into that crown of wires again, I'd be as crazy has he when I came out of it.

No doubt he was complimenting himself about the signal in my body and no doubt he wasn't thinking about the receiver Padarenka and Mikala had forfeited to Lamana and Solvo. He probably didn't even know what had happened to it and, in fact, I had forgotten about it, too, which was just as well since I wasn't listening for the sound of planes, consequently didn't hear them and didn't spend several anxious minutes wondering what Gorwyn's reaction to them was going to be. If he could follow me anywhere in the world, so could Solvo, when he had a mind to.

Maybe Gorwyn was like a weasel and always kept a lookout over his shoulder. At any rate, he evidently heard the drone of the aircraft above the roar of the buggy. I was stumbling along a shallow ditch when the motor shut off. Hoping the machine had overturned, I climbed onto a ridge and looked back, and it was then that I heard the other engine in the sky.

I didn't know whose plane it was but since Gorwyn wasn't being totally indifferent, they probably didn't belong to friends of his, which meant the only way we would find out who piloted them was to wait and see. It was a proposition that could be more expensive and dangerous for him than for me.

He seemed to be thinking the same thing for he got the buggy moving again and plowed hurriedly away in the direction he had come.

It turned out that my signalling the plane wasn't necessary. All I had to do was walk to the nearest flat area, wait for it to convert to a copter and watch it land.

"My daughter?" said Solvo. Naturally he didn't look worried but maintained his dignity and remote expression.

"She muted. I expect she's home by now. And you lied to me about knowing where she was."

"Of course, it was the first time anybody ever did that." Wonder of all wonders, he smiled.

I was flabbergasted when the copter took me to a nearby city of bulging roofs and ultra polite, brown citizens. It seemed I was in Cairo. The real one, not a mockup.

It seemed that the electronic tape inside me was losing its effectiveness after all, and Solvo had spent the last few days pinpointing the source of the weakening signal.

He had a few other things to tell me, such as, several of his people were tracking down suppliers of large apes because that's what sloks were. When taken from D to Earth they became their former docile selves. The process was like ducks and imprinting. Accompany an ape into D and he became your fierce slave and he was also more intelligent than in his own dimension.

After spending much time looking at color cards I selected a blue one and told Solvo where he could find the bodies of the twins. I carefully described the cavern where they were hidden. It wasn't long before his people reported back. The twins couldn't be reached because of the heavy concentration of sloks and hostile goths in the area. Pat and Mike would have to stay dead a while longer.

In the meantime, Gorwyn had escaped in spite of the large number of hunters combing the desert.

"Where do you think he would go?" Solvo said to me, but I had never successfully second guessed my insane acquaintance and said as much.

Solvo flew home in the jet with me. "Don't worry," he said. "Not about anything. But don't mute for a little while longer." He hesitated for a moment before continuing. "Everyone has superiors. Mine forbade me to lock you up for the duration of this situation, otherwise I'd have done so without a qualm. You were the honey that attracted the first real flies, and so you were left to continue."

"What about now?"

"Don't mute and you'll be all right. We'll get them. Another thing I regret is that you can't direct us to the oil camp."

His advice about my not muting wasn't bad but neither was it good. If I muted, the oil camp would be my destination while as long as I roamed Earth I stood in danger of being grabbed by the enemy. No matter what I did, short of staying in jail, I was in some kind of jeopardy. Solvo might not think so but then he had never met Erma.

I presumed he muted to New Mexico after he parked the jet on American soil. As for me, I took a bus to the nearest express office and bought a ticket east.

Croff's niece didn't seem surprised to see me, might even have been pleased. She was feeling talkative and in a good mood and told me all about the earthquake at a nearby shopping center the day before. She was convinced the world was coming to an end.

"What do I care, really?" she said. "They're a trifle. Go ahead and take them, though I can't imagine what you want with them. Don't tell me a girl your age rides a motorcycle."

"Do you hear a copter?"

"Why, yes, I believe I do. It sounds quite close, as if it's right above the house."

A heavy hand was already rapping at the front door as I pulled the goggles over my eyes, which was just as well since it drew the woman's attention away from me and spared her the trauma of seeing me vanish.

Like a wraith I faded into an obscurity so total I might even have lost some of my substance. It was difficult to say. The feeling of solidity was still there but I moved so effortlessly and rapidly I didn't want to take the time to check myself out. It seemed that seeing was indeed believing. In the universe through which I traveled, nothing was stationary but all was in motion. Little bits of matter were as significant as worlds because I could discern them and comprehend the service they rendered.

Here the planets spun so fast they resembled flat disks falling like a never ending row of dominos. The colors of the rainbow were everywhere around me, pastel and glittering, flashing past me like an assembly line of fragile pieces of light. Earth was a revolving coin that enveloped me, appeared to flash on over my head and then was gone as the disk that was Gothland dropped over me only to make way for Waterworld. Nothing on the planets touched me. They moved too quickly, or my molecules dodged too agilely, or it could have been that I had become something other than human.

I saw reality descend like sprinkling rain, scatter like disturbed dust, zoom from an invisible cannon to spread until the infection of tangible things was a milling crowd. Not a creator, but not an intruder either, I drifted through chaos, accepted the proposition that it was sometimes better to take situations as they seemed to be and never mind their actuality. If I could scrutinize a small bit of the impossible, why not go ahead and do it, and if my purpose in putting on the glasses in the first place had been to escape my enemies, did that mean I was bound to do nothing more?

My subconscious must have been overly active because I couldn't make a fast decision as to where I would go first. That I knew the way to everywhere was an understatement. Like a miniature tornado I whirled in space while my thoughts took me first one place and then another, and in the meantime I looked about me.

I saw Lamana and Tedwar in the clinic in New Mexico and Doctor Oregon was standing behind Tedwar's chair while Chameleon bedazzled the boy with her diamond eyes. They were safe and so I looked elsewhere and even moved a millimeter or two but no more because then I would have left the boundaries within which I wished to remain. I could have gone vast distances with a few steps. Now I merely leaned forward a little to see that strange planet where Orfia Kint and her two associates were voluntary captives.

Behind the green double ring was the usual brief oasis leading to a piece of ground enshrouded in what looked like a cumulus cloud. Within the cloud, in a cleared area, stood two men and a blonde woman. The planet wasn't fit for habitation and wouldn't be for eons and so the oasis provided a way station for intruders where they might linger untouched and unchanged. The three were also unknowing. Deep in suspended animation—a condition of the cloud—they stood in relaxed stances and waited. No matter what happened outside their tiny reality, they would go on waiting until someone came and drew them out. Three sleeping beauties whose last thought had probably been an anticipation of the touch that would bring them to wakefulness. As I looked at the woman I experienced an unwelcome flood of resentment.

I didn't enter the double ring but diverted my glance, sought out less threatening objects, located Kisko and Wheaty. To my astonishment I found they were almost like myself.

"Hi, kid," said Kisko. "What's the matter? Cat got your tongue?"

"At least!" I said. "Is this what being nutty has done to you?"

"It was there in my mind all the time but I just wouldn't look. You should know. There're none so blind, etcetera."

"Why should you have such special vision?"

"Jealous because I don't need glasses?" he said.

"Sort of." I gestured toward Wheaty. "What about him? Don't try to tell me he has super vision too."

"I can speak for myself, if you don't mind," said Wheaty. "If you'll notice, I'm tromping on the boss's heels. He's doing everything and I'm just skinning along in his treads. Me, I can't see much no matter where I am."

To Kisko I said, "I assume you could have come out of D long ago. Why didn't you?"

"Actually I haven't had my head together for very long, but I've done considerable observing and now I think it's about time we cleaned up."

Looking askance at Wheaty, I said, "I could have trusted you, couldn't I? It was Deron all along."

"You did what you had to do and you did me a favor. Getting back on the job was the medicine I needed. And we know all about Deron."

We stood almost literally in the middle of nowhere and conducted our chat and by and by we left off remarking about how unusual, sterling and priceless we were and got down to serious subjects. It seemed Kisko had a yen to get into the pipe at the place in Gothland where I found the invisible shield.

"We can't get in," he said. "That shield keeps us out."

"Is that all that's bothering you?" I said and led them straight to the spot. "They added this elbow later," I said, pointing at the inner section of pipe. "The oil flows through it while in this other section they have machinery and weapons. It's probably heavily guarded."

"What good can we do in there as goths?" asked Wheaty.

"Then don't change when you go in," I said.

Kisko looked at me with a jealous expression. "Can you do that? Do you have that kind of control?"

"I think so, with these glasses on."

"But we'll fry like eggs if we go in there as people!" said Wheaty.

"Just copy everything I do," I said. "Stay behind me and take part of the universe with you as protection. See? Pick it up in your hands."

"It's like trying to grab fog!"

"Gently," I said. "Put your hand out and hold it still. Feel that? It's light but it's there. Now hang onto it. Spread it all around your body. Got it? Okay, let's go in now."

They read us coming in. One of them was watching a blinking red light, growling and snarling as he tried to adjust his chest holster in order to get off the first shot at us. Our appearance in human form didn't give them too much pause. They were afraid of what would happen to them if they were apprehended. Every goth was ticketed for a long stay behind bars, so they reacted quickly when Kisko, Wheaty and I drifted through their shield and settled down onto our feet on the floor of the compartment as though we were perfectly solid. The sloks knew only that they were being attacked by strangers. Eventually they would be mutated to their less intelligent, original forms and be returned to the zoos, labs and jungles from which they had been taken.

The enemy complement was about half goth and half slok, sixteen or eighteen in all, and each got their shots, slashes and swipes off before we three made a move. It didn't matter. Nothing they did could touch us because though we seemed substantial we were in another field of space. However, we could make contact with their dimension by using the strange matter around us. One by one their weapons were taken up and tossed through metal walls that might as well have been made of air. It was all in the seeing. There were plenty of ways to think and move and we had our choices. If, for instance, I desired to pick up a gun and send it floating through a bulkhead, all I had to do was aim it along a myriad of obvious tracks or courses boring straight through three-D matter. Since there was nothing in its way the gun went into the wall and out the other side.

That didn't make the sloks and goths timid. Probably with visions of Earth prisons in their heads, they attacked us in full force only to end up bruised and battered on the floor and against the walls as we allowed them to move through us. They didn't surrender until we finally ignored them and started doing things with the knobs and dials on their machinery. We left a little bit of our uncanny traveling atmosphere upon each object we touched so that their positions were sealed.

Meanwhile regulators, pumps and gauges in the main pipe ceased operating. Airtight doors slid shut preventing the contents of Waterworld from coming through. The oil flow stopped, at least for a while. No doubt Gorwyn had an emergency backup unit planted somewhere that could open the doors and start the pumps again. The last thing we did before leaving was to place a seal on all the walls and floor.

"See how I do it?" said Wheaty. He made motions with his hand as if he were shoving something invisible away from him, and it probably looked that way to the sloks and goths, but I could see filmy matter depositing itself firmly against a bulkhead. Kisko and I helped him finish the rest of the compartment after which we exited and closed up the seal.

"That ought to hold them until we can send some law in here after them," said Kisko. "I'll get Solvo onto it right away. Oh, yes, I know him. West of the Mississippi there's no bigger or better government outfit." He dusted his hands. "Okay, that's one good deed done. Now what'll we do?"

He couldn't leave 4-D, as he called his present habitat, and expect to get back into it. "It was only a fluke that I got here in the first place," he said as we drifted and observed what went on in that small portion of reality. "My mind was so fractured I was able to sneak in. I felt as if I was about half a centimeter wide so it was like I slid in under the door. But being here was good therapy and it wasn't too long before the illogic of the place made the reality of 3-D turn right side up. Things finally started looking normal again."

"How long was it before you could have come out?" I said.

"A few weeks after I entered, but I didn't because I knew I

couldn't accomplish much back home on Earth so I stayed to see if anything would turn up here. Once in a while I slipped back into dementia and did a little raving, but now I'm all cured."

We went to Gorwyn's mansion and there was no problem involved in our finding it since great and small things sailed under and past our scrutiny as slowly or as rapidly as we desired. In all the memorabilia and forgettable items that we noted, I spied the mansion and suggested we see if Solvo's men or the Egyptian police had put Gorwyn's machines out of commission. I doubted if they had. Solvo would want to save them for later study.

There were guards all around the outside of the house but nothing had been done inside so we floated into the heavily locked laboratory, placed a seal upon everything mechanical after which we headed west once more. I would know how to find the place again if ever I wished to. There was a blue haze across the desert that was easily discerned as I wore the goggles Orfia Kint had devised. It would be easy to find a ring leading here.

It was early evening when we came to rest on slippery ground above the oil camp in Pennsylvania. The pipe still dumped black gold into the tub below which meant that either the last of the oil was running out or Gorwyn had used another energizing unit to continue production. In no way could he have cleared away the seal we placed in the junction in Gothland.

"Let me try something," I said and attempted to pull the big blue ring that trembled and vibrated as it was held in place by the metal pipe. I pulled gently and although the ring didn't come to me it shifted several meters so that the pipe was diverted from the tub and poured its contents down toward the barracks. The workers came running outside only to be caught in the deluge. A dozen or so lost their footing and were swept on down into the valley where they managed to crawl out of the flow and lay panting and gasping on the saturated ground.

"See if you can do that again," said Kisko. "Give it another nudge."

I tried but the pipe was wedged in a shallow indentation in the ground and the ring didn't seem to be able to lift it. "I need Lamana," I said. "She's a friend and an agent and—"

"We know," said Wheaty. "Remember, we kept our eye out for you."

"Uh, oh, look who just came out of the barracks," said Kisko.

Wheaty nodded. "You know, in all our wanderings this is the first real glimpse we've had of him."

Deron had probably been on the defensive most of his life. Maybe psychoanalysis would have divulged the reason for his cowardice, maybe not, but whenever he had a weapon to hand he would most likely use it at the slightest provocation. Today he seemed to prefer an old police revolver that made so much noise when he fired it that those who weren't caught in the flow of oil were petrified with shock. Or their behavior might have been caused by the sight of me and my two friends standing untouched in the middle of the muck with a hazy glow around us.

Adding to their fear was the fact that Deron fired his gun straight at us with no effect. He was too far away to recognize us but, since we kept rising a few centimeters off the ground and then descending, he probably knew we were good targets. As he fired, he came closer, side-stepping independent flows of oil, leaping over or wading through others until at last he was near enough to really see us.

He didn't care about me, gave me no more than a flickering glance, but when he recognized the curly haired man behind me and the hound-dog visage of the last of our trio he suddenly stopped and reacted. His fingers opened and the gun fell to the ground.

Kisko didn't mean to leave 4-D. Perhaps thoughts of the past became too painful for him too quickly. It could have been that the desire to lay hands on the traitor was all at once overwhelming. An expression of longing on his face, he dropped everything that held him out of Earth, took a stumbling motion forward and fell all the way onto the ground of the camp. Wheaty could do nothing but follow him and in another moment both were lying and looking up at me.

"I didn't mean to leave you alone," said Kisko.

"I can bring you back in," I said, and tried, but he wouldn't come no matter how strongly I pulled.

"I guess I don't really want to go back in," he said. "It was a fine place to take the cure and now I've got business here."

"Okay, at least let me help put you a step ahead." I picked up the gun Deron had dropped. I smiled at him as I did so and he gave a squawk of fear and headed down into the valley at full speed.

"Let's get him," said Wheaty, accepting the gun when I handed it to him.

"You're not going to use that," said Kisko.

"On him? No, but I'll use it on any of the others who try and interfere. He's going to sweat it out in a cell before the law gives him what's coming to him."

They didn't need me, particularly after I floated inside the barracks, gathered up all the weapons and threw them in the oil tub. I was grieved that neither Erma nor Gorwyn was there. The last thing I did before leaving was to heave as much electronic equipment as I could into the strongest oil flows and the rest was rendered inoperable by a 4-D seal.

# 23

I MOVED OUT of view of the camp, drifted a few dozen kilometers and then stepped onto a highway in normal D. Putting the goggles in the back pocket of my jeans, I started walking toward an overpass beside which bobbed a few friendly looking rings. I would discover later that four or five hours in 4-D was my limit. If I wanted to stay longer I'd have to become utterly fractured in the head as Kisko had been. Now he was sane and out of the dimension and could never return unless I loaned him the glasses.

Lamana wasn't too surprised to see me. Eating dinner in the clinic's cafeteria, she nodded to me and continued as if nothing unusual had happened or ever would happen. "I made it easy for you to locate me by coming here and staying," she said.

"Tedwar?"

"Downstairs. Locked up, I'm afraid. He's in bad shape. Chameleon found out what's wrong with him."

"Don't tell me. I already know. Can you see to it that he isn't released? I promised him I'd help him."

"I hope it works out."

I told her where I wanted to go and she agreed to accompany me. Not long after, we both leaped through a yellow ring in Gothland and landed in the oil camp. The black fluid still gushed from the pipe and down onto the barracks. The entire place was deserted. Kisko, Wheaty, Deron and the working crew were all gone, to jail I presumed.

It was easy when we both called the ring at the same time. It rose gracefully into the air, carrying the pipe with it and then we directed it to dart forward, which it did, leaving the pipe suddenly unsupported. The flow of oil abruptly ceased. The ring made a hasty departure straight down into the ground while the loose section of pipe crashed onto the buildings. How the fire started I neither knew nor cared. Lamana and I escaped through the first blue ring we saw while behind us Gorwyn's brilliant plans went up in smoke.

"I'll meet you at the farm in five or ten minutes," I said to Lamana and left her. Traveling through D for a few seconds, I stepped into Gothland again. Choosing a familiar labyrinth, I loped down its length to a crevice jam-packed with a couple of people I knew. There wasn't a goth or slok in sight. Thankfully the deterioration process in the dimension was extremely slow so that it wasn't overly unpleasant to take a haunch in my jaws and haul one body topside. Within a short time I had both corpses lying beside a smoking volcano on the surface. Calling a yellow ring, I laboriously shoved the twins through onto good old mother Earth.

They cried because of their bad memories, laughed with relief at being alive, frowned at thoughts of their own idiocy and the fact that once again I had pulled their chestnuts out of the fire.

"We're sick of being killed and then restored but mostly of the first," said Pat. "You have our solemn promise that we'll never again interfere in your life."

"Trouble follows you," said Mike. "Knowing you isn't a good idea. I think maybe we'll go to China and hunt for work. Are you sure Gorwyn and Erma aren't hunting for us?"

"Yes."

"You could have let us follow you. They wouldn't have killed us if you hadn't had your Indian friends take the receiver."

"Bye, bye," I said.

For the first time they noticed where they were. "What is this place?" said Pat. "Why did you bring us here? I don't see any rings anywhere."

A few drifted here and there but they were the skittish kind and useful only to someone like myself who could force them to settle down for a moment or two. As for the twins, they couldn't control rings which meant they would have to hike more than forty-six hundred meters down Mount Whitney. I hoped the trek took them a year.

So I popped back to my farm to meet Lamana and together we would decide what to do about our problems, but it didn't work out that way because I was careless and walked right into Erma's waiting arms.

"Where are they, flea?" she said after she nearly knocked my brains out with a gentle cuff of her hand. At least Olger hadn't been hurt too badly. Tied to a chair before the fireplace, she had a few burn marks on her arms but I could tell she was in good shape by the contempt in her expression. Lamana sat nearby, untied but dazed. Apparently Erma had started on her just before I arrived.

"Why do you think I worked for that coconut?" said the big woman to me, and I assumed she was referring to Gorwyn. "I meant to get the glasses and have myself some power." Holding me with one hand, she opened my bottom lip with the other. "Don't pretend you don't know all about them. Bass saw you wearing them at the camp. She saw you disappear into D. Where are they? Where'd you hide them?"

Lamana staggered up behind her and crashed a chair down on her head. Cursing, Erma reached back and tried to grab her. Meanwhile I wriggled from the heavy grasp and climbed out a window. There were rings all over the place and as I was in the act of only thinking about one of them, Erma made like a tackle behind me, got me by one foot, brought me down hard and caused the goggles to fly out of my pocket. They landed three meters in front of us where Lamana scooped them up and ran.

For a few minutes we played toss over Erma's head. It was like daring a runaway tank and I knew that sooner or later this huge killer would get the idea that if she broke one of our necks, the game would stop.

"Here comes a fat blue one!" cried Lamana, tossing the glasses over Erma's head.

I caught them, feinted to the left and then darted to the right. It wasn't an entirely successful move because the big woman in the red dress was neither dumb nor slow. I stepped in the way of a strong gust of body odor before her reaching fingers took hold of my thigh. Bellowing in pain, I yanked free and ran. Heavy footsteps pounded behind me as I caught up with Lamana and then the two of us, or maybe it was three, tumbled headlong into Gothland. At least the glasses were left behind and I would pick them up when I muted back onto Earth. Or maybe I shouldn't have felt so relieved, after all. Erma had only to knock me out or kill me and then shove me through a yellow ring and the goggles would be there in my hand.

Three of us went tumbling down a scorched hill of tar, lava and brimstone. I was a big goth, Lamana was a medium-size one while Erma had to be the biggest monster I had ever seen. Her fangs were at least sixteen centimeters long and her paws looked like round pillows fringed with daggers. She took one look at me and snorted.

Deliberately I ran away from Lamana. Erma didn't particularly want her but would no doubt kill her at the first opportunity, besides which this chase wasn't going to end in a snout to snout confrontation if I could help it. There was no virtue in inviting defeat.

Erma came for me and Lamana followed us for a while but soon fell far behind. I leaped and scrambled up and over the smoky terrain as athletically as I could but still the giant behind me gained ground. Not intentionally did I enter the labyrinth since the jagged entrance looked like a hole leading to some high rocks, but once inside I found the way barred except for a narrow tunnel. Thinking it might become too small for Erma to follow, I sped into the darkness only to find that the corridor soon widened. She almost caught me as I entered an amphitheater but I was accustomed to playing in those surroundings and knew there should be a hidden tunnel above the one I was just exiting. Erma took a chunk out of my flank as I made a quick right turn and leaped for sloping rocks.

The labyrinth wasn't as small as I hoped but it slowed my enemy a bit and allowed me to reach a three-way fork. I turned left and experienced a thrill of triumph as I saw a green ring drift through the rock wall and hover in my pathway. But then I knew my victory wasn't all that complete as the sound of big paws slapping stone came close behind me. Erma had also taken the left fork.

The ring remained where it was and I dived through it in a hurry. Mutating into a tiny swimmer, I darted toward a large cluster of seaweed and wound my way as deeply into it as possible before Erma grabbed it and shook it to pieces. Obviously she had known exactly where I had gone. Naturally she couldn't know which section flung me with it and so while she demolished first one and then another I tried slipping away by moving above her. Cunning, crafty and ever on the alert, she saw me and plunged upward through the water.

It wouldn't have mattered to me what color the ring was floating just to the north of me. I entered it quickly, not caring that its purple hue really wasn't alluring, nor was I fond of its oval shape.

I muted back into human form except that I was now unusually hairy. In fact I was decked from head to toe in a natural fur coat. Also I was wading knee-deep in an icy stream while a blizzard howled around me. The sky was dark with driving sleet, the stream continued to be freezing cold and in the meantime Erma made loud splashing noises behind me. I guessed she grew weary of the chase. Impatiently weary, not tired.

Sloshing along, I suddenly ducked as a boulder-size rock flew at me. It hit Erma but I was too busy to be amused. Either this planet rained stones as well as frozen water or it had natives who resented our intrusion.

I never saw the planet's people which was just as well since I hadn't the time or presence of mind to appreciate them. Altering my course, I plowed upstream until it occurred to me that Erma probably couldn't see any better than I in the raging storm. Locating a particularly shadowy spot, I paused and waited, shielded my eyes and watched as a huge and hairy creature lumbered past me. Just seeing her made me shudder from more than the cold. Bad enough without fur, Erma now looked worse than my old acquaintance, the lummox, who used to be on Lamana's mountain.

She might have been half blind but her hearing was just fine, and she proved it by changing course and following me. I plunged toward the place where we had first entered the dimension, stopped and blinked sleet out of my eyes while I hunted for the ring. It was no longer there but another one was, a small blue specimen that suited me well enough. Anticipating a tight squeeze, I stuck in my arms and head and then grunted in surprise and dismay as the thing expanded and dumped me off an escarpment in Gothland.

First my mind had tired and gradually every physical form I assumed during the chase became weary. Now as I loped up a smoldering hill of cinders and red rock I knew what exhaustion was. Erma was not going to let me mute to Earth and grab the glasses. She must have been tired too but the lure of much power evidently lent her extra stamina. She came after me like a juggernaut bent on my destruction.

I tried running my legs off while I ran out of ideas. As a matter of fact I wasn't thinking too clearly throughout all that stampeding and muting. Conceivably I could have stayed on the lookout for a ring that would take me to Lamana's clinic or even to Solvo's office. Of course both places might be empty, so I wouldn't be any better off, but it made no difference since I never thought of them. There wasn't time.

Just as I was giving serious attention to the idea of dying, I saw a ring on the top of a low escarpment. Normally I wouldn't have given it a second glance since I knew very well what lay between its ugly gray boundaries. Having already been that way once before, I knew it was a doorway to a world where fliers, sphex and huge, smelly glots lived.

Erma raked me with a claw as I hurtled off the incline and dropped into a shallow tar pit. She jumped in after me. Being smaller and lighter, I could wade faster than she, reached the shore ahead of her and made as if to climb the mountain again. She bit off a piece of my left rear paw.

Now I was more than ever determined to reach the gray ring for I was all out of opportunities. Erma still wasn't all the way clear of the tar pit so I stopped long enough to kick her in the head. As she fell backward, I braced myself and leaped for the top of the escarpment.

There was no need for me to look to see if my pursuer still followed. I could feel her breath on my haunches, hear her pant as she anticipated my death and, trying to make the best leap of my life, I went into the gray dimension fast and hard, hoping she would do the same. She did.

Dinglo, or some monstrosity exactly like the one I had known, squatted in the valley with his heavy lidded eyes looking for all the world like twin pools of mud. He stank like a thousand corpses. Fliers worked on his body to keep him healthy while mites hovered above him in thick clouds.

I zoomed into the gray sky directly over the valley, needing no time to adjust to my new body. Owning a set of strong wings, I used them to bank sharply to the left, and the movement was made just in time to evade an endless banner of a tongue that roared out of Dinglo's mouth. The dripping weapon stretched greedily for me, flicked back into the cave as it missed and then emerged again as Erma burst into the dimension.

It's hard to say what she saw in her last few moments of life. She was a large flier with powerful wings but she was also human and needed a few spaces of time in which to orient herself. Of them she was deprived. The glot knew a tidbit when he saw one and Erma screamed loud and long as she stuck fast to the red banner. One moment she was a writhing, shrieking flier and in the next she went into the trap like a bird into a cuckoo clock.

Shaking, shivering, shuddering, nauseated and full of regret that I was alive, I ignored the fliers who came to investigate me, soared high toward a yellow ring and entered its enveloping folds. I went home, from one menace to others and perhaps the new ones would be my last.

Lamana sat on a fence at the farm, waiting for me. She would never be as blank faced as her father and I read the anxiety in her expression as she stared behind me while I walked toward her.

"She's gone," I said. "Permanently. Dinglo."

She gave a slight shudder. "My father called. He's located Gorwyn on the campus at Mutat. Raving mad."

I hadn't done any work in my human form but I was tired. "Let's call him back and finish this."

It took us only a few minutes to arrive at the school and there we waited for Solvo's copter. He brought Tedwar and Bud Jupiter with him as I had requested.

Gorwyn hunted for his lost goggles in the grass of the campus. Sometimes he scrambled on his hands and knees, parting blades with great care, while at other times he leaped about and stamped the ground with rage. Now and then he raced across the lawn to a new area where he began his search anew. He looked nothing like the sedate scholar I had known but his face was a weird and frightening mask of glaring eyes, pinched nostrils and slack jaw. He needed a shave, shower and change of clothes. He needed a new brain.

Not having all the facts, I could only guess how he had inserted himself with Orfia Kint and her colleagues at the university. Most likely he had simply walked in and asked for a job, and why wouldn't he be given one when he probably knew more about rings than anyone living? Who else but an expert and a genius could poke an oil pipe through a pair of rings and make them stand still for it? It was too bad Croff hadn't been a part of the inner group for then he would have known everything, or most of it; he would have told me about it and something might have been done sooner.

Gorwyn merely bared his teeth when he saw me after which he resumed his insane hunt for a pair of goggles he had never owned and which at that moment rested in my pants pocket.

He reacted differently when Tedwar stepped from Solvo's copter, let out an animal-like howl of derision, contempt and fear. Only later did he notice Bud Jupiter who was supported on each side by Solvo's people. Gorwyn stiffened and stood like a statue for a second or two before giving a shriek of rage. With an air of desperation he flung himself down and searched through the grass. Strangely he made no protest as two men lifted him up.

"You promised to help me," Tedwar said to me. He looked around, saw Gorwyn, saw Bud Jupiter, frowned as if he were trying to remember something. "What are we doing here?" he asked.

"If you do what I tell you you'll be all right."

"Why should I trust you?" His tone was rough as his mood changed in a flash. "I never liked you."

"Yes, I know. I should have kicked you around like everyone else did and then you wouldn't have minded me."

I put on the glasses, caught a blue double ring zooming across the sky, halted its progress and caused it to land gently in front of us. I didn't know how clearly he saw it.

"You want me to go through that thing?" he said. "Is that it?"

"Of course she does, stupid," said Bud Jupiter. Momentarily lucid, he let a grin twist his evil old face. "You're me when I was little and this son of a maniac over here is me when I was grown. Any way you look at it, it's me. Let's go." Jupiter took a firm grip on a writhing, whining Gorwyn and kicked him until he stood up.

Tedwar looked at me. "That can't be right. I'd remember a thing like that, wouldn't I? Just because I can't pin down the memory of what happened—"

Jupiter pushed him through the ring before he could finish the sentence. I saw the startled look on his face just before he disappeared. That was the way he went out, too surprised and puzzled to be scared. As for Gorwyn, terror made his knees give way and he went through the ring with Jupiter's boot in his rear.

A rush of horror and grief nearly bowled me over as I stared at the spot where Tedwar had vanished. "Maybe I'm wrong," I whispered to Lamana. "I hope I'm wrong."

Seeming to read my mind, she said, "You aren't. Chameleon got it all out of his subconscious. Don't have too many hard feelings about the old man. As soon as he did it, he wanted to go right back into the ring but Gorwyn ran away. Tedwar followed him."

Bud Jupiter came shambling back onto the campus a few minutes later. He was alone and cackling in amusement. I stood there staring, waiting for Gorwyn and Tedwar to become real and living again, and all the while fear beat a hollow cadence somewhere inside me.

"We did a thing or two in my time, didn't we?" said Jupiter. "Too bad I didn't use one of those other stalls. It would have been wilder if I'd split up ten ways. I think I'll go back in."

They grabbed him.

"I always had a condition, you know?" he said. "From my infancy on. Interfered with my work and finally made a mental cripple of me." Looking at me, he said, "Just before I had my last breakdown I started making those glasses. That other me, that Gorwyn, must have had the upper hand in finishing the job. Nobody but he could have done it. They rightly belong to me."

He was put back into the copter and taken away.

That was the end of another of my enemies. Or was it two or three? Now there was just one left; Orfia Kint.

Having put the goggles back in my pocket, I took them out and used them again, stepped into 4-D and hunted through that alien universe until I found the corridor of the blue double rings. Up and down the hallway I went, sealing every doorway, and when I had finished I was satisfied. No one would be going through double blue rings anymore, at least not while I had anything to say about it.

Solvo and his people did a good job cleaning up the mess. Troops were sent into Gothland and Waterworld to destroy machinery and capture the last of Gorwyn's soldiers. Sloks were rounded up and shoved through rings where they muted back into unintelligent simians.

# 24

IT WAS A DAY much like any other when I put on the goggles and went after Orfia Kint and her sleeping companions. What kind of planet the place would become was impossible to say. Conceivably giant reptiles would flounder here in deep swamps a few eons hence or land masses might never form and the world would remain a flaming ball of gas. It could only matter to a universe that hadn't yet come into existence. For now, I stood on the brief oasis inside the green double ring and wondered what would have become of my life had I never seen the goggles in the carton in the house of Croff's niece. What would have happened if a man named Trundle hadn't gotten scared and mailed his responsibilities to Croff? What if Erma hadn't killed them?

Without the glasses I couldn't see the double green ring that had led the three here, and with them I had to be careful not to drift away. D-4 was like a thousand openings in a winding, confining corridor. Maintaining a predetermined course was arduous.

I had brought a hooked pole with me, something I couldn't have done without the glasses, not that I needed it but I had a decided aversion to the idea of touching any of them. With the pole I made like a fisher, snared around the neck the man whose name was probably Folgay, applied a little pressure and watched as he floated from his foggy environment toward me.

He was blinking his eyes and twitching his fingers as I continued applying pressure so that he went through the ring and vanished into Earth.

Next came the man named Busine. Orfia was last and then I followed them home, deliberately landing well away from them. The first thing I did was take off the glasses and lay them on the ground. When the Kint woman moved toward them or me, I didn't hesitate but backed away. I didn't need or want them. Let them rot for all I cared.

"Where's Trundle?" said Busine, yawning and trying to look alert. "It was supposed to be Trundle who released us." Squinting his eyes and scratching his partially bald head, he said, "What the devil is going on?"

"He's dead," I said. "Appy's henchwoman killed him a long time ago."

Orfia Kint smiled at me, stepped toward me and I kept backing up so that we circled the area like a pair of cautious combatants.

"What about Appy?" said Folgay. He was tall and lean and tried not to seem confused.

"He's gone," I said. "He, Bud Jupiter and Tedwar went back through the blue ring."

"Tedwar? You mean there were three?" Folgay was wide awake now, businesslike and a little alarmed. "You mean everything is all done?"

"Yes, the police are in charge now."

"Daryl, what's the matter with you?" said Orfia. "Can't you see I want to get close to you?"

"There's something odd about her, I believe," said Busine.

"Come and give me a kiss," said Orfia. "I could tear my hair out thinking of you involved in any of this."

"You lie," I said, backing away.

She suddenly looked scared. "Do you think I deliberately placed you in danger?"

"Why not? I might be part of you but you'd consider me as someone out of your past, like an unwanted relative."

"She's off her shelf," said Busine. "I told you she had too much imagination. It's been too much for her."

"One thing's for sure," said Folgay. "She doesn't remember us and I think we can do something about that."

"Don't do anything," I said, preparing to get close to a handy blue ring. I looked at Orfia. "I'm sorry. I thought I'd have the courage to walk through a double blue ring with you so you could get rid of me. I know I'm like Gorwyn and Tedwar. I'm you as a child. You split yourself in two and sent me off to act as a catalyst and get things happening."

"I hired a man to drive you to your uncle's and I'd like to know what you're doing here!"

"Being nuts, I think," said Busine.

"You're my flesh and blood!" said Orfia.

"No doubt," I said. "We're the same flesh and blood, more so than any two people in the world, but I don't care. I want to live no matter what kind of an existence it is." Ignoring her expression, I side-stepped to the ring. There had to be somewhere I could stay and at least be satisfied if not happy. The worlds stertched all around me and I could pick and choose my spots.

Not being very selective, I ended up making camp in a familiar labyrinth in Gothland. They didn't allow me to remain unmolested in the dimension for very long before they sent Kisko after me. I believe he volunteered.

"You don't owe me anything!" I growled, not caring if he misunderstood me, but evidently he knew what I meant or he had decided to be tolerant of anything and everything I said and did.

He had the advantage over me where conversation was concerned because he was wearing Orfia's famous goggles and stood in his human form. "Today you're being rockheaded," he said. "Your imagination has never been normal, but really, this has to constitute some kind of record."

"You trust her?" I scratched on a rock.

"She's that type and she seems to trust me. Why don't you just shut up and listen to me for a minute? First of all, you were hypnotized and sleeping that day when you were involved in the car wreck. You were on your way to Sonny. Ectri. You know. That guy. They're always taking different names for their jobs, remember."

I groaned without sound.

"Gorwyn took the job at Mutat in hopes of finding you, but

you were amnesiac, so he thought maybe seeing Ectri would jolt your memory. He particularly hated your mother, was jealous of her special D talents and the fact that she had been continuing Bud Jupiter's work. Ectri had already been investigated to make sure he knew little about Orfia's work or where she was hiding. Had you arrived safely at his house as you were supposed to, he probably would have taken you to a doctor to try and find out why you couldn't remember anything, and then he would have waited for Orfia to show up. Gorwyn deliberately sent a report about you through Ectri's Washington office and since Ectri's sister and niece, who were both immune to truth drugs, were missing, he came to have a look at you. Incidentally a post-hypnotic suggestion was given you to contact Solvo in New Mexico if you were ever threatened."

"Glasses?" I croaked, even that much effort making my throat sore.

"Their full potential isn't known. That'll be decided through experimentation. Trundle had them and was supposed to visit the hideaway planet every six weeks, the idea being that he should drop hints to police and politicians on the east coat until the honest law here got after Appy and his crews. Which, incidentally, is what got me into the act. They were simply willing to do nearly anything to keep the glasses out of the hands of a maniac. Anyhow, it wouldn't be too difficult for Appy to find one person out of four but it wouldn't be so easy to find just one, and that was why the three hid in the first place. Appy, or Gorwyn, made more than one mistake. First of all, an old maintenance man at the university who had once worked for him recognized him and told Orfia and the others he was Bud Jupiter reincarnated. A little snooping proved he was almost exactly right. Another mistake was in wasting so much time with you. You didn't know that much about the situation. Your mother tried to protect you by wiping what little you did know out of your head. She also turned you against friends and cleaned out your vision of double rings."

"Croff?" I scratched on the rock.

"He was never really all the way in it. He unwittingly led Erma to Trundle. He knew where Trundle's summer place in Vermont was so he went there trying to gain some more information. Trundle was frightened and sent him away without telling him anything. Figuring Erma and Appy were onto his whereabouts, Trundle got desperate and mailed the glasses along with some junk to Croff. Before he could contact Croff and give him instructions, Erma killed him. Later, on Deron's order, she killed Croff because he was trying to help you."

"Didn't Trundle have a transmitter in his arm?"

"He probably got rid of his in about the same way you disposed of Croff's. By the way, before Orfia and the others went into hiding, they tried to find Croff to help him, but he went into D and got lost."

I didn't write anything so Kisko paused for a moment and then said, "How about it? I'm getting hoarse and this is a complicated situation. You can always spend the next year or two listening while your relatives explain it to you."

It took me a long time but I wrote my response on the side of the escarpment: I DON'T HAVE ANY RELATIVES AND I'M GOING TO BE A HERMIT FOR THE REST OF MY LIFE.

"Yeah, yeah," he said. "Hey, that reminds me, I've a recording here I'm supposed to play. Folgay would have done it before but you skipped out too fast."

He fiddled with the knobs on a little box he carried and shortly thereafter three voices spoke out of it, one after another. They all said the same thing and they must have put a great deal into it since their words accomplished some pretty shattering things.

"Daryl, remember," said Busine.

"Daryl, remember," said Folgay.

"Daryl, remember," said Orfia Kint.

Something collapsed in my head so suddenly I almost fell down, though I stood solidly enough on four feet. Old Chameleon had tried to get rid of that wall in my brain and she had been good but still she failed because she hadn't known the correct formula. What was it? "Daryl, remember," said by Busine, Folgay and Orfia, in that order.

So I remembered it all and went back home to see my mother and have her explain everything to me.

Life was different after that and not all of it was unpleasant. I got to keep the farm and Olger stayed to look after things,    I 43 though I was there enough hours of nearly every day to get underfoot. Bandit perplexed us by showing up one day with big Komo and two little ones. In their homeworld the babies are beautiful but in my paddock they can only be described as chips off the maternal block. Funny thing, my horse treats them like his offspring no matter which dimension they're in.

Uncle Sonny's dogs tried to lick my skin off when I visited him. And to think they once terrified me and forced me into D.

I've decided to be an agent when I grow up, and Kisko and Lamana promise to show me the ropes during my summer vacations from Mutat.

Another funny thing, being part of a family and being wanted and needed is fine, but every once in a while I experience a little stab of nostalgia when I remember those other days. Nobody wanted me then but I was as free as a bird.